T0162714

Love, Life or Diamonds

Julie Branken

authorHOUSE®

AuthorHouse™
1663 Liberty Drive
Bloomington, IN 47403
www.authorhouse.com
Phone: 1-800-839-8640

First published by AuthorHouse 9/6/2011

ISBN: 978-1-4634-4471-6 (e)
ISBN: 978-1-4634-4470-9 (sc)

Library of Congress Control Number: 2011914333

Printed in the United States of America

This book is dedicated to

LOVE

Chapter One

IT WAS AUTUMN. LEAVES HAD abandoned the trees and formed golden carpets around the trunks. Bare branches appeared stark and silhouetted against the sky while a soft breeze teased the colorful leaves; scattering them haphazardly into the air. The sun was setting beyond the ocean. The surrounding mountains were lit up with brilliant hues of burning reds, oranges, pinks and purples, suffusing the vault of sky until all was aglow. It was times like these that Jessy's imagination invariably got the better of her when, at this time of the evening, the mountains looked so majestic yet mysterious.

She envisaged hobbits and gnomes walking inside the crevices that were etched in the steep mountain sides, formed by their constant journeys over eons of time. They were singing their merry tunes as they went along, oblivious to the hustle and bustle of the humans below. *Wouldn't it be wonderful if they really did exist?* Jessy sighed.

Jessy knew people who could see into other "dimensions". There was one person in particular whom she remembered with great fondness and admiration – a young man, unassuming, but with a great sense of humor. Jessy had only met him briefly on a few occasions, yet felt drawn to him. During one of those meetings, "spirituality" had come into the discussion. It was then that he told her about the beings of light or as he called them; "Echoes". He noticed that everyone had at least one Echo which hovered around the shoulders of a person. These Echoes spoke to him on a cosmic level and he would get information, from them, about the person. Other times, when he went to sleep, somehow information was downloaded to him – things he couldn't possibly know except for the insights given to him by the Echoes.

Of course this gift was sometimes a curse because he would see the good with the bad. He told Jessy that when an Echo was sitting around the stomach area of a woman it meant that she was pregnant. He could also tell when someone was about to die.

He told Jessy she had one Echo but it was larger and more intricate than he'd ever seen and it seemed to be a conduit of some kind – a facilitator Echo, meant for use by the person. He told Jessy to think of herself as being a "radio receiver"; open to frequencies and channeling. Whereas most people have short-range radios, Jessy seemed to hold so much energy, thereby offering great potential. He suggested she meditate to become more open to things she currently couldn't access.

Jessy was fascinated with the unknown and over the

years had been to many psychics. Some didn't offer much at all, while others were extremely accurate. Jessy's ideas of the universe and life had changed over time. Although brought up as a Christian, she found herself with a strong understanding of the wholeness of life, instead of feeling separate from God. God, to her, represented oneness – God existed simultaneously in everything and everywhere, therefore making all things one. She couldn't describe how she felt, except that she now felt a kind of inner peace.

Although Jessy had a passion for the subject, it wasn't a topic that was candidly discussed; yet it was a topic she found intriguing. There were very few people with whom she could discuss it and she was receptive to anything being possible – if one truly believed in it. She had discovered that it wasn't enough to say, 'I believe' and expect it to happen – but that one had to believe it so deeply that one *knew* it would happen, and it had to come from the heart – where love was the only outcome. This was a concept she had tested and tested, over and over again, until she had discovered the true difference between *believing* and *knowing*. There was no room for the slightest hint of doubt. It had to be complete, like blind faith.

What frustrated Jessy though was how human beings always required proof of everything. Yet the issue regarding proof of God's existence remains unanswered and unproven. There is no proof other than the private and personal strength one feels about the existence of God.

Just then her chain of thought was broken and she noticed the sound of waves crashing on the rocks below the house. Her home was built into the mountain which overlooked the ocean, like most of the houses in the area. Llandudno wasn't really a town. It was more like a suburb of the town. But it wasn't that either because it was completely surrounded by mountains and ocean. It had no shops or facilities to accommodate all the visitors who constantly visited. It was not only the incredible beauty of the area that attracted them, it was also the famous nudist beach – Sandy Bay – which was only accessible from two points; one was over the sand dunes from Hout Bay and the other was from Llandudno itself.

Holidaymakers and nudists would flock there in the summer time to wallow in its splendor and laze around on the glorious beach. There were no hotels, so one could only make day trips. The locals were always happy to see the visitors go, reclaiming their peace, and tranquility. Developers had tried to get permission from the local council to build a few shops but the Llandudno people had stuck together and insisted they did not want to com-mercialize their beautiful piece of heaven.

Jessy decided to take her dog Scanty for a walk along the beach, something she hadn't done for a while. The walk she wanted to take was about half a mile and it meant climbing over rocks and pushing her way through bushes. She was starting to have second thoughts about it, noticing that the wind had picked up and she could see it was growing into a strong southeaster. Scanty sensed her hesitancy and started to bark madly. He too had missed their walks to Sandy Beach and was determined that Jessy was not going to escape this one.

'Okay Scanty, I know what you are thinking and yes, I would like to call it off.'

She spoke to him as if he were a human and he seemed to understand her every word. Now his eyes looked sad and he gave a little whimper in protest. With that pathetic sad look in his eyes, Jessy went to her cupboard and pulled out the biggest, warmest jersey she could find and flung it over her shoulders. Scanty leapt to the front door with an approving bark as Jessy walked towards him. As she opened the door, she was almost blown off her feet by a gust of wind that came howling through the gap!

Jessy needed to go on this walk as much as Scanty did, so she ignored the wind and boldly ventured out, battling to close the door behind her. She had some serious thinking to do and this was as good a time as any. She knew the beach would be empty, for no sane person would venture out in this kind of weather. The locals knew that when the southeaster decided to blow, staying indoors was the only option, because when it blew, it blew like the devil.

She looked down at Scanty and said, 'Shall we leave the walk until tomorrow? We really must be mad to go out in this weather.' She knew jolly well that he would complain, and sure enough, before she had uttered the last word, the barking started and he ran ahead of her, tail wagging madly.

'Well, I was only thinking of you; I'm dressed warmly but you could get cold out there,' she said, trying to persuade him but enjoying teasing him too. He ignored her and ran on, happy that he had got his way.

As they walked along a beach path, the wind blew her long, golden hair behind her like a bridal veil and the sea spray dampened her soft skin, leaving the taste of salt on her lips; white salty patches dotted her face. Jessy loved the wild wind and the unruly sea. She was grateful for nature and its recalcitrant power. But how long that would last she didn't know; 'they' were coming up with weird and wonderful ideas, daily.

The two of them scrambled over rocks and brushed past the shrubs that covered the path which led to the beach. She felt better already and was pleased she had decided to brave the weather.

Stepping onto the sand, Jessy felt a presence. She wasn't sure what it was or who it was but there was definitely somebody there. She glanced around hurriedly to see if there was any visible evidence of footsteps but there weren't, nor was there a soul in sight. Jessy was psychic and was seldom wrong about her feelings, as long as she never questioned them and just went with her first instincts. She felt rather apprehensive and wanted to turn back but something prevented her. She took a few more steps and stopped dead in her tracks. She didn't know what to do next. Scanty hadn't barked but he was aware that Jessy had sensed something.

The person or whatever had to be in front of them for the wind was blowing onto their backs. Scanty would have picked up the scent if it had been blowing the other way. Jessy scrambled to find a stick and threw it for him.

'Fetch it, Scanty!' she shouted. He galloped after it and brought it back with it clenched between his teeth, wagging his tail proudly. The third time she threw it Scanty didn't go after it but veered off in the opposite direction. He had picked up a scent and ran off barking. Jessy ran after him, not knowing what she would do once she reached him. He stopped beside two huge boulders and barked furiously, not stopping to take a breath. As she approached Scanty, she was preparing herself for whatever it was that Scanty had found. She froze and looked down at the ground. There, lying on the sand was a man – dead or alive she could not tell. There was no movement at all. She moved closer to get a better look at him before touching him. She was concerned that he was dead and that frightened her. She hoped it was someone playing a boyish trick, but in this weather he would have to be desperate to subject himself to this kind of punishment. No. It was no trick. She walked around him very slowly, keeping her distance.

He had dark-brown hair which was matted and un-kempt. She unwittingly began to scratch her own hair. There were at least two weeks growth of facial hair, not quite an established beard. His skin was bronzed by the sun and very dry with salt. Dirt was embedded in his pores. The clothes he wore were close to being non-existent. What was left of them was tattered and torn, as if they had gone through a shredder. She could see his protruding muscles through the torn clothing. He had the look of a fisherman or some sort of laborer.

Scanty was still barking furiously and Jessy shouted, 'Stop that silly barking Scanty; that is quite enough!' Scanty gave a little whining noise and ceased. He lay down on the sand beside her feet, like a scolded child. The stranger had not flinched despite the noise. Jessy recalled her father's face just before he died – his skin had turned an odd, grayish color. She took a good look at his face to see if there was any resemblance in color but she couldn't really tell. He was too dirty to see much at all. She decided the only way to find out was to bend over and see if he had a pulse. With great caution she touched his arm and turned it slightly to find his pulse. It was there all right, but it didn't seem too strong and his arm was cold to touch.

She wanted to call for help but there was no one around. There was no time to run back to get help for she feared he may not last that long. The first thing she had to do was to warm him up, so she took the spare jersey she had wrapped around her waist and put it over him. She grabbed hold of his arm and started to shake it vigorously; trying to stir whatever life was left in him. He was too big to lift so he would have to get up himself if he was to live through the night.

She felt relieved when he groaned, even though it sounded very feeble, but it meant he was awakening and perhaps he would have enough strength to get up. He was obviously in pain and Jessy did not want him to move unnecessarily; well, not until she had established exactly what was wrong with him and whether or not he had any broken bones.

'Can you hear me? Are you all right?' she asked, feeling a bit stupid at the question. There was silence for a few minutes, then, he slowly turned his head in the direction of the strange voice and gradually opened his eyes.

Their eyes met and Jessy felt a strange connection – but there wasn't time for her to question her emotions. His eyes were a piercing blue with specks of darker blue. The wrinkles around his eyes were embedded with salt. Jessy guessed he was about thirty years old, but it was difficult to tell with all the grime and salt that covered his body. Yet, his body was strong with a youthful look about it.

'I'm not sure . . . I can't really feel parts of my body.' He spoke with deep husky voice. Jessy noticed his accent had a hint of French.

'How long have you been here? Your body feels very cold – we must try and get you up and moving so that your body can warm up,' she said. She tried to remain calm and casual but she didn't know what she would do if he couldn't move any part of his body and if he were paralyzed. She thought she must take one step at a time.

He seemed to be thinking and then replied, 'I don't know how long I have been here. In fact, I can't recall anything at all.'

Jessy felt sorry for the stranger and guessed he must have been shipwrecked or maybe washed overboard while fishing out at sea and left for dead. It was a treacherous coastline and ships were always getting wrecked on the rocks. She didn't really have time to think about where he came from or who he was. She had to get him warmed up as quickly as possible.

'We can talk about all this later but right now I want you to try and move,' she said as she grabbed hold of his arm firmly, hoping that he would feel it. He moved very slowly but at least he moved. She did the same with his other arm and then his legs. Everything seemed to be all right, no broken bones, just a lot of bruises and a few cuts here and there.

'You are doing well. Now try and see if you can sit up. I'll help you,' she said.

Jessy put her hands under his arms, which felt all sticky and sandy as she struggled to help lift him up.

'Good, now see if you can get up onto your feet.' She knew she was asking for the impossible but Jessy always did, she expected the best of everything.

Carefully, he started to rise inch by inch, foot by foot, until he was on his feet. But he wasn't there for long. As he tried to stand, he fell down onto his knees. His legs were weak. He groaned as he hit the sand.

'It will take a while but you were up once which means you can do it again.' She was so encouraging. How could he not get up? He looked at her more closely and was caught by surprise. She was so beautiful.

She caught his glance and wondered what was going on in his head. She just hoped he wasn't up to anything but somehow Jessy doubted it.

'Are you ready? We *must* try again; you have to start moving around to get your blood flowing,' she said. She wondered if she should offer to rub his legs and arms, to try and warm them up.

'My body is feeling warmer, but my legs and arms are still very cold,' he replied, as if he was reading her mind.

'Let's put the jersey on you. It might be tight, but at least it will keep some of the cold off you,' she said. The jersey was very baggy on Jessy, but they could barely get it over his shoulders. Jessy then proceeded to rub his legs and arms, trying to get the circulation going. She thought to herself, *here she was, with a total stranger, rubbing his legs and arms!* Under any other circumstances she would have felt very uncomfortable about the whole idea, but she didn't feel that way. He needed her help and she was going to do everything she could to help him. His stare burned through her, but she didn't care. She continued to massage his legs and arms until he said, 'They are feeling better. I can actually feel life in them. Thank you. I think I will be able to get up now. Well, at least I am ready to try again.'

Jessy helped him up once more and this time he didn't fall back into the sand. He managed to take a few cautious and carefully maneuvered steps. But at least he was moving around and the circulation was going. Jessy had placed her left shoulder under his right arm to support him. He was tall and must have weighed about one hundred and ninety pounds.

Now as he tried to walk, Jessy stood behind him and looked at him closely. There was something exciting about him and it made her feel alive. She shocked herself at these thoughts because she didn't normally take to men so quickly, especially when she didn't know the first thing about them. But she had a good feeling about him. The question was though; was she going to take him to her house, or straight to the hospital? *He could stay in the spare bedroom*, she thought to herself.

'I think I can manage on my own, thank you' he said. Just then he turned and faced her.

'Where am I?' he asked.

'You are in Sandy Bay, which is about half a mile from Llandudno, which is in Cape Town, South Africa. That much I can help you with,' she answered. 'Where are you from?' she asked. He looked at her with a confused expression on his face.

'I honestly don't remember anything' he replied, confusion and frustration in his eyes.

'Well, with an accent like that, you are not from this part of the world. You have a French accent, which means you may have come from Mauritius or France, or some other French speaking colony. But you seem to speak English very well,' Jessy said, wondering where he could have learned it.

'I seem to have no memory, so I can't offer you any explanations. I can't even tell you my name. By the way, what is your name?' he asked politely.

'It is Jessica but most people call me Jessy, and you may too if you wish,' she replied, wondering what she would call him.

'I think I prefer Jessica. It has a nice sound to it. That is, if you don't mind?' Jessy smiled in agreement. The only other person who had called her by her full name had been her father. He had died a while ago, so it would be nice to hear someone call her Jessica again. She felt a warm glow as she remembered him.

'I have to be able to call you something. Do you have any idea?' she asked. There was a blank look on his face. Jessy had remembered hearing the name Jacques and had always thought it was a nice name. 'How about

Jacques – would you have any objection to me calling you that?' she asked. He said the name out loud to see what it sounded like and then replied, 'Yes, it sounds fine. You may call me Jacques,' he smiled as he repeated the name.

It was now becoming bitterly cold and the wind was cutting through Jessy's clothes. She could imagine how cold Jacques was feeling. She saw his teeth chattering as he stood there. As she drew closer to him, she could hear them too. The sun had just sunk behind the sea and it was now quite dark.

'We must hurry. It's going to be pitch-black soon. I'll take you to my house and then we can decide what to do. Perhaps once you have warmed up, we should go to the hospital in case there are some other internal injuries,' she suggested, looking to see his reaction and the expression on his face. But there were none.

'That is very kind of you and I appreciate it, thank you,' he accepted graciously. 'It will feel good to be out of the cold. But I don't want to be any trouble,' he said. She could see that he was rather surprised at her suggestion and she knew she was taking a chance. She could have offered to take him to a hospital instead and he was relieved that she hadn't.

'Are you sure you are well enough to walk back, as it is quite a distance?' she asked.

'I'm feeling a lot better. I'll manage anything just to get warm,' he said, wobbling over to her. She placed herself under his shoulder again and helped him along the way. The path they had to take was very narrow and they struggled to keep on it. Jessy was thankful for the full moon since it gave them just enough light to see where they were going.

The wind was still blowing wildly and small branches kept blowing across their path. Jessy's imagination ran amok as they ambled along. At one stage she thought there was something hiding behind the bushes just in front of them. It was only when they approached it that she saw it was a shadow from a huge rock next to the path. Then she gave a little scream, making Jacques jump and wondering what had happened.

'What is wrong, Jessica?' he asked.

She felt stupid. She realized that it was only a branch that had blown in front of them. She thought it was a leopard as they had been seen recently in the mountains around there.

'It's nothing, I just got a fright when that branch blew across our path,' she replied feeling a bit more relaxed. Then, not too much further on, Jacques tripped over a rock and ended up on his knees with Jessy beside him. She hadn't been strong enough to hold him up so they had both fallen down together.

'I'm so sorry. Are you all right?' he asked, hoping she was. Jessy managed to get herself up and felt okay.

'Sure, I'm fine. How about you though?' she asked. Jacques managed to get himself up.

'I'm all right,' he said, feeling a bit embarrassed.

They were soon back on the path again heading for her home. Jessy was relieved as they approached the road. She had had enough excitement for one day.

Then she remembered the *real* reason for her going on this walk. It was to decide what she was going to do about her boyfriend, Michael. He had asked her to marry him. She loved him but she wasn't *in love* with him. Yes, he could give her everything that she could ever wish for. He was rich, good-looking and good company, but Jessy just didn't love him the way she had always *wanted* to be in love and to be loved unconditionally. She admired his strength and capabilities. He owned one of the biggest shipping companies in Cape Town and was admired by many for his brilliance in the business world. He was hounded day and night by beautiful women and knew that he could take his pick of the bunch but deep in her heart, Jessy knew that he was not the one. A man about town for most of his life, he changed his women like he did his clothes, until he met Jessy.

She believed he had been faithful to her for the short time that they had been seeing each other. But she really believed that he would soon tire of her and be off on the hunt again. She had spoken to him about this, and he had said that she was the one he loved and he was prepared to give up everyone else for her. She was flattered, but she did not trust him, and without trust, how could they have a complete relationship? She didn't want to stand in judgment of him, but a friend of hers had told her that she had seen him with another woman. Of course she had challenged him on the subject, but he denied being with any other woman. She never told him what her friend had said to her. She hated lies and always admired people who spoke their minds, instead of hiding between the lines. She sensed a lack of loyalty from him. Most women would turn a blind eye to it because he could give them material things; spending money and lots more, but what Jessy wanted from a relationship, money could not buy and she was not interested in materialism.

They both held different attitudes towards sex and relationships. Jessy was sincere and genuine in everything she did, but Michael had different ideas. Of course she also accepted that men and women had polarized perceptions of life.

Jessy didn't want to judge him as he obviously had his reasons for what he did. She just thought he would be better off with someone who didn't really mind him going off with other women. It was this lack of trust and the constant threat of lies that had prevented Jessy from falling in love with him. If she was honest with herself, she would have to admit it was more than the issue of loyalty. It was a lack of open-mindedness on his part. Michael was always saying, 'There is only one way to do things,' and Jessy of course, believed that many different paths could be taken to reach the end result. There wasn't only black and white, but a whole spectrum of colors in between and so many roads and avenues to be taken to reach a destination. Jessy viewed life in this same manner. She believed that we are all on a journey, each taking different roads but each ultimately seeking the same destination, whether it be God, Universe or whatever one wished to call the Creator or Source of all.

Michael was an agnostic and therefore didn't believe in anything greater than himself. Because of this, he was often rather condescending about Jessy's belief system and often threw snide remarks around when she commented on spirituality. So it wasn't just the honesty; there was so much more. Jessy would and could not, live with a man who stunted her growth. She wanted to grow with her partner, each stimulating the other and honoring the other's path. She believed there was no right or wrong religion, no greater, nor lesser. Each was and is, as important as the other. Jessy knew what she wanted and it wasn't Michael.

Well, the decision was made and she had known it for a while. She was giving up the material things in life for genuine love, trust and everything else that went with it. She hoped that one day she would find it but she wasn't holding her breath. She was now twenty-five years old and had heard and read so much about "falling in love"; when one's heart would pound wildly and one's knees would weaken with passion and desire. Some have even said that it felt as if the "earth moved under their feet". Perhaps this didn't happen to everyone and maybe Jessy just happened to be one of those.

As the two walked side by side, Jessy could feel the pace slow down and she tightened her arms around him, feeling his flesh on the palm of her hand. His skin was clammy and rough and felt cold. But it wasn't long before she felt the warmth under her hand. 'Do you think we could stop for a short break? I am feeling rather weak,' he asked quietly.

'Of course, let's sit down on those rocks up ahead,' Jessy suggested. As they sat in silence, it occurred to Jessy that he had probably not eaten for a long time; hence the weakness.

After a few minutes, with only the sound of the wind howling and Scanty faithfully panting next to them, Jacques said, 'I have rested long enough; let's get out of this wind and cold.' And with that, they both stood up and continued.

As he spoke, Jessy thought how beautiful his voice sounded, like angels. She could sit all night and just listen to him speak.

As they approached the steps to her house, Jessy could hear the phone ringing. She didn't rush. If it were really important, the caller would phone back later. But whoever it was, wasn't giving up. The phone continued to ring until she opened the door and walked inside. It must be something important, so she helped Jacques down in front of the fireplace and then dashed to answer the phone.

'Hi sexy! We are all at Sue's house waiting for you. Have you forgotten about the dinner party? The food has been ready for the last fifteen minutes and we can't delay it much longer or Sue says it will be ruined. Are you on your way out the door?' the voice on the other end of the phone asked. The dinner party had been planned for weeks and it wasn't like Jessy to forget something like that. She was always very punctual. Normally Michael picked her up, but she could remember telling him that she would come along on her own. She had to get things prepared for her jewelry exhibition and was not sure how long she would be. She felt guilty but wasn't really in the mood now to leave her present situation to go off to a dinner party.

Generally, the talk at these dinners was invariably the same topics; how much money this one or that one had made during the week, or what new toy had been purchased. She found the current turn of events far more exciting.

'I'm sorry Michael, I forgot all about it, I have had so much on my mind. I really haven't had time to think of anything else. Please give my apologies to Sue and go ahead and start your meal before it is ruined. I'll speak to you in the morning,' she said.

There was silence at the other end of the phone. She knew that he was upset, especially as he was now on his own. This was just unheard of for Michael as he was used to having some gorgeous girl hanging off his arm.

Perhaps Jessy was being too hard on him and perhaps he really would miss her. Whether she had just become neurotic about him she would never know, but she wasn't really going to wait to find out. Perhaps he would change but she believed a leopard never changes its spots. When he spoke, he sounded very sad about her not making it.

'I understand, sweetheart; I'll give you a call tomorrow. Have you thought about what I asked you the other day? I won't hang around forever,' he teased. That was another thing – Michael wanted to live with her before she married him but Jessy didn't want that. She wanted to marry her husband-to-be and that was that.

'I'll speak to you tomorrow about it. Enjoy your meal – bye for now,' she said and hung up. While this conversation was going on, she watched Jacques get up off the chair and walk slowly around the room. He was studying each of the paintings on the walls. Jessy had collected more than thirty original paintings by different artists. It was something she really appreciated and it was obvious that he had an interest in art too. She stood for a while and watched him before walking towards him.

'Do you like art?' she asked.

'I have always had a great admiration for artists who manage to capture the emotions and essence of life. You have some very fine work here,' he replied, not turning to face her, but continuing to admire the art. Jessy found herself lost in his words: "capture the emotions and essence of life." *What exactly did he mean?* She felt drawn to this curious stranger. He seemed to stir her inner being. *What was that all about,* she wondered?

'Yes, these are some of my favorite pieces. I'm glad you like them. We can continue this conversation, but first I think it would be a good idea if you took a hot bath. It will warm you up and clean you up too, and then we can decide whether or not I should take you to the hospital. After all, you can't go there looking like you do,' she said. No sooner were the well-intentioned words out when she realized how insulting it must have sounded.

'That sounds great. I'm sorry. I must smell terrible! When you've been like this for days, maybe weeks, you no longer smell yourself. I do apologize,' he said, running his hands through his sticky hair and looking embarrassed.

'It really doesn't matter since you're very close to smelling clean again.' And with that she headed for the bathroom and Jacques could hear the sound of running water. Jessy shouted out to him, 'I think a bath is better for you than a shower. It will warm you quicker and it will relax your muscles and weary bones. If you don't mind I will put some soothing salts into the water.'

'What a wonderful idea,' he called back. Jacques felt excited at the prospect of having a clean body again. It had been such a long time since he'd had a bath. He could already feel the hot water engulfing his body, warming and healing it.

'Why don't you jump in the tub while I go and find some clean clothes for you to wear', suggested Jessy.

She went into her bedroom and searched for some clothes that her brothers had left there. She was sure they wouldn't mind. They were about the same size as Jacques so they would fit. Her brothers would come and visit her and sometimes stay overnight. They loved to fall asleep to the sound and smell of the ocean. They invariably left some piece of clothing behind, and Jessy would wash them and put them away, ready for their next visit. She hadn't always remembered to return them and sometimes they would sit in the spare room cupboard until she had one of her clean-outs and stumbled upon them. Today she was glad that she hadn't returned them. She walked to the bathroom door and knocked gently.

'Jacques, I have put some clothes outside the door. They should fit you,' she said.

'Thank you Jessica,' he replied. He wondered where she had found some men's clothes. He had noticed a few pictures around the room of different men, so perhaps they were some of her boyfriends. No ring on her finger, so she wasn't married. Was it possible that someone as interesting and attractive as her could be single?

Jessy heard the muffled 'thank you' as she walked down the passage, heading straight for the kitchen. They both needed something to eat. Jessy hadn't had time to have lunch, so she was rather hungry herself and was sure that Jacques was starving. She busied herself with making a meal, thinking about the day's events and how bizarre but thrilling it all seemed. She wondered who this mysterious man was and where he had come from. This life journey certainly was an ongoing adventure; one never knowing from day to day what or who may come into your life.

Chapter Two

Jacques lay in the bath feeling warm and refreshed. He couldn't remember the last time he had such a long soak in a bath. It was sheer luxury. He wallowed in the ecstasy, feeling every pore on his body opening and releasing the dirt that had been trapped inside.

He thought about Jessica and how kind she had been to him. He didn't want to think about what lay ahead or of the consequences of this meeting with Jessica. All he could think about was how attracted to her he felt.

She was attractive, perhaps even beautiful, with the most incredible eyes. They were a sparkling turquoise blue, a color that was unique. Her hair was long and silky. It hung down to just below her waist. It was thick and soft to the touch. She seemed to have everything. How did he get so lucky, or unlucky, depending on the way one looked at it? He was beginning to think it was bad luck. His daydreams were broken by Jessica shouting, 'Have you gone down the plug hole?'

Jacques must have been in there for a long time for the skin on his hands and feet were white and wrinkled like an old man. He washed his hair which was full of grime and dirt. The smell must have been terrible yet she didn't complain, not once.

'No, I haven't. I'm still in the land of the living. I won't be long. I'm really enjoying the soak,' he shouted back, before dunking his head under the water and then reluctantly easing his clean body out of the tub.

She didn't hear everything he said but just picked up a few words here and there. She had left a razor, toothbrush and toothpaste on the side of the basin, as well as a towel. The blades looked new so he presumed they were for his use. He decided it was time to get rid of the itchy growth that was around his chin and mouth. He opened the door and poked his head out, just enough to see the clothes Jessy had laid on the ground. He picked them up and disappeared behind the door. Jessica had given him a pair of jeans, a long fleecy shirt and some thick warm socks. He tried them on and they fit him like a glove.

He was now ready to take on the world, feeling clean and human again. As he walked into the kitchen, Jessy lifted her head and was about to say something but instead, she just stared at him. She couldn't believe this was the same man she had picked up from the beach just a few hours ago, half dead.

He was gorgeous. The blue in the shirt brought out the color in his eyes. His hair was long, black and slightly wavy with small curls falling around the sides of his face. He had shaved off the beard but left the moustache. He could have been a movie star. He was striking, but in a very rough, rugged way.

Jessy felt light-headed and her legs buckled beneath her. She thought she would collapse. Her heart was pounding madly and she didn't know what had hit her. She tried to pull herself together. What was happening? Jacques wondered what was going on too. Jessy continued staring at him with a silly look on her face. He wondered if he had perhaps left some shaving cream on his face. He lifted his hand to his mouth and ran it across it. But still, she continued to stare.

'Is there something wrong with me? You are looking at me in such a strange way?' he asked, with a furrowed look on his brow. Jessy pulled herself together and felt embarrassed. She quickly looked down at what she had been doing.

'I'm sorry; I didn't mean to look at you in any particular way. I was just deep in thought before you walked in. Sometimes, it takes me a while to come back to reality,' she said, hoping that he would accept that explanation.

'Those clothes you are wearing are a good fit. I hope you don't mind, but they belong to one of my brothers. They are always leaving their things here. But they are clean; I washed them,' she said, trying not to blush any more than she was already. But Jessy felt the blood rushing to her cheeks. She kept looking down at what she was doing, hoping that he hadn't noticed.

'They *are* a good fit and I am grateful for the use of them. I think I would look rather silly in one of your dresses,' he replied, trying to make the atmosphere a little lighter, for which Jessy was thankful. He walked towards the sink where she was working.

Once she had regained her composure she asked, 'Would you like to go to the hospital? It might be wise to have a check-up, to make sure everything is fine.' He was now standing next to her and she could hear and feel his breath on her shoulder. It made her quiver, arousing her very being. She took a few steps away, pretending she had to get something from the cupboard on the far side of the kitchen. She needed the time to pull herself together, all the while hoping he hadn't sensed anything.

'Thanks, but I really am feeling great. There really doesn't seem to be anything wrong with me other than an empty stomach,' he replied, a cheeky grin on his face.

'That food smells so good. Is there anything that I could help you with?' he asked.

'Why don't you pour us both a glass of wine? It's in the fridge. The glasses are above the fridge in the glass cabinet, that is, if you drink wine?' she asked.

'That sounds great,' he replied and headed for the fridge. As he walked, he noticed that the kitchen had been designed rather well, with plenty of cupboards all around. It had a center isle which contained an oven and plenty of work surfaces on either side. The decor was in earthly tones, with lots of handmade pottery.

The floors were handmade clay tiles, making everything very homely and inviting. The wine glasses were crystal and elegant. While he poured the wine, Jessy popped the food into the oven.

'Let's go through to the lounge and make a fire. It is

really nippy tonight,' suggested Jessy, pulling her wrap tighter around her shoulders.

'Would you like me to make the fire for you?' asked Jacques politely.

'Thanks for the offer but I really enjoy making it and besides, I don't think you should overdo it until you get your strength back. You just sit there and enjoy the break,' she replied.

So Jacques did as he was told and watched her. She was confident in every move she made. The newspaper was tied in a knot, after it had been rolled up, which would help it burn longer. Then the dried pine cones were placed on top, giving the logs plenty of time to catch light. They were a good substitute for small pieces of wood. Everything was placed according to size and thickness. As she picked up each piece, Jacques could see her take a quick look at it before putting it on the fire. It seemed like she threw the whole lot together, but it was done with such care and certainty. When she took the match to light it, Jacques knew there was no doubt whatsoever the fire was going to burn. He sensed an inner strength about her and with that thought, he sat back to watch it turn into a blazing fire.

She looked so beautiful as she sat there watching the fire catch alight. Her hair cascaded over her shoulders and down to her waist, falling in soft curls as it lay on her breasts, giving them shape. Her complexion was clear and fresh; with no sign of make-up. She had a natural beauty about her, something that make-up could never give. He felt a burning fire of passion inside of him, but he controlled it, wishing that he could smother her with love and hold her close to him. Jessy felt him staring and she turned to face him. They caught each other's gaze and held it for a few seconds, then quickly looked away.

'I must compliment you on the fire, Jessica. I couldn't have done a better job myself,' he said smiling.

'Well, thank you, at least we will be able to enjoy the evening without freezing. Besides, you must keep warm. How are you feeling?' she asked, becoming suddenly very concerned about him.

'I am feeling wonderful. Well, I will be once I have sampled that delicious smelling food. I have been getting whiffs of it all night. I am really hungry and when you turned your back in the kitchen earlier, I was tempted to try a sample! I restrained myself, but I don't know how much longer I can keep this up,' he said honestly.

Jessy jumped up. 'I nearly forgot about the food in the oven!' she said and ran out of the room, heading for the kitchen.

'Well, aren't you hungry?' she shouted out to Jacques. He didn't need to be asked twice; he was there in a shot. Jessy walked over to the light switch and turned them down. She beckoned Jacques to take a seat, lit the two unusual African candles that stood in ebony candlestick holders. Jacques was immediately swept up by the romantic atmosphere she had created. The fire gave off a lovely, reddish-orange haze and the candlelight silhouetted the room, throwing a multitude of patterns onto the walls.

The two strangers both felt the warmth of the atmosphere and relaxed, enjoying the peace they each felt inside. Entrées were stuffed mushrooms which had been grilled and topped with cheese. Then they moved on to the Moussaka, which was delicious.

Jacques couldn't help wondering how she had managed to escape marriage. It was now apparent to him that there was no sign of a male living in the house.

'That was a scrumptious meal Jessica. I can't remember the last time I ate so well,' he said and with those words they both started to laugh. They really shouldn't have because amnesia is serious, but it was hilarious given the situation.

'I really didn't mean to laugh at that,' Jessy said, 'but it's the way you said it.'

'You don't have to apologize. I also find it quite amusing.' he said and they laughed again. She felt so relaxed being in his company and felt as if she had known him her whole life. There was a familiarity about him and she didn't know where it came from but she was sure that he felt it too. They polished off the bottle of wine and finished the meal with Irish coffee which they enjoyed in front of the fire.

'Jessica, tell me something about yourself. I would really like to know something about *you*,' Jacques said.

'I would rather we talked about you, but I appreciate that that is an issue at the moment. Well, where shall I start?' she asked, feeling a bit self-conscious.

'Let's start with your family; where you came from and how you have got where you are now. That should keep you busy for a while,' he replied. He just wanted to watch her and if she did all the talking, then it gave him an excuse to do just that.

'Well, I am one of six children, four brothers and one sister. We were brought up in Zambia for part of our lives and Australia for the other part. I left school at the age of fifteen without finishing my "O" levels, which were the minimum requirements. I went to a boarding school in Zimbabwe and didn't enjoy it at all. I then attended a Technical College and completed a secretarial course, in Zambia. As soon as I acquired a job, I decided to work for a year and save, in order to travel overseas. I went to Europe for a year. I adore traveling, so, I would work a month in London, make some money doing temp jobs and then go over to France, Germany, Spain, Austria and more. It was really a very happy time in my life. At the end of that year, I decided that the weather was too bad in Europe and headed back to the sunshine.

'I came to Cape Town and completed a course in designing; something I had always been interested in. When completed, I was offered a job with one of the biggest jewelry shops in the city. I worked there for three years learning as much as I could. I enjoyed every moment of it. Then one day, I had an altercation with my boss and walked out. He wasn't a very kind man and he was rude to all his staff. The only reason I had stayed there was because he was seldom at the shop. Most of his time was spent flying around the world buying gemstones and going to European jewelry exhibitions. Another reason I left was because of his dishonesty. I couldn't take any more of his lies.

'I had become very friendly with all the suppliers and especially with a chap called Klaus. He was like a father to me, especially when my father died. He taught me a great deal and when I told him I had walked out, he offered me a job. I was tempted, but I didn't want business to get in the way of our relationship. Klaus works in a different way to me, and I didn't want those differences of opinions to come between us.

'So, I decided to go it alone. I had saved a bit of money so I bought all my own gold and all the tools I needed, which weren't that many since I already had accumulated a lot over time. I had been making my own pieces at home for friends and relatives for many years and I had also become quite well known at the shop where customers had started to ask for my pieces. Once I was on my own, I was commissioned to design pieces for a number of wealthy people. Klaus helped me as much as he could, but most of the work had to be done by me.

'I worked through the night and into the early hours of the morning most days and every weekend for months at a time. Where I managed to get all the energy from I don't know. How I stayed awake is also a miracle because if I don't get enough sleep I become very bad tempered. I guess I was, just loving what I was doing and everything else was unimportant. My friend, Megan, says that energy is a universal gift of life and that there is abundance for everyone to channel into, whenever we need it. I suppose that is what I managed to do. There was no sense of time passing. It seemed to stand still, and I became a part of it.

'After about six months the workload became too much for me and one of the girls with whom I had worked with, decided she had also had enough at the other shop. I bumped into her one day and said that I was looking for some help. She jumped at the opportunity to work with me again. We decided we needed a small shop so that our work could be on display. From there it grew bigger and bigger.

'I love it and I must confess that I drive the women who work for me crazy. I am always working and doing something. They are constantly reminding me that it's lunchtime or time to go home. I find myself going to work on holidays and sitting in the quiet of the shop, absorbed in creativity. I seem to get my most creative work done at that time. I suppose one day I will slow down. I can't remember the last time I took a holiday, which I suppose will catch up with me sooner or later.

'I was getting so busy that I had to have an even bigger shop, so Klaus suggested that I open one up in a more central area, right in the busiest part of town. That's what I did and I have never looked back. I now live comfortably, and that's about it,' she said. She didn't believe she had told him so much about herself.

Jacques had been listening to her closely, trying to picture each movement she had made through those years. He had thought she had been left all these worldly possessions, but she had worked for them. He suddenly felt great admiration for her.

'But you know what? Some of my most exciting times and best memories were in Zambia with my friend Zeke. There were nine teenagers in our crowd and together we did some great things. We would sometimes disappear into the bush to the sunken lakes which were believed to be bottomless. No human being had ever been to the bottom of them. Zeke loved diving, so he would spend most of the day in the water enjoying exploring the different caves and tunnels. He had, on many occasions, tried to get to the bottom, but even with his equipment he couldn't. We made sure that there were always two who dived together because the caves were very narrow in places. People have been known to get lost and never return.

'Some of us would spend the day fishing for our evening meal and others would go and look for wildlife, as there was an abundance in that area. At night, we would sit around a campfire, enjoying a good old sing-song and chat until the early hours of the morning. The fire had to be kept burning all night as there were a lot of wild prowlers. We didn't fancy the idea of waking up in the morning to find that one of us had been eaten, or taken away in the night! It was so intoxicating, smelling the untouched bush smells and listening to the different animal noises, cries, and seeing the sky full of brilliant stars above us. Those were my favorite times, in the bush, with nature.

'Some days were spent at the local boating club. We would go water-skiing on the dam which was man-made but one of the biggest in the country. It was full of crocodiles and every now and again we would hear that one of the local people had tragically been taken by a crocodile. We would actually see the crocodiles but it didn't deter us from skiing. Fortunately none of us were ever attacked – we always believed it wouldn't happen to us. Naive perhaps but it was a way of life. When we fell off our skis, we would have to wait five to 10 minutes treading water until the boat turned around and came back for us, which was so risky, I'll admit but it was a great feeling.

'There *was* one terrible incident that I will never, ever forget. We had all gone down to one of the rivers and had spent the day swimming and just generally embracing the outdoors. The place was called The Rapids, which was rather apt. The river was very strong in places and the rapids would go hurling over the sharp-edged rocks. There were quite a few people around that day. Just downstream from us were two little boys playing in the water, trying to catch some fish. Their mother was sitting on the side of the bank, knitting. She had told the boys on several occasions not to venture too far into the water. The boys had been good and had done as they were told. I love kids and I found myself watching them from time to time. Then I went cold with sudden horror. The boys had been splashing around and one had gone in up to his hips, trying to escape from his brother. They were teasing each other. Out of nowhere a crocodile appeared. It all happened within seconds. Before I could even scream, the crocodile had lifted its mighty tail out of the water and flicked the boy, flinging him some twenty feet into the air. The crocodile lay in waiting with his mouth wide apart, ready for the kill. The little boy was shouting and screaming for help. Their mother looked up just in time to see her son land right in the crocodile's mouth. We were all up and running, but there was nothing to be done. The crocodile and the child had vanished under the water.'

'The mother ran into the water after them but where was she going to look? The water was dark in color and you couldn't see a foot below the surface. We dived into the river, but there was no sign of anything. The mother was naturally in a terrible state and we tried to console her but she was hysterical. Our hearts went out to her, I don't know how she would have coped.

'We heard days later that someone up the river had found part of a child's arm on the river bank. We take these lives of ours for granted, not appreciating that life is a *gift* to each and every one of us,' she said solemnly and quietly.

Jessy shuddered in her chair as she recalled the incident. Her hands were sweating and quickly she changed her thoughts.

'Don't stop now; tell me more of these stories' Jacques said, hanging on her every word. Jessy blushed, but continued.

'I recall the time we went to one of the local game parks for two weeks. We were the only visitors there so we had undivided attention. We were served a good, healthy farmhouse breakfast in the morning before our sight-seeing tour of the game park.

'It was truly magnificent! The atmosphere was fresh and wild. The animals roam freely and the air is pure. A peace and serenity exists that isn't found anywhere else and one feels that everything in nature belongs to everyone. We watched hyenas hunting down a herd of small game. They were both skillful and fast. They planned every movement and every member of the pack had his own job. They knew which animal they were going to attack. They would separate and isolate their prey and even though to some it seems cruel and barbaric, it is exciting to watch. It is the way of the bush and there is no place for the weak and the slow. The animals know and understand this law. It is the survival of the fittest. One day, we came very close to being attacked by a lion. As we approached the lion and lioness lying in the thick, long grass, the driver slowed down and beckoned us to be very quiet and still. He slowly lifted his hand and pointed to the lions saying, 'There has been a fight between two lions. They were fighting over the lioness. See the blood around his mouth. That means there is a wounded lion lurking around here somewhere. Be on your guard!' The Land Rover had no doors or roof, so we were an easy sitting target.

'Before we knew what had happened we heard a loud growl. The lion had managed to get up, and was now behind us, heading straight for the Land Rover. The vehicle was stationary, which meant the lion was approaching rather rapidly. But the driver, being familiar with lions and the bush, reacted quickly. He managed to drive off just in the nick of time. Adrenaline was pulsating through our veins – I really thought that was the end of us. *Eaten by lions, never to be seen again.*' Jessy spoke with such exhilaration in her voice and was quite breathless. Then she became aware of all the talking she had been doing and suddenly stopped.

Jacques had been listening to her stories of the bush and the wildlife and he wanted to hear more and more. It was as though he had been transported into another time and place, experiencing it for himself.

'Have you remembered anything about yourself yet?' she enquired, hoping it was her turn to be transported into his world.

'Nothing, I'm afraid, but I'm sure it will hit me sometime soon,' he replied, sounding very positive about his recovery.

Jessy had felt him staring at her all the while she had been speaking and became very aware of the strong vibrations between them. They talked into the early hours of the morning, both feeling great contentment in each other's company; both feeling a great pull to one another, like magnets, yet somehow managing to control their emotions. After all, they had only met a few hours ago.

Jessy felt on top of the world, yet she also felt as if the whole world around her had just been pulled out from under her feet. Her heart pounded wildly; she got goose bumps each time he touched her. She was out of control and it frightened her. Was this the thing they called 'love', and could it be happening to her, so quickly? Jacques never made a pass at her and she respected that. She just hoped it wasn't because he did not find her attractive, but because he was a gentleman.

Jessy was definitely a romantic and her friends always ragged her about the crazy ideas she had about meeting someone and falling madly in love. Having the friendship, the physical attraction and having a lot in common wasn't that easy to come by these days. Most couples tolerate each other's nonsense, either because they are too scared of being left on the shelf, or sometimes because they do not want to be lonely and need to be with someone. Loneliness is a terrible thing to some people. They need company around them because they think they cannot cope on their own.

Jessy wasn't interested in all that nonsense. She knew what she was looking for and would wait a whole life-time until it came along. She had dated many men but they became casual friends. There wasn't anything special about them. They didn't have that 'something' that she was looking for. Her friends were always trying to match-maker her but failed.

It was now half-past three and Jessy found herself yawning. She *had* to go to bed if she wanted to function coherently at her exhibition. She looked over at Jacques who was also looking tired. The wrinkles around his eyes were exaggerated by his weariness and dark shadows lay beneath them. But his eyes were bright and shining. His nose was sharp and his chin was strong and dimpled. His cheekbones were high and he had an aristocratic look about him, which made Jessy wonder where he had come from. It was obvious he wasn't just, anybody. The way he spoke and handled himself made her think that he probably came from a good background. His shirt was open, revealing thick dark hairs on his chest. His arms were bronzed and powerful. She finally had to tear her eyes away from him. The attraction was far too strong. She ached to be in his arms but she had to control herself.

'Jacques, I must go to bed now. I have a very busy

day tomorrow and I'll need whatever strength I have left in me to handle tomorrow's events. So please excuse me,' she said in a tender soft voice.

'I could do with some sleep myself. I thank you again for your kind hospitality,' he said in return and smiled.

'Let me show you where you will be sleeping tonight,' she said. Jacques got up first and then put out his hand to help Jessy up. As their fingers touched, shocks went shooting up their arms but they both ignored it. As Jessy took his hand and got up onto her feet, she looked up at him. It was just too much for both of them. Jacques bent down and kissed her gently on the lips. Jessy should have pulled away, she knew she should have, but it just felt so right. Here she was, taking this stranger into her house, and yet she felt as though he had lived with her all her life. The kiss was gentle and their lips moist, and as their tongues intertwined, they both felt a very deep love inside of them. Jacques ran his hand through Jessy's hair. It was soft to the touch and smelled so sweet. His hands moved slowly down her back, feeling the gentle curves of her hips and then her bottom, which was firm and youthful. He so badly wanted to make love to her but he didn't want her to think that he was taking advantage. Jessy melted with each movement of his hands. She ran her hand over his hairy chest, feeling the muscles of his body and then slowly, she ran her hand around the inside of his shirt. She wanted him, but she too didn't want him to think that this was something she did all the time. In fact, Jessy couldn't believe that she was even in this predicament, but right now, she didn't care. They kissed long and hard and when it came to an end, Jacques opened his eyes and looked at Jessy.

'I'm sorry Jessy, I really promised myself I wasn't going to do this, but I just find you unbelievably attractive,' he said and before he could say anymore, she put her finger up to his mouth to quiet him.

'You really don't have to apologize; I am equally to blame. But quite honestly I think we both know what we're doing and there is no need for anything else to be said,' she murmured, looking deep into his blue eyes.

'You're right,' he murmured and then they walked towards the sleeping area. His room was the second on the left.

'Please make yourself at home and I'll see you in the morning,' she said as she continued to walk down the corridor.

'Goodnight and sweet dreams,' he said as he closed the door behind him. He lay on the bed thinking about her and his situation. She was both mentally and physically attractive. She had a certain charisma about her. She was quietly spoken but said her piece. She must have known she was all these things but she hadn't made her vanity her world. She always had time to listen to others. Jacques found himself falling in love with her, even though he knew it was not timely under the circumstances.

He had tried all night to keep his distance and not touch her. He was able to control himself tonight but it frightened him, knowing that it could not last. But control himself he must. He had to keep reminding himself of what was more important right now. His mind was active and he knew he wouldn't be able to sleep, even though he was physically exhausted. His mind turned to the elusive word 'fate'. Was there such a thing that brought people together for a purpose? And with that thought, he eventually drifted off into a deep, much-needed sleep.

Chapter Three

Jessy woke abruptly to her noisy alarm clock buzzing in her ear. Not the sound she wanted to hear on this particular morning. Her head was feeling thick and fuzzy and for a few seconds she wondered if last night had been a dream. She dragged herself out of bed feeling tired and haggard; not in the mood for speed as with each movement, her head ached. She wasn't used to drinking so much wine; normally, one glass was enough for her.

She put on her dressing gown as she did every morning before venturing into the kitchen to make some coffee. As she passed Jacques' room she noticed that his door was open. She peeped her head around and saw that the bed was empty. Now she really did wonder whether last night's events had taken place. Her heart sank with disappointment. Suddenly her aches and pains disappeared. She longed to see him again and to believe he was real.

She went through to the lounge and there he was, lying

on the carpet in front of the dead fire, fast asleep. Returning to his room, Jessy took the duvet cover off the bed and gently covered him with it. He looked so peaceful.

Jessy had her coffee, got dressed and wrote a note for him. She was already late; she should have set her alarm clock for an earlier time but knew that the ladies at work would cope. There were certain clients of hers who expected to see her there, demanding her full attention. She couldn't really complain as these clients were the ones who had made her business the success it was.

She jumped in her car and drove along the windy road that led to the city. The smell from the ocean filled her nostrils and the waves crashed loudly against the rocks. The wind had dropped and the ocean was calm but still murky. A few fishing boats had set off for the day's catch. As she drove past Oudekrall, she noticed a couple of divers swimming past a wreck which had gone down many years ago. She chuckled to herself, wondering what they could possibly hope to see in those murky waters.

There was very little traffic on the road. It was too early for the average working person to be heading for work. Jessy preferred to leave at this time so that she didn't catch the morning peak hour to work. She took her time savoring every sight she saw along the way. One never grew tired of the natural beauty. Sometimes there were baboons that would come down from the mountains and sit on the side walls that were built to stop cars from going over the edge. Tourists would stop and feed them but Jessy had heard of people who had been attacked by them so she would drive past them slowly and admire them from a distance.

She tried not to think about Jacques but struggled. *Who was he and where had he come from?* Jessy wanted answers. He couldn't just appear from nowhere and not remember a thing, or could he? Should she phone the police and see what information she could get from them? Maybe they had heard of someone who had fallen overboard. She had the radio on in the car and listened to the news very carefully but there hadn't been mention of any accidents. Normally the news was excellent when it came to reporting local events.

She suddenly felt sick. *What if he regained his memory and remembered he was married with children?* Jessy wanted him to be happy but she didn't want to lose him. This was a very selfish thought. Why was she even thinking along these lines, after all, she had only just met him! She reprimanded herself for being so naïve and vulnerable. She felt ashamed of herself for thinking such things too. What will be, will be – a motto she had always lived by. She reminded herself of a poem that she had once heard:

> *Look to the day*
> *For yesterday is already a dream*
> *And tomorrow, only a vision*
> *But today, well lived*
> *Makes every yesterday*
> *A dream of happiness*
> *And every tomorrow*
> *A vision of hope.*
> *Look well therefore*
> *To this day.*

With those words, she gave up all thoughts of tomorrow. She decided to take it day by day and perhaps not try to get too involved with him until she knew more about him. She couldn't stand the thought of falling in love for the first time and then losing him, especially after she had waited so long for someone like this to come along. If she were to only have a taste of love for a short while then at least she could say, 'I have loved and been loved.'

With that, she was brought back to the world at large with cars hooting and impatient drivers, frustrated with how slow the traffic was moving. There were people everywhere, rushing off in all directions like ants, when an object has been put in their path, sending them into a complete frenzy not knowing which direction to take. Why she was part of this rat race she had never understood. But she had promised herself that it wouldn't be forever and the day would come when she could go and live in a small village on a farm or on the coast. But for now she lived this life because she loved her work and she could only move when she was financially secure. She could see the light at the end of her tunnel and as long as it stayed there she was happy. *Let's face it,* she would tell herself, *life is what you make of it.*

Jessy drove directly to her shop and parked in the space reserved for her. Opening the door of her shop, a feeling of accomplishment swept over her. She felt proud of herself and it made her feel stronger than ever. She didn't want to win any business award of the year; she just wanted to feel that she had done what she had set out to do. She knew what she was talking about when it came to jewelry, and it showed.

The front of the shop, which was the display area, was about three hundred square feet and was surrounded by showcases filled with a vast variety of exquisite hand-made pieces of jewelry. The decor of the shop was in a traditional olive green with a touch of deep rose, dusty pink, and cream. There was a lot of wood which gave it both style and class. One entire wall was full of portraits of royalty and the jewelry they had worn over the centuries. Jessy had copied many of the pieces and they were for sale in the shop. There were pictures of Kings and Queens, with exotic crowns which were worn in those bygone days. She had had the pictures enlarged so that people could appreciate how beautiful and each piece was.

Jessy also had a selection of jewelry that wasn't out of the reach for the man in the street. When a customer purchased a piece of her jewelry they knew it was a one of a kind. She only ever made one piece and never re-produced it. That's what people liked about her work; it really was unique. When you walked into her shop you felt like a million dollars, even if you were only there to buy a small pair of earrings. Everyone was treated equally and they received excellent attention from her assistants. She felt that that aspect was so important.

Michael had sent a lot of business her way for which she was grateful. When she first opened, Jessy had invited many of his friends and they were eager to see for themselves as Michael had been most complimentary about it all. So, between word of mouth from her existing clients and Michael's clients, Jessy had managed to build up a small clientele. He had supported her through the tough times while she tried to get it established. She did in fact love Michael but it was in a friendly manner. He was really a very kind man and willing to help anyone at any time. It was just that she didn't love him the way she wanted to love someone; especially after last night. She now knew that *real* love existed – or was it possible for some and not others. This 'falling in love so quickly' is what she was now questioning.

Jessy hoped that once she told Michael she was not going to marry him, they could still remain friends. She knew he would be waiting for an answer and it was only fair that she should tell him as soon as possible. She had promised she would make up her mind and give him an answer by the weekend, which was the day after tomorrow.

Jessy walked into the shop and could hear noises in the back room. It had to be Melodie; she was most particular, as was Jessy, at having everything ready in plenty of time.

'Good morning Melodie,' said Jessy as she walked in.

'Hi there, Jessy,' was the faint reply from the back.

'I thought you were going to be at the exhibition room setting everything up. What are you doing here?' asked Jessy, now beginning to feel concerned.

'Well, I *was* down there. Everything *is* ready, but we forgot about the special display you wanted to set up. So, I thought I would come here and collect it for you. I wasn't sure if you had done that intentionally or whether you had forgotten,' she replied, walking through to meet Jessy.

'You're a honey! I actually *had* forgotten and that is

why I have come straight here. Is there someone down at the exhibition watching our stall?' she asked.

'Yes, I took Peter and Cindy with me this morning and left them there to finalize a few matters,' replied Melodie.

'Well then, let's get my favorite pieces together and we can head on out,' said Jessy.

Jessy had designed some thirty special pieces over the years which she had never shown to anyone, except Melodie. She had made them during different periods of her life which reflected how she had been feeling at that time. They were unlike any of her other pieces; dissimilar in style and one could even say they were rather outrageous in their own ways. She had never wanted to display them until now and was not quite sure why she had hesitated. Perhaps it was because she hadn't been ready for criticism from anyone but now she actually didn't mind. She was, in a sense, bearing her soul to the world through her work, and she felt good about it. Melodie had loved them but she was an artist herself and had an understanding of the passion and creative work that had gone into them.

The two girls boxed everything up and were heading for the door, when the phone rang.

'I'll get that Melodie and then I'll catch up. Don't wait,' said Jessy.

'Great, I'll see you there,' she replied and headed out the door. Jessy ran to the phone and picked it up.

'Good morning, Jessy's Jewelers,' she said gaily.

'Hi there, poop face. What time is your exhibition

starting? I really don't want to miss it. Come to think of it, I haven't embarrassed you for such a long time. You really must be missing it. Well, put your mind at rest I haven't forgotten how,' said the voice on the other side.

'Don't you even think about it today Zeke or I'll never speak to you again! I don't think you realize how important today is to me,' replied Jessy anxiously.

'Well, you see, that's the whole reason why something different must happen so that you will never forget today,' replied Zeke teasingly.

'Please Zeke, not today,' Jessy said, almost begging him not to do anything stupid. But she knew him better than that.

'What time does it start that's all I want to know? I haven't seen you for such a long time so I thought I would sneak out from work for a couple of hours. I am dying to see your new creations,' he said in a more sane voice.

'It starts in thirty minutes and I was just walking out the door. Where have you been?' she asked.

'Well, you know me, here and there. I'll tell all when we meet this morning. Bye for now,' he said.

'Bye,' replied Jessy and hung up the phone. She ran out of the shop, headed for her car, jumped in and drove to the exhibition.

As Jessy drove, her thoughts turned to Zeke which in turn, warmed her heart. He had been like a brother to her. They had grown up together and over the years a strong bond had been formed. They could go anywhere and do anything together. They loved each other. He wasn't good-looking but one would have to go a long way to find a gem like him. He had such an adventurous spirit and a great sense of humor. Zeke had everything Jessy had always dreamed of except one truly important aspect – there just wasn't that physical attraction between them. She had sometimes wished and hoped that one day it would happen, but it never did. They had been friends and buddies for fifteen years. He was like her soul mate. She loved him more than anyone else in the world, except her family. They both thought if they felt like this, then surely they could feel the same about someone else, only in a passionate way.

Possibly that's why she hadn't found anyone at all because she was always comparing everyone to him. Zeke had an incredible love of life, something which nobody else had ever shown her. He did what he wanted to do regardless of what anyone thought. As long as it didn't hurt anyone he did it. They really did have some fun times together. People would turn their heads and give them such dirty looks while other eyes would light up jealously, wishing they had the courage to be themselves and to join in the fun. Zeke and Jessy didn't give a hoot about other people's reactions; they loved life.

She enjoyed reminiscing about the good times they had spent together, especially recalling the first time they had met and how stupid and immature she thought he was. But by the end of the day her impression had changed completely. She had judged him on sight, but once she realized how genuine he was Jessy loved him from that moment. She had never had so much fun before. The day ended with Zeke throwing her into a very large pond in the middle of one of the parks in the center of Salisbury, Rhodesia (now Harare, Zimbabwe). She had felt anger surge through her body and had wanted to throttle him but knew she had pushed him too far and she deserved what she got. He didn't take any of her nonsense as other men had done. When he realized she was a good sport and did not have a tantrum about it, he jumped into the water himself and helped her out like a true gentleman. But before he did, they decided to have a head-on water fight. They laughed so much she nearly wet her pants! The friend who had introduced them was in hysterics. From that day on the bond had formed, never to be broken by anything or anyone. They seemed to be on the same wavelength and often when Zeke was thinking something, Jessy would echo his thoughts. It was too consistent to be just a coincidence. What was it when people could read each other's minds? Was it possible perhaps, that Jessy and Zeke had channeled into the Collective Consciousness? There was a renowned prophet called Edgar Cayce who was known as the 'sleeping prophet'. He had lived in Virginia Beach, Virginia and from an early age, was able to channel into the spirit world. He would put himself into a trance and was able to answer all sorts of questions about health and illnesses, and yet how did he know all of this? His main objective in life was to help people, especially children.

The question is – where did this information come from? Many people believe in a Collective Consciousness where every thought and action is recorded and one day reviewed by us at death. It would appear that Edgar Cayce had a gift and he helped many people and never once asked for payment. When someone offers their services to humanity and never asks for anything in return, he/she is a true soul of the universe, here to serve mankind. He was surely a great teacher to us all. Perhaps on some level Zeke and Jessy were able to connect into these mysterious, unseen dimensions where people subconsciously know what the other is thinking. As the years went by, their bond grew stronger and stronger.

Well, Jessy thought to herself, *that's enough daydreaming for one day.* She found a parking spot and entered the building. As she had expected, everything was ready. Melodie was a star and Jessy was very fond of her. Melodie had been working for Jessy since she opened the shop and they had never had an argument in all those years. She was thirteen years Jessy's senior and had helped her a lot but she lacked whatever it took to be really good at designing. Perhaps it was confidence in her own ability that was her downfall. She was worth every penny Jessy paid her and Jessy knew it. When Jessy couldn't make it to work for some reason or another, all she had to do was to pick up the phone and call Melodie. She didn't have a second thought about work after that because she knew the shop was in very capable hands. She was wonderful with the customers as well as reliable and honest.

She walked straight into the hall and began talking to her waiting clients. She mingled for a while but was on the lookout for Zeke. There were a lot of comments flying around about Jessy's new exotic jewelry. Some were complimentary and some were rather taken aback by the variety and change in her work. Some of the responses were derogatory but Jessy never took them personally because she had a great respect for each person's taste and perceptions of life. The morning, on the whole, was good and many pieces were sold. A lot of orders were placed. There still was no sign of Zeke, and then, just as she had given up and most of the people had left, in he walked. They saw each other at the same time and smiled.

'I didn't think you were going to make it,' she said as she embraced him.

'Well, here I am. I wouldn't have missed it for the world. I've missed you,' he replied.

'It's nearly over but perhaps we could go to lunch,' she suggested.

'Those were my thoughts exactly. How about, I just take a quick look around here. I promise, no funny tricks, and then we can meet at our favorite place at one thirty,' he suggested.

'I'll be there,' she replied. They walked and talked as they wandered around and then Zeke left. When everyone had gone and the exhibitors were packing up, Jessy flopped into one of the chairs. She was glad it was all over. She had sent Melodie back to the shop to open up for the rest of the day's business. After a few minutes Jessy walked over to Cindy and Peter.

'I'm going to the shop. Could you finish off here please?' she asked.

'Sure,' they replied.

'You go off; we'll cope just fine,' Cindy added. So Jessy did just that and headed for the shop. She arrived at the shop door, opened it, and walked in. The aroma of freshly brewed coffee filled her nostrils. She saw Linda in the front shop busy arranging some of the showcases.

'Morning Linda,' greeted Jessy.

'Good morning. I've heard that the exhibition was a great success,' replied Linda with a smile on her face.

'Yes, I think it went very well,' Jessy replied as she walked through the door to the back workshop. There was Melodie and a few of the others sitting down and enjoying some coffee. They all looked up simultaneously.

'Hello, everyone,' called Jessy.

'You are just in time for some coffee; it's a fresh batch. Would you like some?' asked one of the assistants.

'Hmm, that sounds great; it was the first thing I smelled when I walked in the door. Thanks,' replied Jessy.

'Jessy, Michael has phoned you three times this morning. I told him you were still at the exhibition and that you weren't expected back until later,' said Melodie.

'Thanks, I'll call him when I get a free moment,' Jessy said.

Jessy sat with them at a central table which was their meeting place. They all chattered about the exhibition and other things that were going on in Cape Town. Although Jessy was there she found that she wasn't really listening. She finished her coffee and placed the cup down on the table. Standing up, she then flung her handbag over her shoulder and said, 'Well, thanks for the coffee. I am now on my way out; if anything urgent comes up I'll be at lunch and then at home,' and with that she slipped out the door.

'Bye Jessy, have fun!' everyone shouted behind her. They all thought the same thing; most unusual. Jessy never usually just left like that. They normally had to throw her out of the shop to send her home. Everyone looked at each other one by one, each in turn shrugging their shoulders.

'I don't know what's happened but I sure am thankful for whatever it may be. She needs some sort of personal life so let's hope there may be some truth in those words,' said Melodie. Everyone looked at her enquiringly for she was the closest to Jessy. If anyone knew, it would be her. They all waited for some kind of explanation from Melodie but it was not forthcoming. So after a few patient minutes had passed, they returned to their work, still wondering about Jessy.

Chapter Four

JACQUES WAS WOKEN BY SOMETHING wet and rough licking his cheek. He lifted his hand, ready to give whatever it was a good slap. But just in time he opened his eyes and realized it was only Scanty. For the first few seconds he wondered where he was and what was going on. Then he slowly woke up and remembered Jessica and how he had ended up in this strange house. There was a blanket on him and he knew that she must have put it over him while he was sleeping. What he couldn't understand was why he was lying on the floor in front of the fire. He could remember falling asleep on the bed but he didn't remember going into the lounge. Maybe he had just had too much to drink. He wasn't used to drinking and it must have gone straight to his head.

'Good morning Scanty, what do you want? How about a nice walk along the beach?' he said as he patted him on the head. Scanty wagged his tail wildly. Jacques moved his body and it felt rather stiff and sore. He decided to lie down for a while longer. He had put on Jessica's jersey before falling asleep and he could smell her.

He found himself dozing off only to be woken up by Scanty again. Scanty was relentless; Jacques should never have offered to take him for a walk, and he was already regretting it. He stroked Scanty as he made himself comfortable, sprawled across Jacques' chest. His face was facing Jacques'. He lay very still, pretending to be asleep. But every now and again he would open one eye just to see what reaction he was getting from Jacques. Jacques looked up at the grandfather clock that stood close to the front door. It was already eleven thirteen but he decided to have another few minutes rest before making a move.

He could hear the waves crashing against the rocks. It was a relaxing and soothing sound, one that made him feel peaceful. The sun was shining through the window filling the room with a purple haze, creating a mystic air. It was like walking through a mist with the sun shining through, but it was a purple mist. There was a large crystal hanging in the window, and as the sun kissed it, hundreds of rainbow lights collected on the ceiling and walls, displaying the chakra colors. It was so calming and Jacques found himself drifting off into the spiritual world where time was non-existent.

He was aroused and brought back to earth by Scanty scratching himself. He looked at the clock again thinking that he had only just popped off to sleep. But the clock said twelve forty nine and this time he forced himself to keep awake. He stretched his weary bones and muscles, and then pulled himself up into a sitting position. The room was a sun trap, warm and cozy. He still had Jessica's jersey on so he took it off. Jacques noticed a white envelope on the table where he had placed the jersey. His name was written on it so he picked it up and opened it.

'Jacques, please make yourself at home and help yourself to some food from the kitchen. I'll be back around six o'clock this evening. Have a good day and don't take too much nonsense from Scanty. I know what he can be like when he gets a bee in his bonnet.' Jacques read it out loud. 'Did you hear that Scanty; Jessy says you are to behave yourself today.' He lifted his eyes from the note and looked down at the dog. Scanty, of course, had that, 'You must be joking!' look, all over his face. But still Scanty lifted his head and propped his ears up, at least showing some respect for what Jessy was saying. He understood every word that Jacques had spoken. He barked twice, in disgust, at the idea of Jessy thinking he would be anything but good. He got up and walked like a drunken old man in the opposite direction. He really didn't want to hear any more of it. Jacques continued to read the rest of the note.

'You will be getting a visitor this afternoon at about one o'clock. Her name is Betty and she is my maid. If you are going out you will find a key on the entrance table. Don't worry about Betty, she has her own key and will let herself in. I have also left her a note explaining your presence in the house. She should be finished around five o'clock. See you later,' signed *Jessica*.

Jacques placed the note back on the table and decided to take a shower and shave. If he was going to have company he had better get a move on. Just as he was about to open the door, Scanty barked at the rattle of keys in the front door. Jacques walked towards the living area, but before he could say anything he heard a scream. He had obviously startled Betty.

'Who are you? What you doing here? How did you get into this house?' Betty shouted at him, backing up towards the door as she spoke, obviously ready to make an escape if it was necessary. Jacques smiled at her, hoping to calm her down before she headed out the door to perhaps call the police, which was the last thing he wanted to happen.

'Please, I don't want to hurt you. I am a friend of Jessica's. She has left a note for you on the table', he said and turned and picked it up to hand it to her. Jacques continued to explain his presence as she started to open and read the note. 'I am staying in the house for a while. Please don't be afraid,' he said in a quiet voice. He could see her starting to relax once she heard Jessica's name mentioned.

'My name is Jacques. I am pleased to meet you. Jessica has already told me your name is Betty. Hello Betty,' he said.

'Hello, Mr Jacques. I am sorry I screamed but I have never come into this house to find a strange man before. Miss Jessy didn't tell me anyone would be here,' she said apologizing.

'Please, hmm, just carry on with your work and pretend I'm not here,' Jacques said. She nodded in acknowledgement and headed for the kitchen.

Betty started to collect all the dirty plates and stack

them. She couldn't quite make out what was going on. *Where had this man come from? Was this Miss Jessy's new boyfriend?* Perhaps she would get some more details if she went to the bedrooms, so she did. As she passed the spare room she noticed that the bed had been slept in. So perhaps this man *was* just a friend because he hadn't spent the night in Miss Jessy's bed. She then went into Jessy's room and picked up the coffee cup which was always on her bedside table. She took it back to the kitchen and noticed that the dining room table was still set. There were wine glasses and coffee cups on the small table next to the fire. The duvet cover was lying over the couch. She then began to think that maybe they had slept in front of the fire. She couldn't decide what was going on. But whatever it was, she was happy for Miss Jessy. It was about time she had something in her life other than work. Betty had met Mr Michael, but she wasn't that crazy about him. She wasn't quite sure why because he seemed to love Miss Jessy. But, she had seen how Miss Jessy looked at him and it wasn't with an overwhelming sense of love.

The room smelled of stale smoke from the fire so she opened a few of the windows. The wind had dropped and it was a rather lovely day. She saw Jacques head for the kitchen and he began to rattle some crockery. Betty walked towards him.

'Mr Jack,' she couldn't quite pronounce his name but Jacques didn't mind. 'Would you like me to cook some breakfast for you?' she asked.

'Thank you Betty, but I really don't want to put you to any trouble,' he replied.

'Trouble? Oh no, no trouble for me; you see I like to cook. Miss Jessy has taught me how but I don't often get the chance because Miss Jessy likes to cook herself. Please, Mr Jack, if you hungry I cook breakfast for you,' she said excitedly and in her broken African-English.

How could he possibly say no to her. He was hungry and she was dying to cook.

'That would be lovely, thank you Betty. I must admit, I could eat a horse,' he replied laughing. 'Betty, do you think there would be time for me to take Scanty for a walk?' Jacques asked.

'Yes Mr Jack, you take Scanty for walk, he would like that. I still have lots of things to get ready. I must tidy this mess up first before I can start your breakfast'. It was better that he got out of the house and out of her way. He felt rather uncomfortable just being there. With those words he saw Scanty's ears prick up and out came an approving bark. Before Jacques had reached the door, Scanty was there waiting.

'You really do like your walks, don't you Scanty?' Jacques said as he opened the door. He looked around him and couldn't believe how beautiful it was. The sea was straight in front of them and the mountains were on either side. There wasn't a breath of wind and the sun was shining brilliantly. It was a magnificent winter's afternoon. He knew he was going to enjoy this walk as much as Scanty, if not more.

They didn't go to the beach where Jessica had found him. Instead, they went to the beach closest to the house. This was obviously a more popular one, with people swimming and others playing ball. Jacques picked up a small stick that was lying on the rocks and he threw it towards the ocean.

'See if you can fetch that Scanty!' he called. Scanty went off after it, picked it up and brought it back to Jacques. This game went on for a while, but Scanty soon got bored with it and headed off on his own. Jacques lay down on the sand. It was cold even though the sun was warm. As he lay there he could feel every part of his body coming back to life. It was as if his body was being recharged.

While he was enjoying the sun his thoughts returned to Jessica. He decided that he should do something for her. He was also feeling very guilty about the whole situation, but he could not let her know why. *Why couldn't she have just been a normal lady, and someone he did not find attractive?* He really didn't like the idea of what lay ahead, but as he saw it, he didn't have much choice.

His stomach was starting to rumble so he shouted for Scanty. They made their way back up the rocks and to the front door. He had forgotten to take the key to get back into the house so he knocked on the door.

'I was wondering when you would return. I have your breakfast ready for you. Sit down, I'll bring it to you,' she said as soon as the door had been opened. She had a wonderful bright smile with shining white teeth.

'Thank you Betty; it smells delicious,' Jacques said as he made his way to the table which had been set so beautifully. Fit for a King! He could see that she was really enjoying herself and he was pleased that he could oblige her. He sat down and poured himself a glass of fresh orange juice which looked and tasted as if it had been freshly squeezed. It was so refreshing that he drank it down and poured himself another one. He had no sooner finished that when Betty walked in carrying a hot plate of food in one hand. In the other was a plate with freshly made toast. She placed them down in front of him. As she did, Jacques noticed that she had a scar down the left side of her face. It was a nasty one and must have been a deep cut to have left such a prominent mark. Her skin was not black, but a tone lighter. Her eyes were a dark brown and her nose and cheeks were covered in small freckles giving her a very girlish look. Her nose was broad, but the tip was slightly pointed. She had very unusual features. Her hair had small tight curls and was dark in color. He liked her. There was happiness about her. As she placed the food on the table, Jacques got a whiff of it and couldn't wait to devour it.

'It smells really great; thank you Betty,' he said enthusiastically. She didn't walk away, but stood there to see what his reaction was to the first mouthful. He sensed that so he carried on with his meal. After the first bite he smiled and made an approving noise.

'This is *really* good,' he mumbled in between mouthfuls. Betty's whole face lit up and her smile beamed from ear to ear. She was now satisfied at the outcome and turned and walked back into the kitchen. Jacques could hear her banging and clanging as she went about her work. Every now and again he would make little approving groans at how wonderful the meal was. She had cooked bacon, pork sausage, mushrooms, French toast, fried tomato and eggs. Betty brought a freshly brewed pot of coffee in.

'I thought you would like some coffee Mr Jack' she said as she placed it on the table.

'Thank you Betty; that's just what I feel like,' he smiled.

As Jacques finished eating Betty was there ready to whisk the empty plate away from him.

'That really was delicious Betty. The best breakfast I have had in a long, long time,' he said, and that was not a lie. He hadn't eaten like that for years. He could see that she was delighted that there wasn't a single morsel of food remaining on his plate.

'Miss Jessy taught me when I first came here. She was so very busy with all her work she didn't have time to cook, and if I didn't make something for her she just didn't eat. She didn't seem to notice if it was morning or night. I cooked lots of hot meals for her. I would come in, even the days I don't work here, just to make sure that she was eating. I love Miss Jessy like my own; she's a real nice lady. She never once shouted at me and I have done some pretty silly things. But Miss Jessy, she just smiled and say, "It doesn't matter Betty, we can fix it. Accidents happen all the time." She then turned and walked away. Jacques got up and started to help her clear the table.

'No, Mr Jack, please, that my work. You please leave it for me. Thank you,' she said with a no-nonsense tone. Jacques got up from his chair and went over to the couch. He sat down next to Scanty who was now fast asleep. He noticed that the house had already been cleaned. She was good at her job and seemed happy with the work she did. Jacques turned on the radio that he had noticed earlier sitting near the front window. It took him a while to find a station that he understood. A lot of it was in different languages. He finally found a station that had some music he recognized. He flopped back into the chair and fell asleep. When he eventually awoke, he looked at the clock; it was now four o'clock. He stirred and got up out of the seat, looked in the kitchen for Betty, but she was nowhere in sight.

'Betty, are you still here?' he called out.

'Yes Mister Jack, I'm here,' she said, poking her head around one of the doors. Jacques walked towards her. 'Betty, is there anything around the house that I could fix? Something that maybe Jessica hasn't had time to get repaired?'

'Well, Miss Jessy *has been* wanting to get the garden tap fixed. It seems to drip, drip, drip, all the time. She doesn't hear it that often because it is normally the gardener who waters the garden. I know she has just forgotten about it,' she replied, wondering why he was asking such a question.

'I can take a look at it and see if I can stop the drip. Can you please show me where it is and where your tools are kept,' he said, pleased that he could do something for Jessy.

'Yes, certainly, come this way. There are lots of tools in the garage. Miss Jessy bought them all at once. She decided she was going to learn how to fix her car and anything that went wrong around this house. But that didn't last very long because as soon as something went wrong, she was too busy to find the time to do it. So she just called in other people to do it,' she said, leading Jacques into the garage which was accessed down a spiral staircase. It was a large garage; perhaps four cars could fit inside.

The sun streamed in, making it a perfect room for an artist or in this case, a jeweler. One wall was nothing but sliding doors. Betty led him to the other side where Jessica had the tools that Betty had been talking about.

'Here are the tools. Now come with me and I'll show you where this tap is that drip, drip, drip,' she said. She walked to a door on the side and unlocked it. She opened it and they walked out into a back garden. It was beautiful. He stood for a few seconds looking up. From there he couldn't see another house. The garden had been landscaped in such a way that even with all the elevated houses going up the mountain, nobody could look into the garden. There were magnificent old trees that had vines growing up their trunks. There were many varieties of shrubs that he had never seen before. Flowering plants bordered the edges, giving splashes of color everywhere. There was a birdbath set at the back of the garden where the birds were splashing and bathing themselves. It was like a secret garden, where one could escape and revel in the peace and solitude. Betty turned around to see where Jacques was.

'Come this way Mr Jack. The tap is in the middle of the garden,' she said. Jacques started to follow her again. They went through an archway that was covered with a flowering rose creeper, then past a bench which was under a large tree.

'There Mr Jack, there's the tap,' Betty said, pointing to it. It was hidden behind a large shrub to the side of the bench. Jacques walked over to it and noticed the continuous dripping. He was sure he could fix it if he could only find a washer.

'I must go back to my work, Mr Jack. You call me if you want me for anything else,' she said, looking at him.

'Thank you Betty. I'll go back to the garage and see if I can find what I need to stop the drip, drip, drip you talk about,' he replied, smiling to himself about her descriptive language for the leak. She turned and walked away. Jacques sat down on the bench while enjoying the serenity. He could still hear the roar of the sea below him. But the sound of birds was closer. He noticed a few squirrels playing in one of the nearby trees. As he sat there he could hear the rustle of leaves on the ground. He turned his head towards the house; it was Jessica. He hadn't even heard the car drive up the driveway. He jumped up to greet her but before he could say a word, she said, 'Hello Jacques. Betty told me you were in the garden. I believe you are going to fix the dripping tap that I have neglected for so long,' she said smiling.

'Hello Jessica, I didn't hear you arrive home. Well, I thought I would take a look at it. I'm sure it's just a washer that needs replacing so if you have the right part, the job will be done. I wanted to do something to return the kind hospitality you have shown me,' he said.

'Thank you, Jacques. That would be nice. How has your day been?' she asked.

'Well, I took Scanty for a walk to the beach and then ate a wonderful breakfast that Betty cooked for me,' he replied.

'She said you seemed very hungry. Let's go inside; it is starting to cool down,' Jessy suggested. So they both walked back towards the house, chatting about the day's events as they went along. Once inside they could smell the food that Betty had prepared for their evening meal. It made them both feel rather peckish. They arrived just in time to meet Betty who was getting ready to leave.

'Goodbye, Miss Jessy. Mr Jack I'll see you on Monday. I have put your food in the hostess trolley so it will keep hot until you are ready to eat,' she said.

'Thank you Betty. Have a good weekend,' replied Jessy.

'Bye Betty, and thank you for looking after me,' said Jacques.

They watched her leave and then went into the lounge and sat down. The sun was just starting to set over the ocean. The sky wasn't yet orange and red, but there were signs of it changing. Jacques didn't want to miss it. They sat in silence and watched as the sun became bigger and bigger as it dropped, changing from white to yellow to orange. The sky was gorgeous, portraying all the colors of the rainbow. If one had to try and capture these colors in a painting, it would look too false as they were so brilliant. This was truly a beautiful place and Jessica was very lucky to live there. The sun disappeared and dusk quickly set in as well as the cold air.

They decided to make a fire so Jessy agreed that it was

Jacques' turn. It was now about six fifteen and pitch-dark. The fire was made and they could feel the warmth from it. Jessy found a bottle of wine and proceeded to opened it.

Jessy told Jacques all about the exhibition and about her friend Zeke. She had been out with him since lunch-time. She had so badly wanted to tell him about Jacques, but she knew that would have been a bad move. She in fact, had not told anyone. She knew that they would have called her insane for taking a stranger into her house. Knowing Zeke the way she did, he would have been up to her house quickly to check out this 'Jacques'. So she had not mentioned him at all. But she had had a wonderful time with her friend and was glad that they had had lunch together. Zeke had sensed there was something on Jessy's mind but soon discovered, no matter how much he quizzed her, she wasn't sharing.

'There is something wrong or should I say different about you. I know you will tell me when you are ready but the nosy side of me would like to know now. I know you too well so don't deny it. I was wondering if you wanted to go to Sharon's party tonight. We could go straight from here. We haven't had a good dance for a long, long time,' he had said. She told him she couldn't and it was then that he knew there was something going on. So Zeke went to the party by himself and Jessy went home. She really would have loved to have gone to the party with him, but she wanted to go home to see Jacques.

'I'll pop in and see you next week. Drive home carefully,' he said. He kissed her on the cheek and said goodbye as she jumped into her car. Jacques listened very carefully as she spoke about, Zeke. He knew that she loved him very much and he felt glad that she had such a good friend.

Jessy started to feel quite exhausted. All the excitement of the day had suddenly gotten to her.

'Jacques, I really have to go and have a long bubble bath before dinner. Can you wait that long before we eat?' she asked.

'Sure, that's fine with me. I can wait; take as long as you want,' he replied. He watched her carefully as she got up to walk towards the bathroom.

She wore a navy blue skirt with a slit up the back seam. Her legs were long and slender and as she walked, the tops of them were revealed, giving Jacques a quick glimpse of each leg as she moved. Her hair had been put in a bun on the top of her head. As she walked, she slowly took out the pins that held it in place. As she removed the last one, her hair fell down her back. She shook it loose and it draped her back like a shawl, right down to her waist. He felt aroused. It looked soft and silky, and he longed to bury himself in it, smelling and touching it. Suddenly everything kicked into slow motion as he watched her walk towards the bathroom. Time seemed to stand still. Then he heard the sound of water, and Jessy walked back into the lounge, picked up her glass of wine and then disappeared back into the bathroom.

Chapter Five

BETTY HAD SET THE TABLE for them before she left, so there was really nothing for Jacques to do but keep the fire burning. He watched the flickering flames dance around the wood. Sometimes there were blues, sometimes whites and yellows. Fires really did have a hypnotizing effect on him. He didn't notice how long Jessica was taking because he had drifted off into his own little place where time didn't matter.

He pondered upon this thing called 'time'. Was it just a man-made concept? It seemed that time could be made to stand still, and at other times, fly by. He had experienced both. It was of course not a universal concept, but depending on one's frame of mind at any given moment it could be both. When one watches time it stands still. Yet, when one is so involved with something it flies by. His friend Dave once told him a story about an experience he had had during one of his karate lessons. Dave was attending a karate camp, and three groups took off on a hike, one after the other. The hike was three hours long. There was a guru in Dave's group who was leading his team. Dave kept looking back every so often to see how the other groups were doing and everyone seemed to be walking at the same speed. Then, sometime later, the strangest thing happened. Dave turned to check on the other groups, but none of them were in sight. He thought that perhaps they had stopped for a break. His group continued on the hike and when they came to their destination they arrived half an hour early. The other groups came in half an hour later. When Dave questioned his guru, he was told that "time is an illusion and when one thinks of it like that, one can make it stand still or speed up". Then, on the way home (the drive was four hours long and they did not travel any faster than normal) they actually arrived in *three hours*. So the question is, "Can time be slowed down if we know how?" Jacques often wondered about the "unexplainable". *Was there something the average layman just didn't grasp or never even knew existed, when in actual fact, it was open to everyone who only looked.*

He heard a door open and saw Jessy walk down the passage and into her bedroom. She only had a bath towel wrapped around her. Minutes later she came out of her room and walked towards him. She wore a satin tracksuit in multiple colors of pinks and blues. The colors suited her. She looked fresh and alive. As she walked towards him, he noticed that the satin clung to her body, revealing the outlines of her feminine figure. Her breasts were full and firm. Her nipples were still hard and protruding. She wore no bra and it showed. She was slim but shapely. He tried hard not to stare, but he couldn't stop looking. She noticed his stare and felt his attraction to her. She pretended not to notice.

'Shall we eat?' she asked, feeling self-conscious.

'Good idea,' he replied rather too enthusiastically and went through to the kitchen to help her. They removed the dishes from the hostess trolley and laid them on the table.

'I've got no idea what Betty has cooked. Let's take a look. Do you eat everything or are there some foods that don't agree with you?' she asked Jacques.

'I haven't yet found a food I dislike, well normal foods that is. I don't think I could bring myself to eat sheep's eyes,' he smiled.

'No, I couldn't either,' Jessy said, pulling a face as she spoke.

'It looks great,' he said and started to place a bit of everything on his plate.

'Well, she doesn't cook a large variety of foods but the meals she does produce are generally really tasty'. They talked all through the meal about a variety of things. At the end of the meal Jessy sat back in her chair.

'Jacques, have you remembered anything yet?' she asked in a more serious tone.

His face became rather grave and she knew she shouldn't have asked. She didn't want to upset him but something had to be done about it.

'Not a thing. At times I thought that things were

starting to appear. I get a flash of a place, but it just disappears again. The visions were too quick to be understood or make any sense of,' he replied sheepishly.

'It will come back, I'm sure. It just might take a while. Do you think that perhaps you should go and see a doctor? Maybe they can give you something to help the process along,' Jessy suggested.

'I'll leave it a few more days if that's alright with you. It's strange; I know how to fix the leaking tap. I suppose it's like, knowing how to walk and talk. Those sorts of things are embedded in you and become automatic even though we don't know how or why.' Jessy nodded in agreement with him. She sensed that he didn't want to talk about it so she dropped the subject. There was something troubling him, but she wasn't sure what it was.

'Let's go and sit in front of the fire, but first I'll put some coffee on. Would you like some?' she asked as she got up from the table, gathering some of the plates before walking through to the kitchen.

'Thank you,' he replied and followed her to the kitchen, carrying as many of the items from the table as he could. While she busied herself with the coffee, he finished clearing the table and then stacked them all in the dishwasher. As they sat and drank their coffee, Jessy just couldn't resist asking Jacques another question.

'Jacques, is there something troubling you that I could possibly help you with?' she asked. She knew he was worried about his memory but it wasn't that alone.

'Jessica, I don't know if I should burden you with my problems. I have caused enough trouble already. But

I really don't have anyone else to talk too. If I ask your advice, will you promise not to talk to anyone about this, not even your good friend Zeke?' he said confidentially.

'I promise I won't tell a soul, and if I can help I will,' she said, looking pensive.

'Just wait here a minute, I'll be back,' and he got up and walked towards his room. Within a few seconds he returned. He was holding an old leather pouch which he placed on the coffee table in front of him. It was about ten centimeters wide and fifteen centimeters high and it was obvious that there was something in it. It had been tightly packed and looked like one of those early pouches in which the gold-diggers would carry their gold. The leather was dark in color but had faded in places from normal wear and tear. Jessy couldn't decide if it was because of the dirt that had collected over the years, or whether that was its natural color. It was also very cracked, which would indicate that it was either extremely old or had been submersed in water for a long time.

She watched Jacques as he loosened the two draw-strings that held it together. It took him quite a while to undo them. They were very secure and it took him quite a while to undo them. Someone didn't want whatever was inside to come out. Jessy sat there fascinated and intrigued. She found it hard to control herself. She wanted to grab it out of his hands and undo it as quickly as possible. The excitement was just too much for her. Jacques finally opened it and lifted it up, deliberating before tipping the contents out onto the table. Brilliant multi-colored sparkles came pouring out of the pouch. Jessy could hear the clink, clink, clink, as they fell and landed onto the surface of the glass table.

Jessy's eyes grew bigger and bigger. She could not believe what she was seeing and didn't know what to feel; excited or frightened. She stared down at them for a second, then slowly lifted her hand and placed it in the middle of all the stones. As she touched them and felt their cold, hard surface, she knew then that it wasn't a dream. She picked up a few and held them in her open hand. Then she picked up each and every one with the other hand, inspecting them very carefully before placing them back on the table.

There in front of her was a magnificent variety of uncut diamonds. She didn't have a great knowledge of the value because they were uncut, although what she could see, from the color and the sizes, there was a large fortune right in front of her very eyes. She had never seen so many at one time, especially of that quality. She could only surmise that these quantities and qualities existed only in places like De Beer Diamond Mines where such gems were an everyday occurrence. Even when she had trained in some of the smaller shops she had never seen so many. She lifted her head and looked Jacques straight in the eyes. He held her stare.

'Jacques, where did you get these from?' she asked and picked them up in her hands again, trying not to show that she had a lump in her throat. She also tried to hide the fact that she was feeling uneasy about the whole situation.

'Jessica, I don't know. When I was washed up on the

rocks the other day, I discovered the pouch around my neck. Where they came from I have no idea, but that doesn't change the fact that I have them. What am I supposed to do with them?' he asked in a pleading voice.

'They are very strict in this country with people who are caught with uncut diamonds in their possession. With this amount on you they could put you away for life and throw away the key. You could hand them over to the authorities and tell them the whole story in the hope that they would believe you, but I doubt it,' Jessy suggested.

She had a terrible feeling that maybe Jacques had actually stolen them. He couldn't remember anything so it was a possibility. Jessy didn't want to believe he was that sort of person. A thief! They couldn't go to the authorities, not until he could remember where he got them. Even better still, how he managed to have them in his possession.

'Do you think they will believe me if I go to the authorities and hand them over? Surely they can't do anything to me?' he said, hoping she didn't think it was a good idea.

'Well, to start with, they could keep you in custody until they establish where they had come from. You see, if they *have been* stolen and you are in possession of them, then legally you are responsible for them. It won't matter to them whether or not you can remember. All they will be concerned with is how you got them,' she said in a firm, convincing tone.

Jessy got up and walked around the room for a few minutes. Jacques could see that she was deep in thought. She came back and sat down again.

'Jacques, I don't think we should involve the authorities just yet. Let's leave it a few days and see if you start to remember anything. In the meantime, we must think of other solutions that we might be forced to put into action,' she said.

'Well, if they are going to cause a lot of problems for us both, I would rather just throw them into the ocean and pretend they never existed,' said Jacques convincingly.

'That would be a silly thing to do as they are extremely valuable. Besides, we might discover that you own a large diamond mine somewhere and they are legally yours. Don't worry, things will work out,' she replied, trying to sound happy about her decision and that drastic measures were not necessary. She was starting to feel conscious of the stones and wondered what would happen if they should get caught. Perhaps this whole thing was a set-up.

Jessy had closed the curtains earlier and was now feeling rather relieved that she had done so. There was silence as they both stared at the diamonds; their minds reeling with all sorts of emotion. Just then there was a loud knock at the front door. They both jumped into the air. Jessy gave off a scream and quickly covered her mouth with her hand. She could feel the perspiration building up all over her body. The adrenalin was pumping madly through her veins and terrible images of jail flashed into her head. Perhaps it *was* a set-up and the police had been watching them. Maybe they had even been taping their conversation. She had openly advised him not to go to the police. She looked straight into Jacques's eyes for an answer but she got nothing back. He seemed as surprised as she was by the knock.

'Who could that be at this time of night?' she asked in a tight, quiet voice. Jessy never got visitors this time of the evening. This was just too much of a coincidence.

'I have no idea; perhaps it is one of your friends,' he replied rather hopefully.

'Jacques, put those stones away, in a safe place. Remember that what we have discussed tonight is not for anyone's ears other than ours. If anyone should ask you what you are doing here, you are visiting from Mauritius. My friend Pierre sent you over and I said it would be fine for you to stay here for a while,' she said. She looked over at Jacques and noticed that he had a startled look on his face. She hesitated for a second, wanting to ask him if he was all right, when the knocking on the door started again. Jacques picked up the stones, once he got over the initial shock of hearing Jessy say the name Pierre. He packed them safely back into the pouch and hid them away in his bedroom. Jessy walked towards the door, hoping that whoever it was wasn't expecting to be invited in. The knock came again, but this time it was louder and faster.

'I'm coming!' shouted Jessy. She opened the door gingerly, wondering if now her life would change forever.

'About time, what took you so long to get here?' asked the voice as she walked straight into the house. Jessy breathed a sigh of relief at the first word she heard. She knew it was her twin sister Patricia, even before she saw her.

'Patricia, it's you! This is a surprise. What are you do-ing on this side of the world? Why didn't you tell me you were coming?' asked Jessy. As Patricia brushed past her she noticed Jacques and stopped. Jacques looked at Jessica and then this other person. He couldn't believe his eyes. They were identical and he wondered how on earth he was going to know who was who. Jessy watched Patricia eyeing Jacques and knew that she could quite easily feel the same way as Jessy did about him. Patricia started to give a little cough, prompting Jessy for an introduction.

'Oh, excuse me. Patricia, I would like you to meet a friend of mine, Jacques. Jacques, I would like to introduce you to my twin sister Patricia,' she said. They both walked towards each other and shook hands.

'I am pleased to meet you,' he said in his French accent.

'The feeling is mutual, I can assure you,' Patricia said in a sweet admiring voice. Jacques looked into her eyes, but he could see that they didn't have the same warmth that Jessica's had. Patricia used her looks to get what she wanted and that was obvious to him. Jessy felt perturbed at the fact that Patricia was behaving the way she was, but it was something that had happened many times in their lives. Patricia had often made a move for Jessy's boyfriends but invariably Jessy forgave her, and Patricia had always promised not to do it again. Jessy believed that she really didn't know she was doing it until it was too late.

Jessy had always been the one who accomplished whatever she set out to do. On the other hand, Patricia seldom did; mainly because she just didn't have the staying power and determination that Jessy had. She was always getting into fights at school, and more often than not, they were caused by Patricia. Jessy put her arm around Patricia and led her towards the couch. Although they had had their differences in the past, the fact remained that there was a strong bond between them, so strong that hate and jealousy could never break it.

Patricia held a great deal of anger inside her; almost like a negative streak that would often rear its ugly head when she least expected it. She had tried to fight it all her life and there were times when she truly despised it. Jessy had seen it so often in her, and felt sad at her struggle. She had never spoken to her sister about it because it was too delicate a subject, and to admit to having such anger would probably be too much for her to handle. Patricia had learned to cope with it, and for some reason, chose to ignore it rather than get help.

Jacques sat down in the armchair across from them. Jessy and Patricia did most of the talking. He sat and listened to them reminisce about their childhood, the fun and mischievous things they had gotten into, and managed to get away with because they were twins. People battled to tell the difference between them. Only their closest friends knew them apart.

They hadn't seen each other for six months. Patricia had been transferred to Johannesburg and was travelling on business. She was only there for three days but hoped she would be coming down more frequently.

'I was just about to make some fresh coffee; would you like some too Patricia?' asked Jessy.

'That sounds wonderful; I thought you were never going to offer,' she replied. Jessy got up and went to the kitchen to make the coffee. Patricia turned all her attention to Jacques.

'So, where are you from?' questioned Patricia in a polite manner.

Jacques had to be very careful about what he said. He didn't know a lot about Mauritius. Not even enough to fool her if she had been there and knew the place. The fact that Jessy seemed to know quite a bit meant that Patricia might have also been there. Perhaps they had visited there a lot when they were holidaying as children. What was he going to do? He had to go with Jessy's story and trust that she knew what she was thinking when she told him what to say.

'I am from Mauritius. I met a friend of Jessica's over there and he asked me to come over to drop off a few things for her, so here I am,' Jacques said. He answered very confidently with no hesitation of doubt about what he was saying.

'I've heard it's a very beautiful island. Jessy has been there but I haven't had the opportunity. Perhaps I'll drop in and see you sometime,' she said. Jacques breathed a sigh of relief.

'Sure, I'll leave my address with Jessica,' he replied smiling. That was a close call. Patricia didn't even know anyone who was from there.

'Do you like living in Johannesburg?' he asked, changing the subject quickly.

'No, not really, but it won't be for much longer. I

plan on going on a world trip next year. That's if all goes according to plan,' she said. Jacques got the feeling that there was more to this little visit than he knew about. *Why did she make it sound as if he knew what she was talking about?* He became suspicious. He would have to keep a beady eye on her.

'Well, I think you will enjoy that. It's something many people would like to do and never get the opportunity. But, if you can afford to, than that is great. Have you done much traveling?' he asked.

'No, I'm afraid I haven't. I was supposed to go to Europe with Jessy years ago, but I got involved in something and had to cancel the trip. I think I'll always regret not making the effort and changing my plans,' she replied, with sadness in her voice. Just then Jessy appeared with the coffee.

'There you are, fresh from the pot,' said Jessy. Jacques sighed with relief. They drank the coffee and then Jacques got up and looked at them both.

'I am feeling rather tired and I'm sure you ladies have a lot of catching up to do, so if you don't mind, I'll bid you au revoir,' he said.

'That's fine, au revoir Jacques,' said Jessy. Patricia also bid him goodnight and Jacques made his way to his bedroom. No sooner had he closed his bedroom door when Patricia turned her head towards Jessy and in a whisper said, 'So, where did you find this hunk and are you involved with him?' she asked inquisitively.

'No, I am not involved with him. He is a client of Pierre's and yes, he is a hunk, but this is business. You should know me better than that,' replied Jessy, closing the subject and moving on to other topics of conversation. Patricia didn't push the subject because she could sense that Jessy wasn't ready to share any information at this point.

They talked into the early hours of the morning about the "good old days" when they were growing up. Patricia told her that she could only stay the night because she would have to leave in the morning. She had a few things to do up the coast, but she would be back in a few days. Then she would have to head back to Johannesburg.

'Will Jacques be here when I get back? That should be by Tuesday,' she enquired.

'I really don't know what his plans are. You will have to wait until you come back to find out,' Jessy said. They gave each other a quick hug and both went off to bed.

Jessy tossed and turned all night despite feeling exhausted. Her mind was too active to allow her to drop off to sleep. She found herself thinking of all sorts of ways to help Jacques. After a while, she decided the only way to get rid of the stones was to have them cut. Then, at least they were legal and Jacques couldn't get put into jail. There was however, another big problem. It wasn't that easy to find diamond cutters who would cut those stones without asking any questions. They might have to spread them out and cut them over a long period of time. Once cut, they could then be sold off individually or set into jewelry. She would have to speak to Klaus; he was the only one she could trust. If word got out that there were uncut diamonds floating around, there would be trouble.

Klaus was respected in the jewelry business world and he had many contacts overseas. She knew he would have a solution. She just didn't want him to get involved if he thought they were taking too big a risk of being caught. If that were the case, then the only other thing to do was to throw them into the ocean.

She wondered why she was doing all of this for Jacques. She hardly knew him, yet she was prepared to risk all. It must be either stupidity or love. Gradually she drifted off to sleep.

Chapter Six

Jessy's alarm woke her. She rolled over and turned it off; sorely tempted to go back to sleep. She didn't have anything to do at the shop today. Well, nothing that was that important. But then she remembered Patricia and she had promised to wake her up. Besides, she wanted her out of the house before she could get her hands on Jacques again. Jessy really had to give Jacques a more detailed description of Pierre and his business in Mauritius, just in case Patricia started to ask more questions. She knew her well; too often Miss Patricia had gone snooping around in other people's business. They must be able to collaborate their stories.

This time they were lucky but they might not be the next time. She jumped out of bed and went to wake Patricia. They both dressed, had breakfast together and then Patricia headed off for work. She had rented a car which was parked outside. As Jessy walked her to the car, she was shocked to see she was driving a Porsche.

'Gee Patricia, that's a fancy car. Surely the firm doesn't hire cars like this for you,' she said admiring the car.

'Well, yes they did. They said I could have whatever I wanted, so I did just that. Isn't she beautiful? She drives so well.' She opened the door and slid into the front seat, almost banging her head on the ceiling as she got inside. They said their goodbyes and Jessy went back inside. As she walked upstairs to the front door, she wondered why Patricia's company would let her hire any car she had wanted. Had Patricia gotten a promotion that Jessy didn't know about? It was unlike her not to tell Jessy. Her company had hired cars for her before, but there had always been a limit on her spending. As she walked inside, her thoughts of Patricia drifted away. She was about to gather her things together and head out when she heard noises coming from Jacques' room. He walked out, still looking half-asleep.

'Good morning,' she said to him.

'Good morning; is Patricia still here?' he asked.

'No, she isn't. She left a few minutes ago. I think we got lucky last night. She doesn't seem suspicious at all. We will have to discuss a plan later,' she replied. Jessy started to smile to herself.

'What are you smiling at?' Jacques asked, giving himself a good stretch.

'Just thinking about last night and the terror I felt. It seems kind of funny now, but it wasn't that funny at the time,' she said. And with that Jacques and she both started to laugh. They eventually calmed down.

'I've been thinking about it a lot and I think I will ask a good friend of mine if he could get the stones cut. That way, at least you can still keep them until you remember where they came from. What do you think?' she asked, feeling quite good that she had come up with such a good plan.

'That sounds great, but I don't have any money to give you,' he said looking embarrassed.

'Well, that's easy enough; you can pay for it with some of the stones. I really don't know a lot about the cost of cutting diamonds, but I know that your stones are worth a fortune,' Jessy replied.

'That would be great! I just don't want you or your friend to get into any trouble,' he said breathing a sigh of relief.

'Well, that's why I must talk to Klaus first. He will know which path to take. Now that's enough about that. Would you like some coffee? It's still hot,' she asked.

'Thanks, I'll just go and get some clothes on,' he said, turning his back and walking away.

Jessy was sitting on the seat at the bay window which overlooked the ocean, drinking her coffee and deep in thought when Jacques walked towards her.

'What are you thinking about Jessica?' he asked politely.

'I was thinking what a beautiful place this is. There's not a day that goes by that I don't look out over the ocean and thank my lucky stars. I honestly love it and never take it for granted. I have lived in Australia and seen a lot of Europe, but my heart always returns here. The country has lots of problems, but I can tell you, so does most of the world. If it's not one thing, it's another. I suppose it depends on how you look at life and the problems that exist,' Jessy said pensively.

Jacques sat and listened. He hadn't really thought about the situation. They sat in silence for a while, enjoying the view and the peace.

'Well, how would you like a trip into Cape Town? I have to go and see Klaus this morning, to see if he can help us. Now that I know you are "rich", perhaps you could buy yourself some clothes and whatever else you need? I'll lend you some real money until you get sorted out,' she said laughing.

'I would like that very much. I've heard that Cape Town is a beautiful city, built beneath Table Mountain. Don't ask me how I know that, but I do,' he added quickly before she could ask him if his memory had come back.

They got ready and drove to town. Jacques sat very quietly, admiring the scenery as they went. They were soon in the heart of the city and Jessy parked just outside the shop. She had given him some money just before they left the house, as well as a map of the city, just in case he got lost.

'I'll meet you back here in about an hour,' said Jessy. She could see he was looking at the street signs to see exactly where he was.

'Sure, that's fine, I'll be here. I take it that this is your shop. Should I wait inside if you are late?' he asked.

'Yes, this is she. That's a good idea because I'm not sure if I will have to wait to see Klaus. Sometimes on Saturdays he has clients in his shop,' she replied. They both smiled at one another and went their separate ways.

Jessy watched him as he walked down the street. He walked straight. His strides were long and confident. His arms moved very little as he strode along. His body was firm and muscular and her heart pounded wildly. Within minutes he had disappeared into the crowd. She turned, went into the shop and said her good mornings. She told her staff that she was expecting someone called "Jacques" to arrive and should he get there before her, they were to give him some coffee while he waited. She went into her office and picked up the phone and phoned Klaus. He was happy to hear from her and they arranged to meet in twenty minutes. That was just about enough time to walk up to his shop.

'I'll be back in about an hour,' she told her staff.

'Jessy, Michael phoned again this morning and wanted to know where you were,' said Penny.

'Thanks, I'll phone him when I get back,' she said. She walked out and headed up towards the top of town. It was about ten blocks up but it wasn't worth taking her car because she knew she would battle to find parking space. Besides, she enjoyed the exercise, something she didn't get too much of these days. She had forgotten to check her answering machine at home and thought to herself that she must really make an effort to return his calls. She would do that this weekend, definitely.

Town was buzzing with people and cars. It seemed like the whole world was shopping today. Klaus worked in the upstairs of an old building that should have been demolished years ago. But it was an exquisite piece of old architecture. It was now on the restoration list of buildings that the city had undertaken to help finance. It was a wonderful idea, and it helped keep the age of the city intact. Sometimes the council came up with good ideas, but on the whole they really didn't do as much as they should. She arrived at the door and rang the buzzer.

'It's Jessy,' she sang as she leaned into the buzzer. The door flung open and she walked up the narrow staircase, closing the door behind her. At the top of the stairs she entered a passageway and turned left. Klaus' office was the second door on the right. She felt happy as she walked inside.

'Good morning everyone!' she called as she walked past his employees and straight into his office as if it were her own. Jessy knew everyone there and they knew that their boss regarded Jessy as his "daughter". He was sitting at his workbench, so she walked up to him and kissed him on his balding head. She had been doing that for years. It was one of their "things".

'Hello Klaus,' she said happily.

'It's lovely to see you; where have you been lately? You have such a sparkle in your voice; what have you been up to?' he asked mischievously. He had grown to have a good understanding of Jessy. She felt as if she couldn't hide anything from him; he was so perceptive about many things.

'Well, as a matter of fact, I *have* been up to something but you can't meet him yet. I am keeping him all to myself,' she said with a cheeky smile on her face.

'As long as you aren't talking about that Michael chap,' he replied, not getting too excited about it.

'No, no it's not. But I *have* come for some advice,' she said, backing up towards the office door and closing it. That pricked his curiosity. He carried on with his work, pretending not to take her too seriously. He had one eye supporting his magnifying glass as he inspected a pile of stones in front of him. .

'Please Klaus, this is serious,' she said. He immediately took the glass out of his eye socket and looked up at her. He smiled, trying to make her feel a bit more comfortable. Two large dimples appeared on both his cheeks, giving him a smile and the whole-world-smiles-with-me look. Klaus was a down-to-earth kind of guy with no hang-ups and no airs and graces. A no nonsense person and she loved him to pieces.

He had come to this country twenty years ago from Denmark, not being able to speak a word of English, but he knew a great deal about stones and jewelry. He had worked with his father in a workshop in Denmark, had started at the bottom and worked his way to the top. He knew everything there was to know about metals, stones, gems and everything pertaining to jewelry. He had a passion for his job and it reflected in his work. Jessy knew that he was the finest jeweler in town. She was always getting him involved in sideline deals. He did them mostly for Jessy for he really didn't need more work.

He loved the unknown about her. He never knew what she was going to do next; the things she would come up with and get him involved in. He would chuckle to himself every time he recalled some of them. *What was it, this time?* he thought.

'Well Klaus, you know me too well. I have come to brighten up your day.' He could tell by the tone in her voice that this was not just one of her normal deals, this sounded different.

'This doesn't sound like one of your normal deals to me, but with that sparkle in your eyes, what am I to think? Come on, don't keep me in suspense any longer. Spill the beans,' he said, feeling intrigued. She had his attention!

'I would like to know how easy it would be to get rid of a large quantity of uncut diamonds. If difficult, then how easy would it be to get them cut?' she asked, observing his facial expression at the mention of uncut diamonds. He was silent for a few seconds and then he looked at her with a small frown on his face.

'Jessy, I don't believe I am hearing this from you. You know how dangerous it is to be uttering those words. Without the necessary documentation, it wouldn't just be the normal fines inflicted upon you; it would mean life imprisonment. I hope you are talking hypothetically of course. Tell me what is going on before I tell you anymore,' he said. Jessy could feel the tension building up between them. He was obviously extremely concerned about her and understandably. For a split second she wondered what on earth she was doing asking such stupid questions. She must be mad! She knew nothing about Jacques and there she was, asking her good friend to help her, putting years of his hard work and toil on the line. She was confused and bewildered with the emotional feelings that ran through her.

'Klaus, I don't want you to get involved in something dangerous. All I know is that I have a friend whom I must help. I just thought you could put me in touch with someone who could help him,' she said. As she spoke, Klaus could sense that she meant what she said. This person must be very special to her and that was good enough for him.

'Little one, I will help you, but before I can, you must show me the stones. It is very difficult to do anything before I know what I am dealing with. There are ways and means to get rid of everything, but your friend must be told to keep very quiet. Can he be trusted, and are you sure this isn't a set-up? How well do you know this person?' he asked with concern.

'Klaus, I haven't known him long, but I feel as if I have known him my entire life. This must sound crazy but it's what I feel and I know this isn't a set-up' she said with tenderness in her voice.

'Well, that's fine with me; if you think it's safe and he can be trusted, then so do I,' he said.

'Thank you Klaus, I knew you would understand and help me,' she said, putting her arms around his shoulder.

'I'll bring them for you to see and then we can discuss everything,' she said, now wanting to change the conversation.

They moved onto a lighter topic and Klaus ordered them some coffee. The two friends talked for a while and then Jessy excused herself and went back to her office. She looked around very carefully as she left his place, just in case someone had been watching Klaus' office. He had been "busted" a few times in the past, but they never found anything suspicious about his business. He was an honest man and had a good reputation; she hoped that she wasn't about to tarnish it.

As Jessy left the office, Klaus was left with a sick feeling in the pit of his stomach. He had to remind himself that Jessy was a good judge of character and that she was also very sensible. He hoped that she hadn't been blinded by love. That sparkle in her eyes wasn't something he had seen before. He loved her and would do anything for her but he would have to check things out very carefully before going into this venture with her. With those last thoughts he went back to work.

Chapter Seven

Jessy was late getting back to the shop. Jacques was already there, waiting for her. As she walked inside, her assistants were not behind the counters, but staring glassy-eyed at Jacques. She felt like chasing them away, but instead walked casually up to them.

'Hello everyone,' she said as she grabbed Jacques by the arm and beckoned him to follow her. Jacques stopped talking, excused himself and looked at Jessica.

The staff could feel the electricity sparking between them. There was something about the way they looked into each other's eyes that had everyone convinced there was magic between them. Yes, they were in love, whether they realized it or not. They had never seen her like this with any of the men she had dated. She was normally so blasé. Jessy could take them or leave them; it never bothered her. They approved of her taste and had to admit he was worth waiting for. Jessy and Jacques walked into her office.

'Did you enjoy your walk around the city?' she asked.

'It was very pleasant and I managed to get quite a few clothes. At least I won't have to borrow anymore of your brothers'. It would have been embarrassing if they had turned up at your house and there I was, wearing their clothes,' he said smiling, and rather relieved that he didn't have to explain to her brothers *why* he was wearing them. It might have resulted in some awkward questions that he did not want to answer right now.

'Are you hungry? It is such a lovely day. I would like to take you to a very special restaurant,' she said excitedly.

'I'm starving; it sounds good, let's go,' he said, lifting up all the shopping bags. She picked up her handbag and they walked out of the office together. While on their way to the restaurant, Jacques looked seriously at her.

'Jessica, there's just one thing. I insist that I pay for the meal,' he said in a grave tone. Jessy was just about to say that that would not be necessary when she looked into his eyes and knew that she must accept his offer gracefully. She really didn't mind paying for the meal, but she stopped herself. She understood that it was important for Jacques to feel that he was in some way contributing to this relationship, or whatever they could call it. She realized that he was a proud man and he really needed to do this.

'That would be lovely, thank you Jacques,' said Jessy politely.

They drove up the mountain until they could drive

no further, parked and walked a short distance to a cable car. They jumped inside and it was not long before it started moving up towards the top of Table Mountain. Jacques didn't say a word. He could see for miles in front of him, right out to sea. Jessy pointed out some of the local sights from the air.

There was something different about her and Jacques couldn't quite figure out these intense emotions of love that he was feeling towards her. She was sensible, reliable and capable, but there was a certain wildness within her which contradicted what one really thought about her. He found it intriguing and attractive. He was starting to believe that she was a law unto herself. Jessy was looking out over the mountains and as she drew closer to them, they seemed to fill her with an energy, giving her strength. She felt as if they were alive, almost giving them a godly presence.

The cable car arrived at the top with a bang. They were ushered out and then ventured over to the restaurant. It was a lovely stone building with ivy which clung to the walls. It was busy inside but luckily Jessy spotted a free table near the fire. They lost track of time and were oblivious to all that was going on around them. Nobody else seemed to exist except themselves. The waiter had to interrupt their reverie to settle their bill as the last cable car was ready to leave. They apologized, hurriedly paid the bill and left.

They drove home still talking and laughing. It was starting to get dark. Jessy made a fire and they sat in front of it, still continuing their conversation. They discussed what Klaus had told Jessy. She was going to phone him tomorrow to set up a time for them to meet. It would have to be somewhere other than his shop. Somewhere where he could inspect the stones; somewhere where it was quiet.

Jacques thanked her again for her help. Jessy just hoped that she hadn't been blinded by her feelings for him, thereby putting her dear friend and herself in jeopardy. Jacques had said that he would leave it up to her and whatever she decided would be fine.

She sensed that he was watching her every move and gesture. When she had finished talking, and telling him about Klaus, she looked him straight in the eye. They could no longer contain themselves. He leaned over and kissed her gently on the lips; they were soft and moist. He kissed her again, but this time more passionately, feeling the blood rising inside him. He put his arms around her shoulders and Jessy placed hers around his waist. They were both tingling all over and the excitement was rushing through their bodies. His hands slowly moved down her arms, feeling the baby-soft skin. He kissed her neck and her hair covered his face as she moved into his kisses.

There was something tantalizing and feminine about her long hair. It was exquisitely soft and it gave him a warm feeling inside. As he ran his fingers through it, it aroused him and he slowly undid the buttons on her blouse, kissing her as he worked his way down to the last button. Her bra was silky to the touch and he undid the clasp in the front. He slowly moved one side of the bra away, revealing her breast, which was firm but soft.

His mouth moved towards it and Jessy gave a small sigh of enjoyment at his touch. His tongue moved around her nipple. He could feel it harden in his mouth. His other hand was taking off the other side. He then moved towards the other breast and began kissing her gently.

Jessy pulled his shirt up his back. He took it off and she could feel and smell his body. She could feel the strength of his arms and chest. He unzipped her skirt and it dropped to the ground. He slowly slid his hand down to her thighs which were soft to the touch. She undid his pants and as they dropped she could feel his penis, hard and firm. She couldn't remember how long they caressed each other as time seemed to have stood still. She knew he was inside her and each movement was slow and strong. He was on top of her, she was on top of him, until both reached an orgasm together. She had never reached heights like this before.

They lay in each other's arms on the floor. They didn't say anything, still living within the feelings of love. They both drifted off to sleep. Jessy woke some hours later, feeling cold. She got up and went through to the bedroom and brought back a down duvet from her bed. She lay down beside Jacques again and went back to sleep. That night was a night she would never forget. She could now say, 'I have loved.'

They were woken in the morning by the sun streaming through the windows. Jacques woke first and lay looking at Jessy and thinking how beautiful she was. He had mixed feelings about it all. He was feeling sad and happy at the same time.

Jessy opened her eyes to see him looking down at her and she smiled. 'Hi there, have you been awake for long?' she asked. He leaned over and kissed her.

'No, not long,' he said and kissed her again.

At the touch of Jacques' hand, Jessy found her heart pounding and she wanted him to love her. He moved his hand down her back and then around to her breasts. He caressed them gently and she could feel them harden to his touch. Her head went back and he kissed her neck, still fondling her breasts, now with both hands. He moved down to them and kissed one, then the other. His hands moved down between her legs and she could feel the moisture that had suddenly appeared. Their foreplay was both exciting and passionate, each driving the other crazy with love. He played with her tenderly and lovingly. She wanted him so badly that she never wanted it to end.

She found his ear and kissed it passionately, while her hands went down to his groin. She felt his buttocks, they were firm. They made love again and again with an insatiable appetite for each other. They wanted as much of each other as they could get. They felt as if they had known each other all their lives. There was such a familiarity between them. They belonged to each other and they both knew it, even though it was never said.

Jessy had often wondered about soul mates and if in fact there was only one, or were there many? She tended to believe in the latter. She was once told that there were soul groups and lifetime after lifetime they would meet. They would help one another in their soul growth, pushing the buttons to stimulate the necessary options for this growth to happen. Of course, one had to believe in reincarnation to fully grasp that concept. She had read a lot about reincarnation, and thought it made a lot of sense. Why would we think that *this* is the only life, and then we die. What would be the purpose in that? And with those thoughts, she drifted off into the dream world.

Jacques too fell asleep, but this time they were woken by Scanty barking at them.

'Okay Scanty, I hear you. You hungry?' she asked. Scanty barked in reply. Jessy rose and walked towards the bathroom.

'Jacques, I am going to have a bath and then I'll fix you and Scanty some breakfast,' she said before entering the bathroom.

'Great,' said Jacques sleepily. Jessy bathed and then Jacques went through and had a shower. Jessy prepared breakfast and they sat in the back garden to eat. After breakfast Scanty started barking again.

'I think he is trying to tell us that he needs some attention. Perhaps we should take him for a walk,' advised Jacques.

'Good idea,' Jessy said, looking at Scanty, watching his tail wagging from side to side.

They walked down to the beach where Jessy had found Jacques. They walked hand-in-hand, love filling every part of their being. They sat on some rocks and watched the waves roll in. Jacques suddenly felt very blue and wondered where this would end.

'Jessica, I want to say that last night was magic. No matter what happens you must never believe anything different. Please believe me. This comes from the bottom of my heart.' He said it while looking her straight in the eye. She was about to reply when he put his finger up to her lips. Jessy wasn't quite sure what to make of his words. She was glad that he felt the same as her, but she sensed he was holding something back. They sat in silence and Jacques' mind went back in time. He wanted so badly to forget his past and start his life as from today, but he knew that wasn't possible.

Chapter Eight

IT WAS AN EXTREMELY HOT day and the sweat was dripping down Arthur's face. The heat was unbearable in South West Africa but today it was hotter than normal. Arthur sat in his swivel chair, staring out across the bleak stretch of desert. The heatwaves were visibly shimmering above the sand. He could almost see the isolated shoots of grass shriveling up under the burning hot sun, helplessly trying to bury themselves back into the desert soil.

Arthur had been living in Oranjemund for fifteen years and he still had not adapted to the heat. He originally hailed from England and had come to the conclusion that he would never get used to it. He had often wondered why he had wasted half his life in such a hellhole, yet, there were a lot of people who would give their right arm to be in his position. He had reached a time in his life when he knew he had to move on, but didn't want to walk away empty-handed; he wanted something in return. Just then the phone rang and it startled him. He had been expecting a call from a friend in Cape Town. There was an excited voice on the other end of the phone.

'Hello Arthur, it's Dave. I have some great news. I've managed to find just the person we've been waiting for. There is a letter in the post telling you all about her,' he said. There was silence for a second but Arthur knew exactly what he was talking about. They both knew that they could not say too much over the phone. Although Arthur was the manager of this diamond mine, that didn't mean that the phones hadn't been bugged. Security was tight and nobody ever managed to get any diamonds out without being caught.

Most of the workers on the mine spoke very little of the diamonds. The word "diamonds" was taboo to them. Those who were caught stealing were taken away, never to be seen again. Where they were taken to nobody knew and nobody ever came back to tell their story. Some say they were taken to one of the deserted islands and left to die. Others surmised that they were killed and buried in one of the many no-name cemeteries scattered all around the desert. Then there were those who thought that perhaps they had been jailed and remained there for the rest of their lives. But all of those options put the fear of God in them.

'As long as she has lovely legs and big boobs, she'll do me,' replied Arthur. He could picture Dave's boyish face, on the other side of the world, smiling to himself.

'Oh, she's all that and much more. Give me a ring

once you've received the letter. There is a photograph of her in the post,' Dave replied.

'Thanks buddy. I'll call you soon,' he said and hung up the phone. Arthur and Dave had been friends for thirty years. They had spent many long, lonely nights around campfires drinking Old Brown Sherry and plotting ways to make their fortunes. They both agreed, three years ago, that this plan they were about to put into action was their only chance of ever getting rich.

Dave had left the mines and gone to live in Cape Town, with the hope of finding the "right person" for the job. A few times over the years he thought the right one had come along but at the last minute, found dreadful flaws in their character and the whole thing had had to be scrapped. But Dave felt quite sure that this time it was all going to happen. He had scrutinized her thoroughly and had been informed of all the details by someone very close to her.

As Arthur replaced the receiver, he found himself shaking. Whether it was nerves or excitement, he wasn't sure. This is what he had been waiting for, but now that the time was near, he knew there was no turning back once they put everything into play. It was all or nothing, getting rich or going to jail. His thoughts were abruptly interrupted by a heavy knock on the office door. One of his guards walked in.

'Sir, there has been trouble down in the third shaft. Two men have been fighting and one is badly hurt. Come quickly,' he said in a rush. Before Arthur could reply, the guard swiftly turned and ran out the door, beckoning

Arthur to follow. Arthur jumped up and raced after him, leaving all thoughts of his scheme behind him. But before leaving he picked up his gun and pushed it into his holster. As they ran out to the third shaft he questioned the guard.

'How did this all start?' he asked, puffing as he tried to keep up.

'Sir, we aren't sure what happened, but it was Pierre and Wyman,' he replied.

'That figures; those two have been at each other's throats ever since they started working together. I would guess that it was Wyman who started it. Any excuse to throw a punch at Pierre wouldn't slip by Wyman,' said Arthur.

They got into the cable car that took them down to the third shaft. There was silence as they were taken down beneath the earth. As they got further and further into the mine, Arthur smelled the smell he knew so well, and that was so familiar to the workers who toiled down there. It was a rich earthy, stone smell. He could taste it on his lips as it was so strong and fresh. It was a unique smell; one that could only be found in mines that went to such great depths below the earth.

He was rather glad that he didn't have to work down there because he found that when he returned he had a dusty, tickly sensation in his throat. He always associated it with the dust and damp air that was circulating in the tunnels. It really wasn't very healthy, but there was little that could be done about it. Besides, the men got used to it and it never seemed to bother them, as it bothered

Arthur. But for all the negative associations with the mines, whenever Arthur was down in the tunnels, it was an amazing feeling. To be so far down and actually be able to walk inside Mother Earth, never ceased to amaze and excite him. It was something he would never forget and it was something he felt everyone should experience.

He could hear the shouting and cheering as they neared the bottom. Arthur couldn't help thinking to himself that it must be a good fight.

As they hit rock bottom, the lift came to an abrupt halt and jolted them. The tunnels were lit up by the lamps that were placed strategically every five meters down each tunnel.

'This way sir,' the guard said to Arthur as he pointed down the left-hand tunnel. Arthur nodded and the two headed towards the direction of the noise.

Arthur thought, as he walked, that Wyman had been the leader of the workers ever since he had arrived on the mine. That was some eight years ago and he was respected by all, or rather feared. Nobody ever challenged him. He was built like an ape and weighed two hundred and fifty pounds, towering above everyone. Nobody that is, until Pierre's arrival.

Pierre didn't care who or what Wyman was; he had seen how cruel he was to his fellow workers and despised men who took advantage of the old and weak. Wyman had pushed his weight around once too often and this time Pierre wasn't taking any more nonsense. Pierre was six inches shorter than Wyman and weighed fifty pounds less, but that didn't seem to worry him. Pierre saw red and let loose. Within seconds of the first punch there were a hundred miners around them. Everyone was cheering for Pierre. They had been waiting for this moment for a long time and they felt sorry for Pierre. It was obvious that he stood no chance but they admired his courage or stupidity, whichever way you looked at it.

The first blow struck Wyman on his jaw. It was fierce and brutal, but had little effect, with only a small trickle of blood appearing out the left corner of Wyman's mouth. His head moved slightly, and this only served to infuriate Pierre. He felt the adrenalin pumping through his body at the rate of knots. His face was taut with anger and his fists were tightly clenched. He was determined not to walk away, even if every bone in his body had to be broken.

The only advantage he had over Wyman was his speed and agility. Using both of these was the only way he could hope to win this fight. He knew that if Wyman got a punch in, it would be all over; he was just too powerful a man. Pierre ducked the first three blows that came his way and managed to stay on his feet. He led Wyman all over the place, never staying in one spot long enough for Wyman to get in a punch. Pierre caught Wyman in the rib cage, hoping it would wind him sufficiently enough to at least make him curl up in agony. But Pierre couldn't believe it; there was virtually no movement from Wyman. The crowd shouted and cheered at the blow, but it soon died down when they saw Wyman's reaction and the cheers changed to cries of, 'Oh no!' Pierre could feel the crowd's support, but he also could sense they felt that he had no chance. He hit Wyman again, but this time it was a blow just above his eye. Although Wyman didn't quiver, the flesh around the eye was tender and the blood came streaming down his face. Wyman moved his hand up to the cut and wiped the blood with the back of his right hand. He looked down to see his own blood covering his hand. He walked up to Pierre, ready to punch him once and for all. But Wyman wasn't quick enough as Pierre darted to and fro, ducking and diving, avoiding all the punches that came his way. Pierre could see the anger growing inside Wyman as he became more enraged with frustration. He ducked one of Wyman's punches and ran around him, now waiting for another hit. As Wyman turned to find him, Pierre struck another blow to Wyman's face, but still there was no reaction; a small drop of blood ran down his face and dripped onto the ground below. He would have to try and tire him out and then get in as many blows as possible.

Wyman was exasperated at not being able to catch Pierre and get the fight over and done with. He ran around like a fool and still couldn't manage to strike Pierre. But every now and again, Pierre would get another blow in. His fists were starting to split and blood was dripping from them. After the ninth blow to Wyman's face there was a sound of breaking teeth and Wyman's mouth blew up like a balloon. Blood came squirting out and Wyman stopped. Everyone watched as he swirled the blood and saliva around in his mouth. He then spat a mouthful of blood and broken teeth into the crowd.

This caused the onlookers to go wild. They were shouting and cheering enthusiastically. Their cries grew stronger and stronger and with it, so did Pierre's inner strength. For a brief second Pierre turned and faced the crowd. As he turned back to Wyman he felt the side of his jaw being smashed by the oncoming fist. Although Wyman had only caught him on the side of the face, it was enough to send Pierre flying. As Pierre was lifted into the air, he could feel the pain in his face like an explosion of dynamite imploding inside of him. He had been in many fights as a young boy and had fought many men, but never had he experienced the power and strength of Wyman. All Pierre could think was, *thank heavens he didn't catch me with a full punch*, otherwise his whole jaw and face would have been smashed to pulp.

As Pierre landed on the ground he could hear the footsteps of Wyman coming towards him for the final kill. He forgot about the pain he felt because he knew that if he didn't get up now, it would be too late; he would be a dead man. He pulled himself up onto his feet and turned quickly to face Wyman, who couldn't believe his eyes. Wyman was shocked by Pierre's return and stopped dead in his tracks. How could this be possible? Although Pierre's body was starting to feel rather tired and weak, he kept moving, beckoning and teasing Wyman with all the energy he had left in him.

He knew that if he showed any signs of weakness it would give Wyman just that little bit of extra strength and confidence that he so badly needed.

The time was now right for Pierre to go in with everything he had left in him, and to finish him off. The taste of blood weakened Wyman; he felt beaten and wanted to stop, but he had an image to live up to. He had shouted his mouth off and beat up so many men before. How could he now possibly let this man beat him? Pierre caught him in the mouth again, splitting the lip even further, blood covering his entire jaw and dripping down onto his chest. With a quick swing, Pierre caught him in the upper stomach; he couldn't have wished for a luckier punch. It caught his wind and Wyman tucked his arms down onto his stomach. Vulnerable, Pierre lifted his knee up into Wyman's face, and with all the strength he had left in him, aimed for his jaw. On impact everyone heard the cracking of bones. The big man fell to the ground with a heavy thud. The blood was everywhere, all over him. His eyes were swollen and his jaw was worse. Wyman's nose was obviously broken with the last blow and there was more blood pouring out of his nostrils.

Wyman tried to get up but found himself feeling very lightheaded and wobbled as he lifted himself. With all his strength he crawled onto his knees and pulled himself to his feet. The crowd was now unstoppable. They couldn't believe what they had just witnessed and they shouted in unison.

'Pierre, finish him off, finish him off,' they chanted. But Wyman continued to struggle to his feet and get ready for round two. If it had been anyone else he would still be down on the ground, ready to be taken to the hospital. Pierre felt sick; what was he going to do now? He wasn't quite sure, but he walked towards him. Just then he heard Arthur's voice and knew that the fight would be broken up. They cleared a path for Arthur to walk through. He was shocked at what he saw and it showed on his face. He knew both men and he also knew their reputations. Pierre had only been there a few months but the workers had grown to like him and he them, even though he kept very much to himself, looking after and helping his parents as much as possible. Arthur had watched the fight for the last few minutes and was intrigued with the hidden strength in Pierre. He should have been knocked out a long time ago but with his obvious skill of fighting, he had managed to stay on his feet, even if he did look terrible. Wyman was in an even worse condition, with blood streaming from all parts of his face.

It was time to stop the fight before Wyman got beaten up any more. Everyone had enjoyed the entertainment, which was always a welcome break from the everyday sweat and toil. The workers jeered at the top of their voices as they saw Wyman slowly fall to the ground with a thud, a defeated man. Pierre had thrown him a last punch with his left fist. This was the biggest beating Wyman had ever taken in his life and one which he would never forget. Pierre sat down from sheer exhaustion, the sweat pouring down his face. Wyman's blood had been sprayed all over him in blobs. Arthur was rather glad that he didn't have to stop the fight. He could have stopped that last blow, which he halfheartedly was tempted to do, but he too, was enjoying himself.

'Who started this fight?' Arthur asked one of the guards, who was standing near him. But before he could open his mouth to speak, the crowd shouted, 'It was

Wyman, he started picking on Pierre; it was self-defense.' It was obvious who had the most supporters.

'You two guards, over there, pick up Wyman and take him through to the sickbay,' Arthur said, pointing to the two guards standing closest to Wyman, who was now sprawled out on the ground. They both had grins on their faces at the prospect of two workers beating each other to a pulp, especially Wyman. All the guards were very weary of him, even though they had guns they were still on their guard when he was around. One quick blow from him and you wouldn't know what had hit you. They had witnessed his handy work often enough.

'Yes sir,' they answered simultaneously and quickly bent over Wyman, wondering the easiest way to get this massive body to the sick room. They managed to prop their shoulders under his arms and slowly lift him up. His body was covered with sweat and blood and it had a terrible smell to it. As they pulled him away from the crowd, his feet dragged behind him, leaving a big furrow on the ground.

'Okay everyone, back to work; you've had your fun for the day,' Arthur said in a firm, powerful voice, which echoed through the mine. The workers' heads suddenly bent down towards the ground and unwillingly went back to work. They dispersed in all directions, picking up the tools which had been thrown in haste to get to the fight.

Arthur turned to face Pierre, wondering what he should do with him. He couldn't let him get away with this, but he was pleased that he had won. This was proof of Pierre's strength and there and then Arthur made his decision. It couldn't have happened at a better time. Now he had to be careful so as not to draw too much attention to Pierre, and make the other workers suspicious.

'Pick him up, clean him up and put him in solitude for two days, along with Wyman once he has recovered,' he ordered a guard who was standing, waiting for orders. They helped Pierre to his feet and took him away. He had heard a lot about solitude and none of it good. He had kept his nose clean the last six months and he just hoped there would be no problems with his parents. As he passed one of his friends, he whispered, 'Keep an eye on my mom and dad, won't you Phil?' he asked in a pleading voice.

'Sure buddy, I'll look after them,' he said as he watched them take Pierre away. He knew that Pierre loved his parents so much. They were now very old and found it hard to keep up with their work. The elderly were sometimes taken away and never heard from again. That was the last thing Pierre wanted to happen. But as long as their work was completed, they were safe. Pierre then helped them with their workload, once he had finished his.

Anyone caught fighting was taken to solitude and he had known that before he started the fight but he had to do it. There were many old people who were far weaker than Pierre's parents and you could see it in their eyes; they knew that each day could be their last. Most of them had no one to help them with their workload. Pierre felt sorry for them so he too would offer to help them whenever he had an opportunity. The elders in the labor camp loved Pierre very much and appreciated all that he did for them. But he was only one man, with a heavy load of his own to carry, yet somehow he always managed to handle more than his share of work. Most of the workers were convicts and had been sent to this labor camp to work the diamond mines. Some had been there thirty years and had grown old quickly.

Chapter Nine

ARTHUR MADE HIS WAY BACK to his office, called his secretary in and asked for the files on both Wyman and Pierre. She scuttled off to her office and Arthur could hear her rummaging through her filing cabinets. He sat back in his chair thinking of Pierre. He was a striking man with dark hair and sky blue eyes, enough to charm any woman. He had a presence and confident air about him that seemed to gain the respect of everyone. Some people were born with it; it wasn't something they learned. He had an aristocratic look about him and the manner to go with it.

There was a faint knock on the office door and Arthur beckoned Ruth to come in. Nobody else knocked like his secretary. She was a quietly spoken woman of about forty-eight years. She had been married once to one of the guards, but it hadn't worked out and he had been transferred. She decided to remain at the mines. Her face was round and plump to go with her body. Her eyes were a beautiful green, but you couldn't really see them too well for they were hidden by all the extra weight she carried in her face. Arthur was really fond of her and they had never spoken a cross word to each other in all the thirteen years of working together. He often thought that she would have made a good mother as she was such an understanding and caring person.

'I've brought the files you asked for,' said Ruth as she entered the room. She had a smile on her face. It seemed to always be there; like a permanent feature.

'Thanks Ruth,' he said, looking up at her. It had been rumored that she was in love with him and that's why she had stayed on all those years, working side-by-side with him through thick and thin. She had been hoping that one day he would propose to her and they would get married, but Arthur was not attracted to her at all. She smiled down at him kindly and for a brief second he held her gaze, then he turned and picked up the files that she had placed on his desk. She turned and walked away, out of the office. He watched her walk away from him and thought what a fool he must be, if only he wasn't so damned fussy.

Years ago she had been slim and far more attractive than she was today. They could have spent all those years at least, enjoying each other's company instead of being alone. He had taken her out a few times for dinner when she first started working for him. He wanted to get to know her, but only for companionship, and no more than that. Arthur was not a womanizer, but he did enjoy female company, especially if they were interesting to talk to. Nothing had happened between them and he had never promised her anything, other than friendship. He had also hoped there would be some sort of magic between them, or at least something that would bring them together, but from his side there was nothing but respect. It would have been so convenient and easy to slip into a relationship with her but he had been strong enough to resist the loneliness and keep his distance.

He had hoped that she would fall for one of the others, but it wasn't from lack of trying on their parts. He had been approached by many of his colleagues, asking if he would set up dates with her, but she had continually turned them down. It was sad and he couldn't help feeling responsible for the situation but he couldn't blame himself. She had a free will to decide what she wanted from her life.

When she had closed the door behind her, he wiped the sweat off his forehead and opened the file on Pierre Coppack. He was born in Paris, France and was now thirty-five years old. He had arrived in South West Africa with his parents François and Sondrene Coppack. According to the file, they had been caught with drugs in their possession. They had only been in the country six weeks and could barely speak a word of English, particularly the parents. Pierre had picked it up quite quickly and although it was broken, he could still be understood. Their reason for leaving France and moving to South West Africa was unknown to Arthur. Pierre was an architect and his dad was a civil engineer. They were both working for a local company. Two and two just didn't make four. There was something very fishy about the whole situation. They seemed like really nice people, decent people, but what had actually happened?

He cast his mind back to the newspapers he had read. He remembered that Pierre had said that they had been set up and they weren't drug smugglers. There must have been something that someone had conveniently missed in the trial. No doubt it came from higher places, where there was no justice. As he went through the file, he had a sick feeling in his gut and felt sorry for the family. At the time, it was rumored that it *had been* a set-up but the shots were being called from far too high up. Having known Pierre for eighteen months, it seemed highly unlikely that they had done anything to break the law and that the rumors were probably true.

He sat back in his chair, more sweat dripped from his forehead and he pondered whether or not the plot would work and if Pierre was the right choice. He had also read that François and Sondrene were in their sixties, and although still fairly fit, Arthur had noticed a difference in them since they had arrived. Sondrene had lost the spark she had in her eyes on her arrival. Pierre was by her side, as often as he could be, but there were many times when she had to do kitchen work and Pierre wasn't allowed there. She had once dropped a large pot of boiling water and had burnt her arms badly. Pierre often heard them shouting at her, telling her to hurry up and that cut him to pieces every time. He so badly wanted to go in there and just take her away. He blamed himself for the mess they had got themselves into as he had been the one who had persuaded them to come out to Africa, but nothing had gone the way it should. He knew it was just a matter of time before she would be sent off; what would he do then? It was his worst nightmare and a constant nagging he had learnt to live with.

Arthur would use Pierre's parents as his "ticket" to get to him. He couldn't think of any other way. Very little was known about the man and his background. He had read the personal letters that Pierre and parents posted during the time they had been there, but none of these letters were actually posted, instead they were scrutinized by the officers and guards. They didn't want any family or friends making enquires as to what was going on in the mines. This plan would be an out for Pierre, and his family, so how could Pierre possibly turn it down? Arthur suddenly felt excited; after all these years of talking and planning, he would now be able to leave. He just hoped that Dave had all the ends tied up on his side. It was now a matter of waiting.

A smile appeared on his face as he sat looking out across the desert. At long last he would be free from this hellhole and could go and do anything he wanted to. Over the next two days, until the letter arrived from Dave, Arthur would be busy trying to bring everything together, being careful to think everything through. There were so many *what ifs* that related to the forthcoming events that he had to have some contingency plans prepared. He had to have all sides covered because he didn't want to spend the rest of his life working the mines. The letter arrived three days later.

Dear Arthur,

By the time you get this letter I will have spoken to you on the phone, as I know that I will not be able to contain myself. Do you remember me telling you that I had met a girl and that we were having an affair? Well, through her I have managed to find just the right person to do the job. Her name is Jessica Smith. She is very attractive, intelligent and has her own jewelry shop in Cape Town. She is also single, and although there are rumors that she is getting married, I have inside information that she lives alone. We must have someone from your end who is good-looking and a gentleman. If that is possible!

Those are the first things that will get him in the door. He must also have a certain air about him. In other words, he must be strong-willed, have confidence and also have a good sense of humor. I know that this is perhaps an impossible task, but do the best you can. We must make sure that we have something on him that is strong enough to keep him from leaving us in the lurch and running off with our goods. Jessica does a lot of walking along a certain beach called, Sandy Bay, which is close to Cape Town. Perhaps we could use that as the pick-up place otherwise we will have to think of something else. I will leave that all up to you, but I think the beach will serve our purpose. If you need more information about it give me a ring. We are ready on our side to stage it at any time; just let me know when. It is very important that you pick the right person. We must have Jessica believe in him and want to help him. Please send down the credentials for whoever and whatever you propose. I can't wait to hear from you. Take care my friend.

Yours, Dave

Dave didn't exactly give him a lot to go on but he couldn't help feeling that Pierre was the right bloke for the job. It was funny how he had appeared just at the same time that Dave had found Jessica. How fortuitous! Arthur wasn't a religious man but he believed that there were forces that we knew nothing about, so he respected them and gave his thanks to whoever, in his own way.

He would have to wait until Ruth had left for the day, then he could go into her office and dig out the files on all the men he thought were possibilities. It was a big decision to make because if Jessica didn't take to this person, then their whole plan would fall apart. He sat in his chair and re-read Dave's letter, trying to recall and memorize what Jessica's likes and dislikes were. As he sat there thinking about the situation, he heard Ruth banging and clanging which was the sign that she was about to leave. It would soon be safe for him to go snooping in her filing cabinet, something that she didn't like him to do and usually noticed when he had.

Chapter Ten

I~T WAS NOW SIX O'CLOCK~ and Ruth had finished off all her work for the day. When she left, he wandered into her office and carefully went through the filing cabinets to see if he recognized any of the other workers who might also be possible candidates. He chose about four others and then went back to his office and scrutinized them. There were two others who could also be used. Now he had to decide who would be the most suitable.

He sat down and wrote a lengthy letter to Dave, giving him all the details of each man in turn. The other two weren't as sophisticated as Pierre by a long shot but the one, Steven, was better looking and had a gentle appearance. The remaining one, Wyman, was rough, tough and a no-nonsense guy. He could charm the birds out of the trees. He had a foul mouth and a very bad temper which he had learned to curb since his arrival at the mines. Each had his own good and bad attributes. He thought he would see what Dave thought because his girlfriend would know which one was more suited to Jessica. Then they could decide together when the final choice had to be made. He also popped in a photo of each of the men.

Arthur looked at his watch; it was one thirty in the morning. He struggled getting up from his chair; his body was stiff from sitting for seven hours. He was vigilant in returning the files to their correct places, keeping each page as it was. Ruth knew when papers and files had been moved. Arthur took copies of what he wanted in case he needed them and couldn't get access to them because Ruth was around. He switched off all the lights and ambled out into the evening air.

It was rather chilly, which was wonderful. This was his favorite time of the day. He looked up at the stars; there were millions of them. The sky was so clear that he could almost count each star. He walked to his house, flopped onto his bed and fell asleep as soon as his head hit the pillow.

The next day, Arthur reflected on the diamonds and how, each week, they slipped through his fingers. This week's stones were of a good quality, both color and size, but it varied from week to week. He would have to make sure that he had good stones the week of the escape.

The next week dragged and he was wondering why Dave hadn't replied to his letter or phoned him. His heart sank as each day came and went and still there was nothing in the post. Then on the tenth day, when he was at the end of his tether, it arrived.

Dear Arthur,

Thanks for your letter and all the information on the three men. We can't quite decide; my girlfriend and I have been through the letter many times and either Pierre or Wyman. They seem to be a mixture of what we think Jessica would like, so we will leave it up to you because you know them better than us. Just remember, we have to be able to trust them. They must be able to keep a secret. So if either of them drinks then that could be a distinct negative attribute. We all know how alcohol makes one talk. Also, Jessica would never be interested in anyone who smoked. Just one thing! Jessica does like the French accent, so if they are both equal, I would suggest Pierre.

I realize that I am taking a chance having told my girlfriend, but I have no other way of getting all this information about Jessica. She has agreed to the sum of money that we discussed to pay her and she is very happy with that amount. It looks like she is going on a cruise after this is all over. She is a very nice lady, not really my type when it comes to marriage, but we get on well. We also decided that the beach would be the right place to have it all come together; perhaps Jessica could find him stranded there, shipwrecked. Otherwise, you'll have to find some other way to get him down to Cape Town, but that would mean going through customs. Just get the map out, the one I sent you, and look for Sandy Bay. Jessica lives in Llandudno and Sandy Bay is right next to it. She goes there a lot with her dog, not every day, but often enough. I have enclosed photographs of Jessica so that your contact will recognize her. Let me know when and where. Bye for now. Dave.

Arthur looked at the photographs of Jessica. She was very attractive; he just hoped that she wasn't too fussy and had a sympathetic heart. He had already decided that Pierre was the man for the job, and Dave's letter confirmed it.

The following day Arthur summoned Pierre into his office. He had been over his speech about a hundred times and just hoped he wouldn't screw up and go blank when confronted by Pierre. There was a knock on the door and the guards walked in with Pierre by their side.

'Thank you. I will call for you when I have finished with him,' he said to the guards in a commanding tone.

'Yes sir,' replied the guards as they closed the door behind them.

'Please come in and sit down,' he said to Pierre, and pointed to the chair in front of his desk. Pierre didn't say a word, but he sensed that something was up. He only hoped to God that it wasn't about his parents. He remained cool and calm and sat down in the chair, resting both arms on his legs. He was handcuffed so there wasn't too much he could do with them.

Arthur looked at Pierre for the first time, very care-fully. He was extremely good-looking, and once cleaned up and dressed properly, would be a lady killer.

'How long have you been here Pierre?' he asked, knowing exactly how long it had been.

'I've been here eighteen months,' Pierre replied, won-dering what was coming next. He thought his visit to the office had something to do with the fight or his parents, as did all the other workers. They all wished him 'good luck' as he was taken away by the guards. Their faces were serious and solemn as if they knew exactly what he was in for, and they wouldn't have swapped places with him for anything.

That was exactly what Arthur wanted them to believe. The fight couldn't have happened at a more opportune time. Pierre had never been to the 'frying pan' before. This was the term given to it a long time ago by the workers, and an appropriate name it was. It meant trouble when you were called into Arthur's office and Pierre hadn't known what to expect, but it certainly wasn't how he had imagined it to be. It was a rather warm and friendly office with classic art work on the walls, even if they were only prints. Pierre knew a bit about art and had a love for the creative mind. Although it was just a mining office, it was obvious that Arthur had a touch of class. He had brought in large, comfortable leather furniture which was now old and cracking in places. He had been expecting something more along the dark and dingy lines. *There must be a reason for the nickname 'frying pan',* he thought.

He was obviously missing something because he had heard such terrible things about this place. *What was the truth behind it? Was it that life, was in fact, as we perceive it to be or as we want it to be?* Pierre could feel the perspiration building up between his hands. Arthur looked him straight in the eye, and then leaned forward on his desk.

'I have a proposition to put to you but before you say anything, listen to the whole story first. Should you decide not to go along with it, I shall deny any of it.

Should you say anything to anyone and that includes your parents, you would not live long enough to tell this story again.' Arthur got up from his chair and paced the room, wiping the sweat off his forehead.

'I have been watching your parents lately and I can't believe how much they have aged since their arrival here, especially your mother. I fear that any day now they will have to be sent elsewhere,' Arthur said, watching the expression on Pierre's face change. Pierre felt the anger rising rapidly within him. *Who the hell has the right to do such a thing to old people? It was so final, and he knew he would never see them again if they were to be sent off to wherever.* He wanted to say something, but he controlled himself and listened to what Arthur was saying.

'But, if you go ahead with what I propose, then you and your parents will be set free and sent to Australia with enough money to start a new life. You will each be given new passports and new identities,' continued Arthur, his eyes not leaving Pierre's face. Suddenly, Pierre had a twinkle in his eye. *Could he believe what he was hearing?* He pinched his hand to see if this was a dream. Arthur deliberately took short breaks in between each sentence, giving Pierre time to let it all sink in. There had to be a catch to this, and he guessed he was about to hear it.

'But, before all this can happen this is what I propose.' He told Pierre everything from start to finish, then walked over to his chair and quietly sat down, waiting for some sort of reaction from Pierre. Pierre sat very still in his chair, speechless and not making any movement. This was not the reaction Arthur had hoped for. He thought that he would have said 'yes' straight away. He finally had to say something, the tension was building.

'Well, what do you think? Are you prepared to help us or do you want to stay in this hellhole, while your parents get sent away forever?' Arthur asked. Pierre stared at him.

'This is an offer that nobody on this mine would refuse. It is a chance to be free and for me personally, it is even better, because my parents will be able to live happily until they die. It's just that I will find it so difficult to do something so dishonest. Even though it is said that we were sent here because we were involved with illegal drugs, it was not true! We were set up for some reason or another, and why they picked us we still don't know. This will always remain a mystery. I can only surmise that we were a cover-up and a scapegoat for someone else. But you don't leave me much choice. But how can I trust you? How do I know that this is not another set-up and that you won't take my parents and me out to sea and ditch us? If you harm my parents in any way, I will personally come back and kill you,' he said directly and calmly. He liked Arthur, and strangely enough he trusted him, even though perhaps he shouldn't have.

'If you keep your side of the bargain and do your job, your parents and you will be going to Australia together. But should you slip up and report the whole thing to the authorities, you will *never* see them again. Don't think you can outsmart us because I have contacts in Cape Town and they will be watching your every move. Just remember, you are to tell *nobody* about this or they might blow your cover. The whole thing must remain a secret for it to work. We will all be better off.' Arthur was convincing enough for Pierre to believe that it would all happen and he would be free.

'I will let you know when the time is right. I reiterate, please do not tell your parents a thing until we are all on the ship. That is all for now; think about what I have just told you. When you go back to the other workers you know that they will be asking questions and wondering what is going on. Just tell them I gave you a warning about the fight with Wyman. Also, when you walk out of this door, look as if you have been through hell, and that I gave you a rough time or I won't be living up to my reputation and it could cause suspicion,' he said as he walked towards the door and opened it.

'I'll do that,' Pierre said as he got up from the chair.

The guard was still standing outside, talking to one of his pals.

'Anymore of this nonsense and you shall answer to me; this is your last warning!' Arthur said in a loud voice so that everyone could hear him. Pierre bent his head in shame.

'Yes sir,' he mumbled.

'Take this man back to work and bring Wyman to me!' he ordered. The guard quickly jumped to attention and took Pierre by the arm.

'Yes sir,' he replied and walked away.

Arthur was pleased with the progress and had a good feeling about Pierre. He was a good man. Now all he had to do was put his plan into action, after all, he had had many years to think and plan. He must have gone over it and changed it a million times but this time it was *going to happen*. He would have to get a hold of his friend Stan, who had his own fishing company. Arthur knew that he sailed around Cape Town quite often and he wanted Pierre to be on the next trip. He knew that Stan would help him, especially for a price.

Arthur had known Stan for many years; they were drinking buddies. They had grown close and understood each other. Even though Arthur had been stuck up in the desert all these years, he had made some good friends. Perhaps he would never find such sincere buddies – ever again. It was because they were so isolated, they spent many hours together and grew to trust one another. Arthur would find it very different living in the city, where people just didn't seem to have time for each other. But, he would have enough money to buy himself a farm somewhere in the country, anywhere in the world. That had always been his dream – a farm – where he could live in peace. He sat in his swivel chair dreaming of his farm and perhaps even of a wife and children. He was aware that time was passing and if lucky enough, he would have to marry someone younger than himself. Just then there was a knock on the door and Ruth popped her head in.

'I'm just going out for lunch. Are you coming or shall I bring something back for you?' she asked brightly.

'Thanks Ruth, but I am waiting for the guards to return with Wyman, so could you please bring something back with you,' he replied. She nodded and closed the door behind her. Ruth didn't need to ask him what he wanted; she had eaten with him so often that she knew exactly what he liked. She also knew that if he had felt like something special he would have asked for it. Before he did anything else, he had to remember to make a note in Pierre's file, showing that he had been severely reprimanded and that this was his last warning. He then picked up the phone and called Stan.

'Hi there Stan, it's Arthur, can you hear me?' he shouted down the phone.

'Loud and clear, buddy. What a surprise to hear from you; there must be a good party coming up and you're phoning to invite me!' chuckled Stan.

'Yeah, something like that. Can we have lunch to-morrow at our normal place at around one thirty?' he asked.

'Good idea; we are long overdue for a pub-hopping evening. I'll see you then,' he said and hung up. The two met up the following day as agreed. They got through all the usual trivia and then Arthur popped the question.

'Stan, when do you plan on going to Cape Town next?' he asked.

'Funny you should ask, but I'm due to go in three weeks time. Why, is there something special you want me to bring back for you?' Stan asked, knowing that his friend often needed items that he fancied that were not available there.

'Well, it's not something I want; it's someone I would like you to take there. I need you to drop him off near a beach called Sandy Bay. Do you know it?' he asked.

'Are you kidding? It's a nudist beach; it's world famous.

What is your dirty mind up to now?' he asked, looking at Arthur sideways. Arthur was rather shocked. Dave hadn't mentioned that it was a nudist beach. Well, it really didn't matter and perhaps he could use this information to his benefit.

'Why, it gets better and better. Tell me more about this famous beach,' said Arthur.

'It's a small beach near Llandudno, but there is no access to it except over the mountain and sand dunes from Hout Bay, or through Llandudno and across the rocks and bush. Because it's so cut-off from everywhere, it's the ideal place for people to sunbath in the nude with no disturbances from others. It gets busted by the cops every so often, but that doesn't happen too often because it is so secluded,' he replied.

'Would it be possible to drop someone off there without being noticed?' Arthur asked anxiously.

'It couldn't be done with my boat as it's too big and there have been a lot of ships that have sunk along that coastline. But we could put one of the smaller boats into the water and it could take him to shore. It would have to be done at night though because the Coast Guard patrols that coast all the time. But yes, it would be possible. Is that what you want me to do?' he asked.

'Yes Stan. I have a man whom I want you to take there, and then pick up a month later. Also, I need you to keep another three aboard your ship until the pick-up time. Just name your price and please don't ask any questions until later. It will be safer for you that way,' he said.

'Gee Arthur, this sounds rather serious, but sure, I can do it. If you give me their names and passports, I'll get their fishermen passes ready before we leave. It will take me a week or so to get their documents in order, so I'll need their information soon. It's not a problem my friend. You can buy me a couple of crates of beer, some good bottles of wine and just cover the cost of the boat while we are away. I'll have to make an extra trip to go back but it won't be a problem,' Stan said, not questioning Arthur and making it all sound easy and straightforward.

'The smaller boat won't be returning to your ship until the pick-up but we can go through all those details later. Thanks for not asking any questions Stan; I really appreciate it. But I don't know if you will be able to get papers for the two old people, will they be a problem?' asked Arthur.

'I could put them in as kitchen staff, cook and cleaner. I really don't see a problem with that,' replied Stan.

'Now, I want to pay you more than you normally ask for. You see my friend; I will be able to afford it. So just know there will be a wad of money coming your way once we have completed the trip,' he said sincerely.

'I think I have heard enough, I don't want to know what you are up to. But if you have spare cash, I would be a fool to decline such a great offer, and say no. Hell, what are friends for? Now let's stop all this shop talk and get on to more serious business,' he said. They started catching up with all the local gossip.

That was a load off Arthur's shoulders. Now he would have to get the new passports for Pierre and his parents ready. Before he left, he found out the exact date that Stan was leaving. It was June twenty-ninth.

When Arthur returned to his office he sat down and wrote to Dave telling him all the details. Pierre's parents would have to go with them and Dave would have to remain in Cape Town until it was time to pick up Pierre. He would have to make sure that he didn't contact Pierre while they were there. He phoned Stan and told him there would be a fourth person who would handle the drop-off. Stan said it wasn't a problem and that he had never been pulled in by the local authorities. He knew them well. He was an honest sort of guy.

As he was writing, everything seemed to be falling into place. He had a good feeling about this plan.

Arthur sent the letter off "priority mail" so that Dave would get it in the next few days. Now the waiting game began again, only this time he had some organizing to do. He had another friend who would arrange for the three passports and who advised Arthur they would only take four days. It had been a problem getting the passport photographs taken but Arthur had thought of a way around that. He ended up with hundreds of photographs of the mine and of all its workers but had told everyone it was for a current record of the mine. It worked and nobody suspected anything. He even managed to isolate Pierre and his parents long enough to get a few of each of them. Once he had the passports he passed them on to Stan. He mailed Dave's passport to him.

It was all coming together on both sides; the excitement was setting in. Dave had said in his letter that everything was ready at his end and it had been agreed that Pierre's parents could stay in one of the lower deck compartments aboard the ship. The plan was ready to be put into action. Arthur was shocked at what could be achieved with money.

Now he was anxious to see what sort of stones were coming in over the next few weeks. He had decided that each week, if there were some really good ones – some blue whites and pinks – if possible, he would put them aside and keep adding them to the ones he had taken the week before.

Chapter Eleven

PIERRE HAD GONE BACK TO work as usual, but couldn't stop thinking about Arthur's offer. He so wanted to tell his parents but knew it was too risky. The one thing that truly worried him was using this girl called Jessica. He hoped that she would not prove to be a likeable person and that if he offered her good money she would just do the job. The problem was whether he could trust her enough to tell her what he was doing and could she be bought. All he knew was that it had to go smoothly for his parents to stay alive. He would have to play it by ear. Arthur was leaving that up to him. Only time would tell.

He tossed and turned all night, dreaming of what lay ahead, and hoping that he would be able to pull it off. He hoped there wasn't going to be any bloodshed, because he couldn't live with that. Arthur had assured him that that was not an option. But he knew what money did to people and once they got a taste of it, it gave them a sense of false power, making them feel invincible.

He had often wondered why money gave people such illusions of grandeur. Because when he thought about strength, it wasn't something that came from outside, it was something that resided inside each of us. After all, what is it exactly that we take to our graves – money, possessions, cars? No, the only thing we take with us is our soul. So the question is, how do we determine what is right for us, during our short stay on earth? Is it to develop our soul and gain as much growth as we can? There again, how does one class "growth"? Growth differs for each individual. He concluded it was because each person had his own lessons to learn. He wondered what his were, and was he listening to the whisperings that he heard from time to time, or was he misguided by living in a state of fear? On that note, he fell into a deep sleep.

The next week continued as normal with no word from Arthur until one morning, Pierre was called by one of the guards and taken to his parents to say their good-byes. Arthur had promised that they would be taken first and shipped out with some of the others. Pierre held them in his arms as the tears rolled down his mother's face, yet he could see that she was trying to be brave. He looked at her and then at his father. 'Mother, Father, this is not the end. Please trust me when I say we will see each other soon. Please believe me. I know something you don't but we *will* be together again. Don't cry and don't worry; I will see you again, soon. Do not tell anyone what I have just told you,' he whispered to his mother as he held her tight and close to his heart. She was just about to question him but he put his hand up to her lips.

'Don't ask any questions, just go with the others, please,' he pleaded before she could say anything and before the guards became suspicious. His father looked into his eyes, believing every word, but not knowing how it was all possible. Both parents looked at one another and smiled. They weren't sure what was going on, but they suddenly felt calm. Somehow, they knew that they were going to be alright and that they would see their son again. They chatted about a few things and then the guards took them away, along with about five other elderly people.

Pierre knew that the time was drawing near; Arthur was going to make his move any day now. At least he knew his parents were safe. Arthur had promised to take them first and he had kept his word.

A few more days went by and the waiting was be-coming intolerable for Pierre. He missed his parents and worried about them. He knew he had to see them soon or they would start doubting what he had told them. If only he could get a message to Arthur to tell them he was fine. All Arthur had said was that it was going to be soon, but he hadn't said exactly when. Perhaps he didn't know himself.

About a week later, Wyman and he were called into Arthur's office. Arthur couldn't isolate Pierre and so he had to bring the two of them in together, as well as the guards.

'I have been thinking of having a boxing competition

next month. Would you like to be part of it?' he asked them. They looked at each other, a bit startled at what they had just heard. Of course, Wyman had a huge grin on his face and Pierre could sense his longing for revenge. Pierre, on the other hand, wouldn't have agreed if he didn't know it was part of Arthur's great plan. So he gave Wyman a smirk, turned to look at Arthur, and nodded.

'That's fine, I will call in some other contestants and the game can begin. I think we should have this every year; it will be entertainment for all,' he said as he lifted his hand, telling the guards to take them away.

Wyman was really confused by Arthur's strange request, but Pierre knew exactly what was going on. This was his sign that 'tonight was the night'; he knew that he had to go back and pick a fight with Wyman, because that was the only way to get called back into Arthur's office so that their plan could be set into motion.

After their little chat with Arthur they were escorted back to work and Pierre waited for an opportunity to goad Wyman. It was easy; Wyman was a sucker for a good fight. But he didn't fall for it immediately. He was obviously weary after the last fight they had had, perhaps even the thought of going back to solitary confinement haunted him. Pierre had heard from some of his friends that Wyman was just waiting for the precise moment to kill Pierre. Pierre had been watching his back ever since the fight. He knew that Wyman couldn't last forever, but the timing had to be exact and Pierre would have to be the one to initiate the fight. He just hoped and prayed that Wyman wouldn't start the fight before Pierre got the go-ahead from Arthur. He also knew that the guards had been told to keep an eye on both of them.

What could Pierre do to get this man going? He teased him but to no avail. Wyman remained cool, until Pierre said, 'Feeling rather yellow today? I believe it's rumored that you are scared of me.' He taunted him in a belittling voice, loud enough so that the workers around him could hear. He dropped a handful of soil on the top of his head. Well, Wyman didn't know what was going on, but this wasn't like Pierre. Obviously the power of being number one had gone to his head. That was enough; Wyman had had it; it was time to put Pierre's lights out once and for all.

'I'll show you who's yellow,' he growled through tight lips. Wyman swung round and took a shot at Pierre, catching him on the side of his shoulder. Pierre had moved as quickly as he could, but Wyman had been waiting and anticipating this move. Although Pierre had only been caught on the side, he fell to the ground like a baby bird falling out of a tree. He went down and didn't know what had hit him. The pain in his shoulder was burning. All he could think of was that it wasn't his face because it would have meant a cracked cheekbone for sure and that would mess up the escape plan. Pierre managed to crawl onto his knees and he looked up to see Wyman towering over him with a satisfied sneer. Pierre prayed that a guard would come or this could end badly. The crowd was starting to gather but before Pierre got to his feet, the guards were there with their mallets, ready to crack the first person who got out of line.

'Break this up right now; you two have been warned and the boss is not gonna be happy,' shouted one guard as he stood between them. The other two guards held Wyman back. He was ready to stick it to Pierre again.

'Who started it this time?' a guard asked. There was silence.

'It was me,' Pierre owned up. The guard looked a bit puzzled. *Why would Pierre start the fight?*

'Take them both to confinement,' he ordered.

'Everyone back to work,' instructed the guard as he took Pierre away. The guards then reported the incident to Arthur.

'Sir, there has been another outbreak of violence in the mine. Wyman and Pierre have been fighting again,' he reported. Arthur looked at his watch; it was time to close up and go home.

'I was just on my way out but I have time to see one of them. Bring whoever started the fight,' he said, knowing full well who it was. At least that would throw suspicion from Arthur, because how could he have known who had started the fight. He had been in his office all afternoon. The guard didn't answer, nor did he ask any questions. He just nodded and walked out of the office.

On the way there, the guard thought about Pierre and how out of character it was for him to do something like that. He hadn't noticed any change in him since the fight but he had noticed a change since his parents had been taken away. He guessed that he was feeling angry and Wyman was the scapegoat. He felt sorry for the guy as he seemed to have been messed around from all sides.

He collected Pierre and the two walked back to the office in silence. The sun was setting and the sky was filled with many brilliant colors. They reached the office and the guard knocked on the door again. Arthur heard it and knew it was Big Ben, even though he hadn't seen him earlier. His knock had a definite rat–a–tat–tat to it. It was a strong knock so it could only be Big Ben. He was called that because of his size, both in height and width. He looked like the type you didn't ever want to pick a fight with and at all times, went out of your way to agree with him, even if he was wrong.

'Come in,' Arthur said, but before he had finished speaking, the door flew open and in came Big Ben with Pierre being roughly pushed through the door.

'Here he is sir. Will there be anything else? Would you like me to wait and take him to solitude to join his buddy Wyman?' Ben's face took on a boyish, delightful grin at the mention of Wyman's name. Arthur was still looking down at the paper work on his desk. He looked up after a few seconds and saw the guard, standing with Pierre by his side.

'That won't be necessary; you may leave. I will take him back when I am finished,' he said to the guard. This wasn't an unusual occurrence. Over the years, Arthur had done it on a regular basis so that nobody would suspect anything was different.

'Yes sir,' replied the guard. He seemed relieved that he didn't have to wait and work overtime. He walked out of the door, closing it behind him. Pierre and Arthur looked at each other.

'Are my parents safe?' Pierre asked Arthur anxiously.

'They are fine and waiting for you aboard the ship,' said Arthur, happy to see Pierre's expression change on his face as he muttered the words. There was silence for a few seconds, as they both sat looking out the window. It was now getting dark. The office was empty, except for the two of them. Arthur got up from his chair and walked over to the windows, closing all the blinds. This was a ritual he did every night when it got dark. He walked back over to his desk.

'We are all set for tonight. The stones have arrived and they are in the safe. Can you remember all the details we discussed?' he asked, becoming rather serious.

'Yes, I think so,' replied Pierre, wringing his hands together.

'I have written everything down, just in case you go blank and we don't want anything to go wrong, or it will be jail for all of us,' warned Arthur and handed him a piece of paper outlining the entire plot. Pierre took the piece of paper and read it quickly, just to refresh his memory. It was as Arthur had told him a week ago, and Pierre had been over it in his mind a million times.

'All you have to do is pick up that lamp and hit me over the head with it. Knock me out, but for heaven's sake don't kill me. Just make the bump look real so that no doubt can be cast on me.

'From there, you take my van and drive to just outside town where I have arranged for a man to pick you up and take you to the shipyard,' said Arthur, also giving him the password that the contact would say in reply to his password. Pierre looked a bit confused. How could this man think that he could possibly get past the guards at the entrance?

'This is all very good, but how the hell do you expect me to get through the guards? They are not fools; they can see that I am not you, in your van or not,' he said with a tone of reservation in his voice. Arthur confidently walked over to his desk and rooted amongst his keys for the one that fitted his bottom draw and unlocked it. He pulled out a mask. At first, Pierre wondered what he was doing, then Arthur held it up and Pierre couldn't believe it – it was Arthur's face; it looked so real.

'A friend of mine is an artist and he made it for me. It's taken him nearly three years to complete but it was worth the wait. Now, I want this back for a keepsake, so don't go getting your face smashed up,' he said.

Pierre took it from him gingerly, put it on and walked over to the mirror. He could not believe it. With a few adjustments here and there, it would be impossible to tell the difference. It would be dark when he drove through the front gate, so they would never know that it wasn't Arthur. Arthur stood next to him. Even the hair was the same color. The face was detailed down to the last wrinkle and the coloring was so lifelike. Pierre suddenly felt more relaxed and optimistic about the whole scheme.

'Now, as long as you don't speak, you'll be safe. The guards know that I go out every Wednesday night, so they will be expecting me. All I do when I go through is nod my head and lift up my left hand and give them a small salute, like this,' he said, lifting his hand up to the top of his forehead, holding it there for a few seconds and then dropping it down again.

'They know that I always do that, so it will be as normal. I very seldom talk to them, especially if it is William, who is on duty tonight. He is too busy listening to his radio and doing crossword puzzles. I always slow down as I get to the gate, but they generally just look to see it's me and make the hand gesture. They generally lift the barrier before I even stop, so just remember that. Now let's see you do all that,' he said.

So Pierre practiced it over and over again until Arthur was satisfied that nobody would know the difference. He took off the gold ring he was wearing on his right hand and handed it to Pierre.

'It might be the ring that gives your identity away, so please put it on. But remember, I want it back when this is over and done with,' demanded Arthur as lines furrowed his brow.

They then repeated every minute detail; their minds racing from point to point, anxiously waiting for the next five minutes to pass. The mess would be full and everyone would be chatting and too busy eating to suspect that anything was going on. They heard the mess bell ring and the clatter of feet as they headed in the direction of the smell of the food that hung in the air. Arthur and Pierre sat in silence; both filled with thoughts of their own.

'Well, what are you waiting for, hit me and good luck. See you aboard the ship,' said Arthur, feeling agitated at the prospect of what was to come, but there was no option. Pierre felt sick and could feel the sweat dripping down the hollow of his back and trickling down into his trousers. But before he could do anymore procrastinating, he lifted the metal lamp, and with a heavy blow, he struck Arthur on the back of his head. As Arthur stumbled, and slowly fell to the ground, Pierre bent over and felt for a pulse. It took him a few seconds, seconds which seemed like hours and then, he had it; Arthur was still alive. It was a good blow; there was a trickle of blood that ran down his forehead. There was no doubt that Arthur was going to wake up with a hell of a headache.

There was no time to waste. They had changed clothes earlier in preparation and with that, Pierre took a huge, deep breath and walked towards the office door with the diamonds strapped around his neck. He checked to make sure that everything was in its correct place before opening the door. He peered up the corridor; not a soul in sight. On his hands and knees, Pierre crawled quickly up the passage so that he wouldn't be seen by anyone through the windows. He moved like a wild cat stalking its prey, with exquisite precision and slow, silent movements.

The van was exactly where Arthur had said he would leave it and he had the keys in his hand. He got up behind one of the pillars and opened the exterior door. He could hear the security guards chatting to each other. The atmosphere was tense; and he could feel the blood pumping in his ears. He had to practice Arthur's walk; now it was time to put it to use.

Pierre walked confidently over to the van and slipped into it, taking care that he moved like Arthur, slowly and carefully. There was no haste about him so as not to draw any attention to himself. That was quite often the case with Arthur. He would fill his pipe and light it up before he started off on his trips to town, so that's exactly what Pierre did, making sure that nobody was close enough Those were the longest three minutes of his life. *So far, so good*, he thought.

When he had finished lighting up the pipe, he turned the ignition key and started the van. He drove towards the gates, aware that there was a tower in the center of the camp, with machine guns poised and ready to shoot anyone who tried to escape. There were also spotlights that circled the place all night long. He had been careful to wait until the searchlight had passed him before he continued. The guards watched him approach.

Pierre wondered if they would think it was Arthur or not. When he was in clear sight of them he put his hand out the window, lifting it slowly and gave them the usual wave. He slowed down as Arthur had said, but he did not stop completely. His heart was beating heavily, and then he heard the guard.

'Going into town tonight sir?' the guard on duty asked.

Pierre felt shivers travel down his spine. He mustn't speak, so he just nodded as Arthur did, not answering the question the guard had just asked him. He thought he felt the guard hesitate and look at him in a strange manner, but he was obviously being paranoid, as the guard nodded to the other guard in the sentry box and seconds later, the gate was opened. Pierre headed out with a big grin on his face, trying not to get too excited too quickly and stay focused.

He couldn't believe it was happening. His thoughts immediately turned to his parents and he felt enormous relief that they had been shipped off earlier. He breathed in the fresh air and exhaled deeply. Although it was only a short distance from the mine, it smelt sweeter and felt fresher. Now all he had to do was to make sure everything went according to plan. Pierre felt exhilarated.

Chapter Twelve

His mind drifted off without him realizing that the car had taken over and was driving itself. Arthur had programmed it so well that it was on autopilot. The road was straight and only the headlights lit the dirt road. There was a full moon and everything seemed still and asleep, with only the night animal sounds.

He wondered how Arthur was feeling and whether he was still unconscious, hoping that the guards hadn't found him yet. The agreement was that Arthur would lie there until he was found by someone in the early hours of the morning. If he did wake, it would be a cold night for him so he hoped that he slept right through until morning.

Arthur had given him instructions on how to get to his destination. They were clear and straightforward, but Pierre had never been on this road before and didn't have a clue where he was going. *Suppose his contact wasn't on time or even forgot, what would he do then?* He tried to push any negative thoughts out of his mind and concentrate on only positive thoughts. It was a good two-hour drive and he found himself wanting to drop off to sleep, so he put the radio on and listened to music. He couldn't afford for anything to go wrong at this stage of the game. Perhaps he would hear about the heist, but there was no news which meant they hadn't found Arthur.

He looked at his watch; it was not yet nine o'clock. The countryside was bleak and barren with not a tree in sight; all he could see were the mountains looming up in the distance like over-powering demons closing in on him. He was tired from the mental strain and his body cried out for peace and serenity which he wondered if he would ever have again.

Since their arrival in South West Africa, nothing had gone right and not one day had gone by when he hadn't thought about how he was going to destroy the three men who had put him and his parents away. But to do that, he had to have his freedom, and his parents had to be happy and settled. They had told him to leave the past alone and that those men would get their punishment one day, but that wasn't enough for Pierre. He believed that he had to make them pay for the hurt that they had caused his family. They were the type of men you did not mess around with – their only objective in life was to get richer and by any means. Pierre had found out who they were and their names were imprinted indelibly in his mind, never to be erased. It was only by sheer chance that he had discovered who they were.

Pierre had been on lunchbreak and overheard two

men talking about a job that they had been asked to do. One man was telling the other that he shouldn't really be in labor camp, but he had been double-crossed by some evil men. He was told to plant some heroin in one of the apartments not far from where he lived and these men would pay him two thousand rand. So of course, he did. He was paid one thousand upfront, but when it came time to collect the remaining one thousand, his contact person had disappeared. Then, on top of that, the police arrived at his apartment, broke down his door and proceeded to search the apartment. Guess what they found, drugs. He never did drugs and they were not his. So he was sentenced to hard labor for the rest of his life, with no parole. Pierre couldn't contain himself any longer.

'Excuse me, I overheard you talking about a set-up. Could you tell me where this apartment was?' asked Pierre. At first the man just stared at Pierre, wanting to tell him to mind his own business, but Pierre deemed a great deal of respect amongst the men and, so, answered the question.

'If my memory serves me correctly, it was on the south side of town. I can't remember the name of the apartments but I remember the number, it was twenty-five,' he answered.

'What was the street name, can you remember that?' Pierre asked, keeping his cool.

'It was something like White Lily, or White something,' he replied.

'What about White Silk?' asked Pierre.

'Yes! That's it; it was White Silk. How did you know

that?' asked the man, now looking rather confused by the whole discussion.

His mate, who was sitting next to him, interrupted to ask why he hadn't reported these evil men to the authorities when he had been arrested. He had, but nobody took any notice of him and he was found guilty.

'Can you remember the names of these men who asked you to do this job?' asked Pierre calmly.

'Can I remember? I'll never forget them, double-crossing sons of bitches, never! There was Simon Fletcher who, from what I could gather, was the boss. Then there was Andrew Matterson and Steven Mitchell. They're all high and mighty with the government guys. I'm sure there are a lot of drugs that just disappear into thin air but how can anyone ever prove it?' answered the man. Pierre could tell that this man had enough hate and anger for those men, to last him the rest of his life.

'Thank you,' said Pierre. He stood up and started to walk away.

'Hey mister, what is this all about anyhow?' asked the man. But Pierre just ignored him and carried on walking.

So it was true, and there was the proof. The man who had planted the drugs had been double-crossed in the process. Pierre smiled to himself, thinking that sometimes, there was justice. But Pierre knew there was nothing he could do about it. Nobody would believe him and obviously they didn't believe the other guy either; that's why they were where they were today. But at least he now had their names.

He was getting very close to his destination. Pierre could see the lights from the boats bouncing up and down, bobbing in the water. He drove through the small town and headed for the docks which were primitive and small. He parked at the entrance of the second jetty, turned off his lights and sat waiting. It was nearly nine thirty. He was early but he had nowhere else to go; so he just sat and waited. He lit up Arthur's pipe and sat there puffing quietly. It was something he had never done before but felt the need to do so now.

The harbor should have been quiet but there were fishermen walking up and down, some in drunken states, others with girls on both arms, making their way to their floating homes. Pierre was so intrigued with the comings and goings that he didn't notice someone come up to him from behind until he heard a deep, husky voice.

'It's a lovely clear night,' the stranger said.

'It's nearly midnight,' Pierre replied in return, knowing that those were the words he had to say in return. With that, they both smiled at each other and shook hands. The stranger's grip was strong and firm. His hands were huge and rough and belied his short stature. He looked about forty-five and was well-built with sun-bleached hair. A jagged scar ran down the left side of his cheekbone, adding to the somewhat threatening appearance. His skin was dark and leathery from years of sun exposure. Pierre took an instant liking to the fellow and knew that they would get on well. They had both been instructed that neither were to exchange names until they were safely aboard the boat.

'How long have you been here, and did everything go as planned?' the stranger asked.

'I arrived about fifteen minutes ago and so far so good, but to tell you the truth, I can't wait to get aboard the ship and out of this place. My stay here has been a nightmare. Are my parents with you?' Pierre asked fervently.

'They arrived yesterday and I have been taking good care of them. Your mother is not the strongest of people and with all this happening, not knowing what's going on, I was afraid something would happen to her. But your father has been consoling her as much as possible and telling her that you will be here soon. They really are a lovely old couple,' he said with a soft tone in his voice.

'Thank heavens for that; I was afraid something would happen when they were removed from the group and that they would be returned to the mines or shipped off to the islands!' he said, breathing a sigh of relief and feeling his whole body relaxing.

'We must hurry. Get out of the car and follow me but put this on first,' he said as he handed Pierre a fisherman's jacket. Pierre put the jacket on and hid the mask in the back of his pants.

'Your pass is in the right-hand pocket. We'll walk up the gangway and all you have to do is show it to the guy on duty,' said the stranger.

They walked up the rickety gangway which swayed from side to side, casually chatting as they went along. It was the stranger who did all of the talking. Pierre was careful not to speak when in range of people, as he didn't want his accent to be picked up. Nobody took any notice of them because everyone was too busy doing their own thing. As they approached the ship, the stranger looked Pierre in the eye.

'Just walk behind me and look as if you have been doing this all your life. Pull your card out briefly, showing it to him as you go by. Just copy me and there should be no problems,' he said. Once again, Pierre could feel his adrenalin begin to rush through his body and he wondered how much more of this he could take, but he did as he was told and together they strolled up and on board.

He could feel his whole being suddenly fill up with relief and the tension slowly begin to drain away. The world had been lifted off his shoulders, albeit for a short moment. He felt like shouting to everyone, 'I've made it and I'm a free man!' but he knew that was impossible. He had to restrain himself and enjoy the feeling of freedom in silence.

They walked to the top of the gangway and up onto the deck of the ship. It was an old ship, one that had seen many good days by the looks of it. It was rather neglected and badly in need of a good paint, but it had been a beauty in its time. Whether it was just the freedom that gave Pierre this feeling or whether it was the actual boat, he didn't really know and he didn't much care. Right now, it was like being in paradise.

A few men dressed in workmen's uniforms passed them and nodded to the stranger and he returned their greeting. The boat wasn't due to sail until later in the evening, which explained the reason for the quiet deck. The stranger turned and looked at Pierre.

'By the way, my name is Geoff,' he said and offered Pierre his hand again.

'My name is Pierre,' he said in return and shook his hand vigorously.

Geoff turned and started to climb down the stairs. They then passed through a narrow hole in the side of the ship. They climbed down about thirty steps until they reached another deck. Again, they walked along it and then climbed down another set of steps. They seemed to be going deeper and deeper into the hull. Not a word was spoken during their entire journey. They finally arrived outside a red and black door. Geoff looked around to see that there was no one in sight and then knocked on the door three times, waited three seconds and knocked twice again, waited two seconds and then knocked just once. There was a brief moment and then the door swung open. Geoff walked in first, followed by Pierre. Pierre had not seen who had opened the door and then, as he walked in and his eyes grew accustomed to the light, he was filled with incredible joy.

His mother and father were both seated on a bed in the corner of the room. It was a fair-sized room with two bunk beds on either side and another single one on the other side wall. There was a sink, toilet and shower cubicle. It was rather dark as there was only one porthole looking out to sea but it was like living in the Ritz Hotel after what they had been subjected to.

Pierre rushed over to his parents and they stood up and embraced each other. Arthur had kept his side of the bargain and he was ecstatic for them. They sat down on the bed and told Pierre about their trip and how scared they had felt, especially when they were removed from the group. But when they had realized that this was what Pierre had been trying to tell them, they relaxed. Nobody had ever escaped from the mine, so they were overjoyed and relieved when they saw their son come through the door. Geoff stood and watched them and could feel their love for one another. He had lost his parents when he was a small boy and had learned to survive on his own. But, he had hoped that some day he would have a family of his own. When they had finished embracing, Pierre turned to Geoff and looked at him.

'*Thank you* for taking care of them,' he said humbly.

'It really hasn't been any trouble, in fact it's been a pleasure,' he said with a boyish smile on his face. They were staring at him in awe and gratitude.

'You will all have to stay in here until we arrive in Cape Town. We will be sailing in the next couple of hours and we should be there in a few days. I will come in and check on you from time to time, and you will be called when we are close to our destination,' Geoff told them before turning away towards the door. But before he opened it, he turned around to face them again. 'Just a few more things; do not open the door for *anyone*, except with our code. I know that Dave will be coming in to see you and to put you in the picture. He is our contact in Cape Town so he will be able to fill you in with more details about that. Pierre, don't shave either, as you have to have as much growth as possible. I will bring you food each day and please, try not to make too much noise as there is not supposed to be anyone down here,' he pleaded. They all listened attentively and nodded their heads gratefully.

'We will do everything you say, just one question before you go. Have you heard anything of Arthur? Have they discovered that I have escaped?' Pierre asked, waiting anxiously for a reply.

'Not a word, which means that they either have not found him or they are not making it public. I'm sure this place would be crawling with cops if word was out that you had escaped,' he said. Then he turned and opened the door. 'I'll see you in the morning. Goodnight and sleep well, for you will need all your energy when we arrive in Cape Town. There is some food for you on the table. I guessed you wouldn't have had time to eat before you left.' With those last words he walked out of the room and closed the door behind him. Pierre turned and faced his parents.

'How are you both, the truth now?' he asked.

'We are so relieved to see you because we weren't sure you would make it. I can't believe this, it's a dream and a nightmare all wrapped up in one. Can you tell us what is supposed to happen next? We still don't know what's going on,' his mother asked, her hands clasped together in anxiety.

'From here we go to Cape Town where I will be taken ashore to do what I have to do, which should take four to six weeks. If everything goes according to plan, then we will all be given new passports and taken to Australia with enough money to get you your little cottage by the sea; the one you have talked about for so many years. I can remember you telling me about this dream of yours when I was just a small boy. Please do not ask any more questions because the less you know the better off you will both be; it's for your own safety. But I'm confident all will go well and we will be settled in our cottage by Christmas, perhaps even sooner,' he said convincingly.

As he spoke, his parents hung on hungrily to his every word. He could almost see into their minds. His mother was already living in her cottage and his father was walking along the beach or fishing off the rocks, wearing an old tattered fishing hat on his head to carefully protect his bald patch. Then he would go up to the cottage where mother would have afternoon tea ready for him, served on the porch overlooking the ocean, living the life they always dreamed of. *What a dream that would be,* Pierre thought. They deserved whatever happiness they could get. They had had a hard life and it was their time for some peace and comfort.

They continued to talk about the whole adventure while Pierre ate the plate of food that had been brought in for him. It was cold, having been brought earlier when his parents had arrived, but he ate every single morsel. He then had a shower and they decided to call it a night. All three were physically and emotionally drained.

The rocking motion of the boat sent them off to sleep. Movement meant that they had set sail and there was no going back. The beds were not that comfortable but it didn't matter – they were all together, and safe.

Pierre drifted off into a deep sleep within seconds,

only to be woken by a knocking on the door. Surely to goodness it wasn't morning already, but it was. Pierre looked out the porthole window and could see the morning sunlight glittering on the ocean. He got out of bed and moved towards the door with slow sleepwalker strides, tripping over his clothes that lay on the floor. He opened the door just in time to see Geoff, with a big smile across his face, deliver breakfast.

'Good morning, pleased to see everyone is up and around so early in the morning,' he said. Pierre detected the sarcasm in his voice.

'Good morning! I can't believe it's morning already. I feel that I've only just gone to bed,' Pierre muttered in a slow, sleepy voice.

'We haven't heard anything yet, but we really didn't expect to hear from Arthur at all. They will be keeping a close eye on everyone until this whole business is sorted out. Arthur won't take the chance of drawing any suspicion to himself by making outside phone calls, and we have been instructed not to contact him. We will, however, listen to the radio to see if the mines have released any information. But don't worry I will let you know the minute we hear something,' said Geoff as he walked back towards the door.

'Thanks again for all your help,' said Pierre, yawning before he could complete his sentence.

'Well, I can see that it's time I went; don't let your food get cold,' he said again, treating Pierre like a child, but smiling at the same time. With those last words he left the room. Pierre's parents had also been woken by the knock on the door but they had not bothered to get out of bed.

'Come mom, dad, we had better eat our breakfast,' Pierre said as he moved towards their beds. He couldn't decide which was more important, a hot breakfast or sleep. He decided to pull up a chair to sit down.

'Well, I'm up,' said his dad as he jumped out of bed and walked over to the table where Geoff had placed the breakfast tray. Seconds later his mother was up too. They sat around the table and lingered over their food, enjoying their time together. Every scrap of food was savored until nothing remained on their plates. It was a good hearty breakfast. As the next few days flew by, they kept busy by playing cards and doing crossword puzzles. There was a knock on the door on the fourth day. It didn't have the same touch as Geoff's knock, but it was the same pattern, so Pierre went to the door and asked who was there before opening it.

'My name is Dave,' answered the voice on the other side of the door.

'Come in,' said Pierre and introduced himself and then his parents. Dave and Pierre then moved to the opposite side of the room, away from his parents. Dave discussed the plan and gave him details about what was expected of him. He said that Jessica was a lovely person. He hadn't met her himself but he had it on good authority that she was a kind, gentle sort of person, but also knew what she wanted in life. He told Pierre all her dislikes and likes, and where she would go walking and where he must be waiting for her.

Pierre listened most carefully, and couldn't help feeling that he wasn't going to enjoy using her. But he put that thought straight out of his mind because it was either her or his parents. He had no choice in the matter; it had to be that way. They talked for a good hour until Pierre ran out of questions, and then they decided that they had covered everything they could think of. It was time to put the plan into action.

Dave then advised Pierre that they would be arriving in Cape Town the next day and that Pierre had to be ready to move out at around ten o'clock that night. He said Geoff would be in with more details should anything change. He said goodbye to Pierre's parents just before he left the room.

'Oh, by the way, we heard on the radio that there has been a break-out at the mines and that a Frenchman, called Pierre Coppack, has stolen a large number of diamonds. There is a reward offered for any information that might lead to the arrest of this man. There was no news about whether or not it was an inside job, so hopefully Arthur is not a suspect. But they did say that there was an ongoing investigation and that they were confident that the diamonds would be recovered and all suspects would be apprehended,' Dave said in a matter of fact manner, before finally leaving the room. He did not bother to wait for a response. Before his parents could say anything to him, Pierre turned to face them.

'Please, don't ask any questions. I will be back to get you and we will be free forever,' he said. He did not want to talk. He needed to go over everything that Dave had told him, making sure there was nothing that he had forgotten or missed. He knew that his mother was going to ask about the diamonds. She didn't know a thing about them and he was sorry that Dave had said anything. But it was too late to worry about it; the damage had been done and he couldn't undo it. He knew what he had to do and that was all there was to it; whether or not his parents agreed with it or not, he had to follow it through.

While his parents played cards, he lay on his bed mulling over the situation. That night, Geoff brought their evening meal, and after he had laid it on the table, he handed a brown paper bag to Pierre.

'I've got some clothes here for you to change into before you leave. I'll come for you at ten o'clock, so be ready. Your mother and father will stay aboard this ship until you return. Don't worry about them, they will be looked after. You just deliver your side of the bargain,' said Geoff looking at Pierre and waiting for some kind of response.

'I'll be ready, and … thanks again,' said Pierre. Geoff nodded and left. They ate their dinner. Nobody mentioned the conversation that Dave had had with Pierre but there was an air of suspense.

After dinner, Pierre went and showered. He stripped off everything except the old leather pouch around his neck. At first, he had felt the weight but had now grown accustomed to it and in fact, didn't really notice it. He had worn baggy, heavy-duty clothes, so his parents and others couldn't see he had anything around his neck.

He put on the clothes that Dave had left in the brown

paper bag. They were tattered and torn and looked well worn but they smelled clean. Pierre looked at himself in the mirror. His hair was long and he had a beard which had grown quickly. Now with the clothes, he really looked the part. How could anyone not believe that he had been washed up on shore? He was still quite bruised on the shoulder where Wyman had punched him. His shirt was ripped, exposing the badly bruised shoulder.

As he walked out of the bathroom his parents looked up simultaneously and couldn't help but stare. What *did* their son look like? Worse now than when he was working down the mines. Pierre smiled and sat down at the table to join them.

'I know I don't look too good but this is what they want, so, I will be and do, what they say,' he said quickly before his mother could say anything.

She didn't mention the stones or the journey he was about to take. She talked about everything else but that, for which Pierre was thankful. He found himself drifting off and not really paying attention to what she was saying. He had a lot on his mind. He had spent the last few days resting and was feeling strong and healthy which was a good thing, especially for what he was about to go through. He felt his mother touch him gently on his arm.

'Pierre, my son are you all right, I have been talking to you and it's as if you haven't heard a word I have been saying?' she asked with a worried look on her face.

As Pierre turned to face her, he could see where he got his looks from. Her eyes were a sparkling blue and he could see the concern in them. She was still a beautiful lady and when she was young, she certainly would have been breathtaking. Her cheekbones were high; her skin was olive in color, with a clear, clean complexion. It was amazing for a woman of her age to still have this wonderful, vibrant skin. She had a beauty spot on the lower part of her left cheekbone which was very dark in color and smooth to the touch. Her hair was the color of ebony with no signs of grey which was unusual. The color of her eyes was emphasized by her long, dark eyelashes. He had noticed her beauty many times throughout his life but today, she seemed more beautiful than ever and as he looked her straight in the eyes, they held each other's gaze. They did not have to speak. They understood each other.

His father was the quiet one, never saying too much about anything. But if there was something that he didn't approve of, he would let you know. He had a hidden strength that not many people saw but Pierre understood it well. When all was crumbling, it was always his father who somehow, lightened the load. A tall slender man with grey hair and eyes that were dark brown, small in size and slightly raised at the corners. Pierre looked over to him and their eyes met. They smiled at each other, knowing what had to be done and nothing more was to be said about it.

Pierre had often wondered why such a terrible thing had happened to them. His parents had always been honest, truthful, law-abiding people who had never hurt a soul. So why was it, that they were being punished as they were? Pierre wondered about this magical God, and how the universe actually worked.

If he believed that everyone and everything was God, then how could he blame God when we were all God? Do we create a separation, when convenient? If so, then that would justify us blaming God. Then, on other occasions, he believed that we were all one, made up of the same matter as the rest of everything in the universe. How fickle we humans were. Perhaps the truth was more along the lines that we actually create our own reality which would enable each and every one of us to grow on a soul level, learning whatsoever it is that we need to learn in this lifetime. When he thought about that, it made a lot of sense. It would mean that we would all have to be responsible for our every thought, word and action.

Working in the mines had given Pierre a lot of free time to reflect upon his life and how he fitted into the universe at large. He had always believed that they would have a better life in South Africa, so why then, had all this happened? The other question was, how did karma fit into the common denominator? If the two work hand in hand, then how did one know which one was karma and which was creating one's own reality? He supposed he would have to see where life took him before he would be able to reconcile this puzzling dilemma. Maybe *this* was their journey to happiness.

There was a knock on the door. He quickly walked over to his parents, kissed and hugged them goodbye before opening the door.

'It's time to go, come with me. We must hurry. Dave is waiting,' Geoff said as he walked into the room. Pierre could see that he was anxious so he turned to face his parents again.

'You look after yourselves. I'll be back very soon,' he said in a convincing manner. With those last words he disappeared behind the closed door; the image of his parents imprinted on his mind. The question that came to him was, 'would he ever see them again?' He had to remain optimistic and take one day at a time.

Chapter Thirteen

Pierre followed Geoff along the passage and up the same stairs that they had come down, just a few days earlier. It seemed to be very quiet on board and as they reached the first deck, he could see that the sky was dark and covered by fast-moving clouds which screened the stars from sight.

They walked to the other side of the boat and Geoff lifted his hand, pointing to something in the distance. A few miles in front of them, Pierre could see the lights on the coastline. Then he recognized Dave and they moved towards him. He had already put on a lifejacket and was waiting patiently. He turned to face them as he heard their voices and footsteps on the deck.

'Here, put this on,' he said and handed Pierre a life-jacket, similar to the one he was wearing. Pierre took it from him and watched Dave climb into a small boat that was ready for them.

'I'll take care of your parents, don't worry about them. Good luck,' Geoff said as if he could read Pierre's mind. Pierre didn't say a word. He smiled at Geoff, donned the lifejacket and jumped into the boat next to Dave. When Geoff could see they were both secure, he started the wrench, moving the boat up, out and down, until it hit the ocean. It was cold and as they hit the water, Pierre felt some of the splashing waves touch his arms. The water was icy. Dave was dressed in warm clothes with a large jacket on but Pierre only had the tattered clothes that had been given to him. There was a spare jacket behind the seat where Dave sat. He picked it up and handed it to Pierre.

'You had better put this on before you freeze to death,' he said as he noticed Pierre shivering uncontrollably.

'Thanks, this water is icy,' Pierre said as he plunged his arms into the jacket, feeling instantly warmer.

'See that patch of light to the right, the isolated patch? Well, that's where we are headed, just a little to the right of those lights. That area is called Llandudno and just to the right is the nudist beach, where you will be dropped off,' he said as he switched on the engine. The boat started to move away from the ship.

'Yes, I see it,' Pierre acknowledged. The waves didn't look too big when they were on the ship but now that they were in the water they were enormous. Dave was battling to keep the boat going in the direction he wanted to go. Pierre grabbed the oars and tried to help steer the boat. It seemed to work and he continued until things settled down.

'Now remember, she doesn't come to Sandy Bay

every day. But she does come here a lot, so it's important that you keep yourself hidden. I have packed a bag with some food in it, which should be enough for a few days. Get rid of it before you leave. There is a whole mountainside where you can bury it,' said Dave as they traveled through the darkness. Pierre nodded and then sat in silence, watching the lights twinkling and sparkling as they got closer and closer.

'You still have the stones and don't lose sight of them at any time other than when they are going to be cut, remember that,' said Dave in a concerned tone.

'We are nearly there. If there is anything you want to know, now is the time to ask. Once on shore there will be no contact with anyone from our side; you'll be on your own,' Dave said looking at Pierre, waiting for any questions to be asked. Pierre thought for a while.

'The date of my pick-up is the first of August, at one thirty a.m. What happens if I can't have everything ready by then?' he asked.

'If you aren't ready, then we will be back on the fifteenth of August, same time, so by then, your mission *must* be completed. We do not have time on our side because every police officer will be on the hunt for you. Don't forget to lie low and don't go talking to too many people,' Dave said, trying to emphasize to Pierre the importance of the short time he had.

'I will do my best,' Pierre promised.

'Just remember that we have your parents, and should Jessica or someone else try to convince you that the law can help you, think again. You will find that your parents will be dead before they come to their rescue, and I'm sure you don't really want that to happen, so do what you have to do and get out of there,' Dave said. Pierre looked at him and knew that what he had just said was true. Dave wasn't like Arthur. He had a cruel streak in him and he wouldn't think twice about killing Pierre's parents, should Pierre decide to double-cross him. It was a thought that Pierre held close to his heart; a thought that would haunt him until he was safe with his parents again.

'Just one more thing before you go. Take this photo with you. It's a picture of Jessica so that you will recognize her. I know Arthur has given you one, but this is a recent one and a close up, so there will be no mistaking her for someone else. Just remember to get rid of it before she finds you or she will become extremely suspicious. It also has a picture of her dog. His name is Scanty, so study them carefully before you decide that it *is* Jessica on the beach.' He also handed Pierre a pair of binoculars. 'They have night vision in case a situation should arise where you need them. But make sure it is Jessica before you present yourself as near dead on the beach. It could be critical should the wrong woman find you!

'Also, don't forget that we know how many stones there are, the quality, size and color of each one, so don't try to keep any for yourself. You will have to trade some of them so that you can pay to have the stones cut and for you to live, but we know how much that will cost. Don't sell any because that will draw attention to yourself and Jessica. Think everything through very carefully before doing it, it's not just your life you are playing with, it is the lives of many people, including your parents. Arthur has assured me that you can be trusted and I believe him, but I'm not as forgiving as he is,' cautioned Dave.

'I will do whatever I have to,' Pierre said, finding himself starting to get rather agitated with Dave. He maneuvered the boat towards the land as they approached the beach. There were many rocks around and the waves were crashing around them, making it difficult to control the boat.

'Before you go Dave – you are leaving what happens from now on up to me. Is there anything that I have to do, other than get the stones cut? Are there any contacts who might approach me, someone I can talk to about how things are going?' he asked, even though Dave had mentioned earlier that there was no one. Pierre was hoping that Dave would at least have someone with whom he could talk to.

'I'm afraid not. You're on your own to do whatever you must to get the job done. And do it without drawing attention to yourself. I really can't emphasize this enough, and don't forget, Jessica has a boyfriend, so do whatever you can to avoid *his* attention. He is a powerful man and would soon smell something fishy, so stay away from him,' warned Dave. He hadn't really said too much about this boyfriend of Jessica's, only that she had one. Now he tells me to stay away from him. Pierre could sense that this man was going to have to be watched very carefully.

'The tide is low, so we can land the boat. The incoming tide will wash away all signs of our landing before the morning,' Dave said as the boat hit the shore. He then handed Pierre a bag with food.

'This is it. Be careful and good luck. See you in about three weeks time,' he said and watched Pierre jump out of the boat.

'Thanks, I'll be ready,' Pierre said as he pushed Dave back out to sea.

Pierre got soaked and he could feel his feet going numb. The water was truly icy and the cold evening air sent chills through his body. He got back onto the shore as quickly as possible and out of the water. He stood and watched Dave as he headed out to sea. He could see the ship in the far-off distance and knew that Dave would have to hurry if he wanted to catch up to it. Maybe he wasn't going back to the ship. Pierre really didn't know what they had planned. He watched it until it disappeared into the darkness.

Pierre turned and looked around him. He could see very little but he made his way onto the dry sand and then looked searchingly for some sort of cover from the chilling wind. He fumbled around in the bush and finally found himself a rather large rock to nestle against; it gave him protection from the bitterly cold wind and he was sure nobody could see him. Of course, it was late and there was no one on the beach at this time and especially in this weather. He made himself as comfortable as possible and then lay there with only his thoughts for company. He had no idea how long he lay there before eventually drifting off to sleep.

The next thing he knew, he was woken up by the early morning sun streaming down on his back and by the sound of voices. For a brief second he wondered where on earth he was and then it all came flooding back. He stayed still, trying to decipher where the voices were coming from. Then he heard screaming, shouting and splashing, so he knew that whoever it was, they were down near the water. Slowly, he lifted his head to see if he could get his bearings. At least in the daylight he could see what was going on.

He spotted a young couple stripped down to their naked bodies. They were swimming. He shuddered at the thought of being in that chilly water. Obviously it was "love" that had made them crazy enough to get into the ocean. He looked around and could see the rest of the beach; it was deserted. It was a small beach, enclosed on both sides by rocks, mountainsides and ocean, very isolated, and he realized that it was just the perfect place for nudists. Any cop who was prepared to travel over all this terrain was welcome to bust whoever they caught. He was thankful that he had chosen the place he had. It was set well back into the mountainside bush and out of sight of everyone.

As the day progressed, people came and went. He was careful to stay out of sight of everyone but still had an unobstructed view of the beach. There was no sign of Jessica, and with the wind picking up and the cold setting in, the beach was once again deserted. The sun was starting to set over the ocean and the sky was set ablaze with burning colors.

It was strange how time wasn't important now. He didn't have anywhere to go or see, so he could spend the entire day unaware of time. It was rather a nice feeling and perhaps, he thought to himself, perhaps time *was* an illusion anyhow. It was manmade. Did it exist in any other place?

The next day came and went and still no sign of Jessica. Pierre only had enough food for one more day and that was with cutting down his rations. He couldn't help thinking that he wouldn't last much longer out in the cold, as it was beginning to get to him. But there was very little he could do about it, except wait. He thought he might have to search the bush to see if he could find some berries or roots. They would give him enough energy to keep him going but decided he would cross that bridge when he came to it.

It was late on the fourth day, while Pierre was sitting watching the seagulls gliding along on the strong wind that had picked up, that he heard some branches rustling to the right of him. He turned and looked carefully but couldn't see anything. It was a few seconds later when he noticed a woman approaching the beach. Her long hair was blowing wildly in the wind. *Could this be her?* he thought to himself. He moved a little to the left to try and get a better view between the branches. He couldn't be sure but if it was, he had to move quickly down onto the sand. He had looked along that same path so often in the last four days that he thought he knew every bush and stone along the way.

Then he saw a dog. *This had to be her*, he thought. The long blond hair, the dog, it must be. Pulling out his binoculars, he could focus on her, and then was able to confirm that *she was* the woman in the photograph. He watched for a while longer, until he could see her face more clearly. It was her, he was sure of it! So Pierre moved quickly but quietly down to the beach area, being careful not to leave anything behind him. He had buried the bag and leftover food in the earth the day before, so there was no evidence that he had ever been there.

He lay down on the cold, damp sand, hoping she would come his way. It seemed ages before there was any sign of her arrival. He could not afford for her not to see him, he had to do something to catch the attention of the dog. That would be the only hope of him ever being found. He made a noise and hoped the dog would pick it up. The dog was a long way ahead of Jessica, so it would make sense that he would hear it and not Jessica. He picked up a shell and threw it against a rock and immediately heard the dog bark.

It ran in Pierre's direction, barking rapidly. Then he heard Jessica calling after him but the dog wouldn't budge. He stood over Pierre, barking furiously. Pierre was careful not to move and lay rigid, as if he were dead. Jessica's voice got nearer and nearer until he could hear exactly what she was saying.

'Scanty, where are you? Come back here!' she commanded but of course Scanty wasn't going anywhere; he was laying claim to Pierre. Pierre could sense Jessica's presence and could hear the squeaking sound of sand under her feet, as she walked towards him. She didn't bend down to touch him which is what he thought she would do. She was obviously shocked and was being cautious in not getting too close, too quickly. Then he felt her touch his arm. Her hands were warm against his cold skin.

Chapter Fourteen

JACQUES CAME BACK TO REALITY. Jessica was sitting next to him, quietly, each content with the silence that they shared. How was he going to get through the next few weeks without telling her what was going on? He wanted to scoop her up and run away with her, leaving everything behind; somewhere where nobody knew them, so that they could start a new life together. Where was creating one's reality when you really needed it? He had heard that "one cannot be attached to the outcome", so the question was, was he too attached to the outcome? He thought about it, and was sure he was, because he *really* wanted it. It was a hard thing to practice; wanting something really badly, and yet not being attached to it. Still, he sat and tried to visualize not being attached and letting it go, but somehow holding onto his vision. Perhaps those were foolish thoughts, for that could never happen. Therein lay the problem, he did not believe completely in what he thought.

He tried to pull himself together. It wasn't how he felt about Jessica that was important, it was how to get the job done so he could save his parents' lives. That's what counted and nothing else. He would have to keep reminding himself of that and forget what his heart felt, after all, this was their only chance of freedom and he couldn't let an opportunity like this get away.

'Jacques, are you all right?' Jessy asked in a concerned voice. He turned and looked at her. His heart melted again. She was so beautiful.

'Yes, I'm fine, I was just mesmerized by the beauty around me,' he said as he slowly pulled her head towards his lips and kissed her gently. His heart crumbled with every second that went by. There was nothing he could do about it but to live in the moment, knowing that these memories of the love he felt for Jessy, he would take to his grave. It was this love that would get him through the next few weeks. That was something that nobody could ever take from him, this incredible love that he felt for her. He felt fortunate that they had had all these special times together for their time was limited. He could have wept and laughed with such sorrow and joy at the same time but he kept his emotions to himself.

They sat a while longer, until the beach started filling up and then decided to make their way home. As they walked along the path that led back to Llandudno, the sun caressed their faces. It was getting warmer and warmer and was going to be a beautiful day. They didn't say much as they walked; occasionally nodding greetings to people they met.

When they got back to the house, Jessy listened to her phone messages. She was expecting a call from Klaus but there was only one from Michael. She knew she would have to phone him.

'Is that your boyfriend?' Jacques asked, not wanting to sound too inquisitive. Jessy didn't look up from the machine.

'Well, it's a long story but he was and now he's not going to be.' She knew that sounded very strange but that's just how she felt.

'Oh, you don't sound too sure about any of that,' commented Jacques.

'Well, he's asked me to marry him and he's really a wonderful person. There are many women out there who would give anything for a man like him but I've decided to decline his proposal,' she said, now looking up at him. Jacques felt terrible. Was it because of him that she had decided not to marry this man? She'd already said how wonderful he was. She really deserved to be happy. He walked up to her and was just about to say something.

'Please, don't say anything. I had already decided before I met you. You see, there just isn't the magic between us and that is what I want from a relationship, nothing less. We get along really well and I'm actually very fond of him, in fact I love him, but not in the way that a wife *should* love her husband. I have great respect for him and for what he has accomplished in his life but there is something missing, if you know what I mean?

'So please, don't blame yourself. It is my decision and I am happy with it. I must phone him and tell him. I'm sure he will be upset but there are plenty of other girls who would jump at the opportunity to help him get over this,' she said with conviction. Jacques felt relieved that she wasn't blaming him for her decision but he still couldn't help feeling that maybe it wouldn't have gone this way if he hadn't been around. One part of him was happy with her decision but the other side didn't want her to give Michael up and lose her chance at some kind of happiness.

'I must phone Klaus and see what time he wants to meet us,' Jessy continued as she picked up the phone, but before she could dial the number, Jacques said, 'Jessica, I don't think it's a good idea for me to meet him, or any of your friends. We still don't know where I got these stones from and I don't want you or your friends getting into any trouble. So if you don't mind, I will stay here and you can see him on your own.' Jessy thought for a while and then looked at him. 'You're right. I don't mind going on my own. Klaus has to see the stones but he doesn't have to meet you, even though I would like him to. I just know the two of you would get along well,' she said before she started to dial the number.

Jacques felt a wave of reassurance wash over him. It was just as well she had agreed to it because he knew the time would come when this Michael chap would eventually turn up and he would have to make himself scarce.

While Jessy phoned Klaus, Jacques walked into the back garden where the sun was streaming through the trees. Birds were twittering and being warmed by the yellow sun. He wandered through all the nooks and crannies, bending down to smell some of the flowers. Jessy came out to join him and they sat on the bench and talked. She had arranged to meet Klaus at three o'clock in Hout Bay, which was just around the corner; so that meant they had the rest of the day to themselves.

They looked at each other, smiled and Jacques leant over and kissed her. Her lips were sweet and moist. They knelt down on the grass beneath the oak trees. It only took one look. Jacques lay down on his back while Jessy sat on top of him and smiled that cheeky smile of hers. He knew exactly what was going through her mind. They smiled at each other and Jessy stood up and removed her pants. She bent down, unzipped his jeans and pulled them down. Straddling him, she let him enter her. She moved slowly and purposefully. Her skirt covered them both, its fabric soft to the touch. He undid the buttons on her blouse exposing her breasts which were full and firm and fondled them gently as she slid up and down. They came together and then fell asleep in one another's arms.

The garden was really very special and Jessy told Jacques how she had bought the house because of the large trees in it. She had spent many a happy hour there, planting more and more new shrubs and trees every year, resulting in the beautiful garden. She loved gardening and spoke to her plants on a regular basis. Jacques listened to her while she spoke, mesmerized by her beauty and not finding it strange at all that she spoke to her plants. That's why they were so healthy. He believed that just as people reacted to love, so did every living creature, including plants.

Jacques understood and felt every word she spoke. There was definitely an unspoken love and understanding between them, Jacques just knew it. Perhaps they had lived many lives together. He thought that if there was such a thing as reincarnation, then he had been with Jessica before. They spent the rest of the time they had, lying in the garden, making love and exchanging thoughts and ideas.

'I must go. You stay out here and enjoy the peace. I won't be long. Do you still have the stones around your neck?' she asked.

'Yes, here they are,' Jacques said as he lifted them from under his shirt and over his head. Then he handed them to her. Jessy took the old leather pouch from him, kissed him gently on the lips and wandered off towards the house.

'Jacques, have you made a note of what stones there are and how many there are?' she asked.

'No, I haven't. What do I know about diamonds?' he replied.

'I will do that before I leave. We have to know exactly what we have here,' she said, shaking her head as she walked away.

As Jacques watched her walk away, it occurred to him that Jessica could take a few diamonds and he would be none the wiser. In fact, she could double-cross him and take the lot and exchange them for poor quality, or even better still, she could keep them all and there would be no repercussions, because they are illegal diamonds. *But would she do that?* he wondered to himself, feeling uneasy. He knew that what he was doing to her was wrong, but yet, he continued. So, perhaps if she wanted to do the same to him, it would then make them even. It was a thought that he tried to put out of his mind. She wouldn't do that, she wasn't that sort of person; it was just a nagging thought.

Jessy sat at her table and made a note of each stone, the size, color and weight. It would depend on the flaws and the shape, as to how big they would ultimately be cut to. So she just recorded a note of their uncut size. When she had finished she made her way to her car, jumped into it, and headed towards Hout Bay.

She drove through the small village which consisted of only a few shops on either side of the tree-lined street. As she drove around the bend she could see Chapman's Peak Hotel on her left and the Red Sails Restaurant on the right, which was where she was meeting Klaus, and sure enough, there he was waiting in the car park. He had been watching out for her, so as she drove in, he got out of his car.

'Hi Klaus, I hope you haven't been waiting too long?' she asked, looking down at her watch which showed three minutes past three.

'No sweetie, I only arrived a few minutes ago,' he replied as he walked over to the passenger side and jumped into the front seat beside Jessy. She switched on the car and drove up towards the famous Chapman's Peak Drive, one of the most beautiful scenic drives in the world. They said very little as they drove. Klaus enjoyed watching the fishing boats going out to sea and Jessy enjoyed the powerful energy that she got from the mountains.

Jessy pulled into one of the drive-offs on the side of the road. It was on the mountain, not the ocean side, because there were a lot of bushes which would give them more privacy. These areas were used for picnic spots and were very popular, especially in the summer time. If you didn't get there early enough you would never find a spot. It was winter now, so Jessy had the choice of a few picnic areas, but the one she chose was secluded from the road's view.

She pulled over and stopped under a tree and took a good look around. There was no one in sight, so she turned to face Klaus.

'Here they are,' she said as she opened her handbag and pulled the leather pouch from inside and handed it over to Klaus. He took the bag and smiled at her. Jessy watched him as he undid the leather tie and then emptied them into the lid of a shoebox that Jessy had covered with a black piece of velvet. She watched Klaus' face as he inspected them carefully. There was very little change in the expression on his face, not what she had expected, but perhaps Klaus had seen so many diamonds in his life that these were just another batch. Jessy was dying to ask him what he thought, but she controlled herself and sat patiently. Klaus took out his eyeglass and examined quite a few, then he removed the eyeglass and looked over at her.

'Well, what do you think?' she asked eagerly.

'You know enough about stones because I taught you. What do *you* think?' he asked, testing her ability to determine whether or not they were of any value.

'I think they are a very good quality, color and size,' she said waiting for his reply.

'You are right; there are some fine specimens here. I don't know where you got them from, but one doesn't get stones like these from small mines. I hope you know what you are doing because these stones have been carefully selected. There isn't a single poor quality stone amongst them,' he said, looking at her seriously.

'I thought so. They must be worth millions, but can you get them cut? Is there anyone trustworthy enough to do the job?' she asked, seeming a bit concerned and knowing that she was putting Klaus in a terrible position. She knew she could trust Klaus, but did he know someone who would keep this secret.

'Yes, I know someone who will do the job and ask no questions. He does work for me all the time, but it will cost a lot. How are you going to pay for the work to be done? He is an old friend of mine, now retired but still the best I know when it comes to cutting gem stones. It will be a challenge for him to get the best cut out of each stone, and these, well, these he will love working with. He does things with stones that I have never seen before, brilliant. He brings them to life. He is also honest. He is also my dear old friend and we have many secrets between us which are only ours, so this is just another one. Yes, he can be trusted to his death. He is of the old school, which is honesty and honor,' he said with love in his voice. Jessy smiled at him. She loved him dearly.

'If you say he's our man, then I believe you. Now, my friend doesn't have any money, so I can either pay or he will exchange some of the stones for the work,' she suggested.

'Have you discussed payment with your friend and does he know that you have offered to pay?' he enquired, knowing fine and well that Jessy would just offer without telling this "friend". It was obvious she had a soft spot for whoever this person was.

'Well, not exactly. He said to take payment from the stones but if that causes a problem, then I will pay and just take the stones as payment,' she said.

'You are very fond of this person, aren't you? This is a great risk you are taking,' he said, smiling at Jessy.

'Yes, you could say that. I think, for the first time in my life I am in love and it feels wonderful,' she replied with a sparkle and far-off look in her eyes. Klaus felt very happy for her and just hoped that she wasn't blinded by the love she was feeling for this man. He was tempted to say more, but he knew it would upset her and he did not want to spoil the feeling of love that she was experiencing. And besides, it was great to see her glowing, something he hadn't seen too often with Jessy.

'I'm sure my friend will be happy with taking a few of these stones for himself. I will get in touch with him and see when he can do the job,' Klaus said.

'I don't mean to push my luck, but could he do it as soon as possible? The quicker I get these out of my house and cut, the safer we will all be,' asked Jessy.

'I will see what I can do. I'll go and see him tomorrow. He is always at work before anyone else gets there, so I'll go early. I'll take the stones with me and let you know what he says. Perhaps we can meet in that little café near your shop, but I'll phone you and let you know what time I'll be able to get away,' he said and started to pick up the stones and place them back into the leather pouch.

'Thanks Klaus, I don't know how I'll ever be able to thank you. It seems I have said this so often. Perhaps one day there will be something that I can do for you to repay you for all the favors you have done for me over the years,' she said as she leaned over and kissed him on his forehead. He placed the pouch in his inside jacket pocket, making sure that it was secure with the zip closed.

Jessy started back to the parking lot where Klaus had left his car. They said their goodbyes and went off in their respective directions. No doubt, Klaus was headed for the harbor to buy some fresh fish and Jessy, of course, couldn't get back to Jacques quick enough. She looked at her watch; it was four-thirty. She didn't feel as if she had been gone an hour and a half, but she had.

When she arrived home there was no sign of Jacques in the house, so she went to the back bedroom window and looked out. He was sitting on the garden bench feeding the little sparrows, who had taken to nesting in the garden. It was a precious moment and all she could do was just stand and look.

She went into the kitchen and put on the kettle to make some tea to have with the pastries and cakes she had picked up from the Pastry Man on the way home. Jessy set a tray with a tea pot, two cups and saucers, sugar, milk and the pastries, and went out to join Jacques, under the trees. He stood up to help her with the tray as soon as he noticed she was coming, which wasn't until she was almost next to him. He was deep in thought.

'I thought you might like some tea and cake,' said Jessy as he took the tray from her, placing it on a garden table next to the bench.

'That sounds great,' he responded. They sat down and Jessy poured the tea.

'Do you like milk and sugar with your tea?' she asked as she picked up the tea pot and started to pour.

'Milk and one sugar, thanks,' he said. She gave Jacques his tea and offered him the plate of goodies. Jacques took a small cake that looked like it was topped with flaked almonds and Jessy helped herself to an apple turnover.

'Well, how did it go?' Jacques asked, looking at her but trying not to sound too enthusiastic.

'It went very well! I have given the stones to Klaus and he is going to see his friend tomorrow. He says they are of extremely good quality and that they had been carefully picked for that purpose. He doesn't think that they came from a small mine; he thinks that number of stones must have come from a large mine where they would be readily available,' she said, looking enquiringly at him. Jacques wasn't quite sure what to say. *Was she starting to become suspicious, or was she making a statement?*

'Well, I still can't remember a thing. I only hope that I haven't done anything illegal,' he said, returning her look. They sat in silence and then Jacques just had to say something to try and convince her that he wasn't in it for the money.

'Jessica, I don't want you to get into any trouble, or

your friend, so if you want to call the whole thing off we can just throw them in the ocean,' he said with a straight and serious face. Jessy looked down at the cup of tea she was holding in her hand and then looked up again.

'I think we will be all right. I would just like the whole thing to be over with. I have asked Klaus to get the job done as soon as possible, so that we can get on with our lives,' she said.

Jacques couldn't believe his good fortune; she wanted just what he did. The subject was dropped and they carried on with their tea party, trying to put all thoughts of the diamonds out of their minds. Jessy had such a strange feeling in her stomach, a feeling that there was something unsaid between the two of them but she brushed it off and they enjoyed what was left of the afternoon.

'How would you like to go out for dinner? I would love some good seafood. You suggest the restaurant and it'll be my treat,' Jacques said as they were walking back to the house. He couldn't remember the last time he ate in a restaurant that had good fresh seafood.

'What a great idea! I know the perfect place. I haven't been there for a long time, but it is casual dress and the food is superb,' Jessy said, feeling pleased at the thought of having dinner out with him. But there was just one thing she had to do before they left and that was to phone Michael. She really couldn't ignore his phone calls any longer. So, when they went inside, Jacques went for a shower and Jessy walked over to the phone, picked it up and dialed his number.

'Hello, Michael here,' said the voice on the other

side. Jessy was silent for a moment. She was not looking forward to telling him it was over, because she knew that he wouldn't believe it.

'Hi Michael, it's me,' she said tying to sound cheerful.

'Hi my sweetheart, I've been dying to come and see you, but I know I promised I would leave you in peace for the weekend so that you could decide,' he said sounding relieved.

'Thanks, I really appreciate it but you have phoned a lot, so I thought I would return your call and suggest we meet for lunch tomorrow; our usual restaurant in the harbor at one o'clock?' she suggested, not wanting to tell him over the phone.

'I suppose I can wait until tomorrow for my answer, but couldn't you just drop a hint?' he asked with a pleading sound in his voice.

'No, I would rather talk to you tomorrow,' she said trying to be firm.

'Okay sweetheart. I love you lots and I'll see you tomorrow, bye,' he replied.

'Bye Michael, see you tomorrow,' and with that, they both hung up. Well, it had to be done and she wasn't looking forward to tomorrow. As she put down the phone she turned around to see Jacques standing there.

'Are you okay? You don't look too happy,' he said, wondering what was going on. *Had someone found out about him, was that what the phone call was about?*

'I'm fine. I just phoned Michael and arranged to meet him tomorrow for lunch. I must tell him I'm not going to marry him. I really can't keep him hanging on any longer. It's not fair to him or me. It is better I get it over and done with,' she said anxiously.

'Are you sure this is what you want?' he asked, walking up to her and taking her by her hands.

'Yes, I'm sure. I just don't like doing this sort of thing,' she said with sadness in her eyes.

'Jessica, can I ask you not to mention me, because he *is* going to ask you if you have found someone else, and until we find out more about me, or my memory comes back, we shouldn't say anything,' he said with concern on his face.

'I can't lie to him. If he asks if there is anyone else what shall I say?' she asked, knowing that she was the world's worst liar. It just wasn't in her nature to lie and Michael knew that. *What could she say?*

'I'm not asking you to lie, but perhaps you could just disregard the question and say something else to change the subject; it's just for a little while. Who knows, if he thinks that you have fallen in love with someone else, he might come snooping around. Unless you think it's fine to tell him. I will leave it up to you; I really don't want to try and run your life, you have been so good to me, I just thought it may be safer to say nothing,' Jacques said. Jessy thought for a while and decided she wouldn't think about it anymore. She would think of something, if the question came up.

'Well, now that you're nice and clean, it's time for my bath,' she said, leaving him standing there on his own. Jacques couldn't help thinking how well things were going. Now he could sense that there was trouble brewing and he hoped that he was wrong. Perhaps Michael would shock them, decide to accept the break-up and take it like a man. He remembered Dave's words and the caution in his voice when he spoke of this "Michael". Dave didn't seem to be scared of anyone but he certainly wasn't as confident when he mentioned Michael. That was warning enough for Jacques.

Chapter Fifteen

They arrived at the restaurant some forty minutes later. The drive along Chapman's Peak had been lovely and Jessy's entire being was overflowing with energy. As Noordhoek beach came into sight, its beauty never failed to take her breath away. It was a long stretch of white sand edged by turquoise water, with foamy white waves that endlessly caressed and which timelessly crashed onto the beach. On a clear day it was paradise but this day, there was not a soul in sight. It looked so alluring and Jacques wondered why it was empty.

'Jessica, why is there nobody on the beach as it looks so incredible?' he asked quizzically.

'There are very bad back currents and it's not a safe beach to be on. Some walk their dogs but very few of them venture into the water, unless of course, they are the fearless surfers,' Jessy replied.

They eventually arrived at a coastal town, parked and

walked under the railway tunnel and onto the other side to where the restaurant was. They had a drink at the bar and then were escorted to their table, which overlooked the ocean. It was just as Jessy had described; it exuded character and charm, yet was cozy and romantic. The food was excellent, which enhanced the atmosphere, rendering itself for a perfect, loving evening.

Towards the end of the meal, a woman with long blond hair stopped and looked down at Jessy.

'I *thought* it was you. I've been saying to George all night that it was you and that I should go over and say "hello",' she said in a sugary sweet voice, directed first at Jessy and then turned her attention to Jacques.

'Oh, hello Sandy, nice to see you again,' said Jessy politely. This is just what she didn't want to happen. Sandy would be dying to get back to tell Michael that she had seen Jessy with another man. Sandy stood there silently, beckoning Jessy to introduce her to Jacques.

'Well, aren't you going to introduce us?' she asked smiling.

'I'm sorry Sandy; this is a friend of mine from Mauritius, Jacques. Jacques this is Sandy,' she said, hoping that would take care of that and she would disappear.

'Oh really? I go to Mauritius regularly; it's such a beautiful island and a wonderful place for a holiday. I suppose it is even nicer to live there. What brings you to Cape Town?' she asked inquisitively. The more news she got for Michael, the easier it would be to impress him.

'Yes, it is a lovely place to live and I *am* here for a holiday,' Jacques replied warily. Jessy had to think of something. She and Jacques had forgotten to go through the Mauritius trip. She would have to change the subject.

'Do you and George come here often?' Jessy asked quickly, and Jacques breathed a sigh of relief. They both could see that she didn't really want to talk to Jessy, she wanted to know who exactly this Jacques chap was.

'Well, as a matter of fact, it is our favorite spot. We try to come at least once a week,' she forced herself to reply to Jessy. Then she turned her attention straight back to Jacques.

'Will you be in town long? Perhaps we could get together and talk more about Mauritius? We want to go over in the summer, so perhaps you could recommend some spots that we haven't yet visited,' she suggested, wanting to say more. Sandy turned to look over at her table. She could see that George was getting agitated sitting on his own so she lifted her hand to give him a little wave, indicating that she wouldn't be much longer.

'Unfortunately, I am leaving fairly soon, which doesn't give me any free time. Sorry about that,' Jacques said calmly.

'If you leave your address with Jessy I can get it from her, if that would be all right with you?' she enquired.

'Yes, I'll do that,' he said and smiled.

'Well, I must fly. George is waiting. Give my love to Michael when you see him. I'm surprised he isn't with you tonight,' she said, just managing to get the last words in with a little dig of the knife. Both Jacques and Jessy said goodbye and watched her walk over to George, who gave a little wave to Jessy as he caught her glance. Jessy looked at Jacques and didn't know whether to laugh or cry.

'Who is that woman? Is she going to say something to Michael?' asked Jacques nervously.

'You can bet your life on it. She won't be able to wait until she gets home to phone him and to see if he knows about you. She went out with Michael for years, but he never made a move to propose to her, so she broke it off and started dating George, who is a very wealthy man in his own right. I am going to have to tell Michael about you. I can't deny it because Miss Blabbermouth will have already told him. But let's not worry about that; it really has nothing to do with any of them; let them think what they want. They don't know anything about you, except that you are from Mauritius. Michael knows that I have a good friend there, so what can he say, and if he suggests we are having an affair, I will tell him it's none of his business. Now let's forget about the world and everyone in it,' said Jessy quietly and with a smile.

Jacques was quiet and he wanted to emphasize the importance of not letting Michael snoop around too much. Thank heavens nobody knew about the diamonds, or it would be easy for Michael to pick up the phone and find out from the authorities about the latest diamond heists. *Let's just hope that Jessy never tells anyone*, he thought to himself while Jessy was chatting away. He heard a word here and there, but he wasn't really listening. He then dropped all thoughts of the incident and went back to enjoying the evening with her. They laughed and talked all night and once again, when they looked around, the restaurant was empty and the waiters were starting to clean up.

'We've done it again! The last to leave,' Jessy declared. Jacques caught the waiter's attention, which wasn't difficult as he was diplomatically waiting for them to call him. He brought the bill to Jacques and after settling, they made their way back to Llandudno, this time in the dark. As they drove along Chapman's Peak, the night prevented any views of the sea below but because the ocean was so still, they could clearly hear the thunder of the breaking waves against the rocks.

Jessy was expecting to have a phone call from Michael on the answering machine, but there was nothing. She would have to wait until tomorrow to see if Sandy had taken delight in alerting him to Jessy's "friend" from Mauritius. They made love and fell asleep in each other's arms. Jessy woke early, kissed Jacques goodbye and went off to work, leaving him to sleep. She left a note saying she would call him later. When she got to the shop, Melodie was the only one there.

'Good morning Jessy. Did you have a nice long weekend?' she asked with an enquiring tone in her voice, hoping that Jessy was going to tell her all about this mysterious man.

'Yes, wonderful thank you; how about you?' Jessy replied, knowing jolly well what Melodie was up to, but not offering anymore than was necessary.

'Fine thank you, but I'm sure not as exciting as yours was,' she said smiling, hoping that Jessy would take the hint.

'I can't tell you anything about him yet, but I promise I will very soon,' she said, hoping Melodie would stop with the questions.

'Come on Jess, you don't have to tell me everything, just whether or not you are in love with him,' she pleaded, letting out a huge sigh.

'Why should you say a thing like that? You know that I have been going out with Michael and I have only just met this man,' she said, now looking at Melodie with a puzzled expression on her face.

'Well, Michael has nothing on this guy when it comes to your heart. I could sense it the moment I saw the two of you together. The electricity between you was hugely electrifying. I just don't know a better way to put it. There is definitely something going on whether you like to admit it or not and you can't deny it,' she said to Jessy, now waiting for the truth.

'Yes you're right; I love him to pieces and it seems to be mutual, but that's all I can tell you, so please don't ask me anymore questions,' Jessy answered quickly.

Melodie wondered why she didn't want to tell her anymore about Jacques as she was normally so open with her. Perhaps she wanted to get Michael sorted out first before she could commit to this stranger.

'I'm happy; I just wanted to know if what I suspected was right. I'm really so happy for you, but what about Michael?' Melodie asked.

'I am having lunch with him today to tell him that I'm not accepting his proposal and that we should stop seeing each other,' Jessy answered, feeling sad and concerned.

'I'm glad I won't be there; he isn't going to take too kindly to that, nobody, but nobody turns that man down, and especially a proposal of marriage. There are women out there who would kill to be in your position. You do realize that, don't you?' she said with playfulness in her voice.

'Yes, I know that, but we can't always have what we want now, can we?' she said as she wandered through to the office in a melancholic state.

Melodie didn't ask any more questions about Jacques for which Jessy was grateful. The other members of staff were also dying to know, but she didn't offer any insight to her situation, even when they kept dropping little hints all morning about Jacques. Melodie knew that Jessy wanted everything to be kept secret for now, and she would honor that request. So, the morning was pretty normal with everybody working and busying themselves with their tasks. It was soon lunchtime and Jessy finished off what she was doing.

'Melodie, I am going to lunch now; wish me luck,' she said as she took a deep breath at the end of her sentence.

'I wish you *more* than luck,' Melodie said in return as she watched Jessy walk out of the shop.

She arrived at the restaurant on time and knew that Michael would be waiting for her. He was always early. Sure enough, there was his car. There was an empty space beside his car, so she parked there and walked inside where she was greeted by one of the waitresses who recognized her and led her to where Michael was waiting patiently. He stood up as she arrived and walked over to her chair, pulled it out and kissed her gently on the cheek before she sat down. Jessy could feel the hair on her neck stand up. It wasn't a good feeling at all.

'How are you today Jessy?' he asked in a matter-of-fact manner.

'I'm fine thank you,' she returned. When they were both seated he called a waitress and ordered a drink for Jessy and another one for himself, but his was a double whiskey. Jessy felt herself tense up as this could only mean that he had heard about Jacques. Should she say something now or wait until he brought up the subject? She sat there in silence, waiting for him to lead the way into conversation.

'Well Jessy, have you thought about what I asked you?' he asked, softening up a little and taking her hands in his.

'Yes I have Michael, and before I give you the answer, I want you to know that I have so enjoyed being with you and sharing all the good times we have had together. But Michael, as much as I love you, there is something missing, a certain magic. I am so sorry Michael but I just cannot marry you,' she replied gently. Jessy watched the smile slowly disappear from his face, only to be replaced by a frown that bore into his forehead. He didn't reply for a few minutes, but sat quietly and stared at Jessy. He was obviously trying to decide where this was taking him.

'Well, I'm sorry you feel like that Jessy. Why didn't you tell me this a long time ago?' he asked in a berating tone.

'I'm sorry Michael, but I really thought that the magic would appear,' she said, not really knowing what to say and wondering why he was taking this so calmly.

'I don't suppose this has anything to do with that Jacques guy you were with last night?' he asked, now glaring at her.

'I knew Sandy would phone you, but no, it doesn't, and even if it did, it really isn't any business of yours. I'm sorry Michael, but you can't always get your own way,' she said with conviction, ready to take him on if he was going to become nasty.

'Yes, Sandy did, and rightly so too. I think you owe me some kind of explanation,' he demanded.

'I have already told you that this has nothing to do with Jacques. There is nothing between the two of us and I thought we would be able to discuss this like two adults,' she said trying to bring out the business-like logic.

'Well, my dearest, you don't seem to want to get down to the truth. We had a fine relationship until this man appeared on the scene and I challenge you to prove me wrong,' he said defiantly.

'Now, what exactly do you mean by that?' she asked enquiringly.

'If this has nothing to do with him whatsoever, then why are you so protective about him? At the mention of his name you become rather vicious and your whole attitude changes. Now, someone who is *just a friend* of a friend doesn't get that sort of support now, does it? I know you too well; there are hidden feelings you are not telling me about and I can easily find out about this Jacques. I will just contact our mutual friend in Mauritius and find out what he knows,' he said smirking.

Jessy felt the blood rush from her head and she went

quite pale. She had forgotten that Michael and she had been on holiday together and that she had introduced him to Pierre. He was right; it would just take a phone call and then he would know that Jacques wasn't who she said he was. *What could she do? How could she stop him from doing this?*

'Michael, I think you are taking things a bit far; this really has nothing to do with Jacques. This is about us. If you think about it carefully, we aren't really made for each other and I don't get on that well with all your rich friends. I find them to be insincere and I've told you that on many occasions. It's just that marriage is so final and I really have to be one hundred percent sure before I make a commitment like this. Right now, I'm not ready,' she said, trying to keep the whole situation from exploding and getting out of hand.

'I understand my sweetheart; don't make a rash decision now. If you aren't ready I'll wait until you are, and I'm sorry I got a bit nasty. It just doesn't make sense that you would say "no", especially when we are made for each other,' he said, softly.

What was Jessy letting herself in for? This hadn't turned out how she thought it would. Michael couldn't handle the fact that she had turned him down. How was she going to get out of this? Nothing more was said about either the wedding or Jacques. They ate their food and talked about other things. Jessy was glad when it was over, but she had agreed to go out to the theater that evening with him to see a show that Michael had booked months ago. Jessy had forgotten all about it. That meant that he would expect her to go back to his place afterwards and perhaps stay overnight. They always went to his house and very seldom to hers for which she was thankful. But she knew she wasn't going to be able to have sex with him. She was in love with Jacques and she could never do that to their relationship. But how was she going to get away after the show? When she got back to the shop she went into the office and closed the door behind her. She sat down and put her head on her desk. This was all getting too complicated. There was a knock on her door. She didn't want to see anyone.

'I'm busy,' she said.

'Jess it's me, Melodie. Can I come in?' she asked.

'Sure Melodie,' Jessy replied. She could hear the door open and Melodie walked in and came over to her desk. It was obvious that the luncheon hadn't gone too well.

'Looks like you didn't enjoy your meal? he didn't take it too well?' asked Melodie. Jessy lifted her head off her hands and looked up at Melodie.

'Oh Melodie, you don't know half of what is going on, but I am in a real fix. Michael won't take no for an answer and I can't stand up to him, just yet. I know that doesn't sound like me, but please don't ask me any questions. I have a favor to ask of you,' Jessy said. She was looking straight into Melodie's eyes, an expression of concern on her lovely face.

'Sure, what is it?' she asked.

'Michael has asked me to go to the theater tonight. The show starts at eight o'clock, so I will be there about seven-thirty; please phone me there and tell Michael you have to speak to me urgently. Try and sound rather upset, even weepy. Do you think you can do that for me?' Jessy asked.

'I can do that with ease; it won't be a problem,' said Melodie, seeing how upset Jessy was and wanting to help her in any way she could. She knew there was something serious going on. She had never seen Jessy like this before, but she constrained herself from asking any further questions. She was just happy to be of some assistance.

Jessy phoned Jacques to see how he was but had forgotten she left the answering machine on so she hoped he had heard it. She left her phone number and asked him to return her call. He never phoned back so presumably he hadn't heard the message. Maybe he was out with Scanty? She wanted to talk to him so badly. She needed some advice about Michael, and although Jacques was involved as well, she knew he would look at it with a level head. Jessy was too emotionally involved with both Michael and Jacques.

She decided to leave an hour before closing time. She reminded Melodie of their plans but before she left the phone rang and it was Klaus. He asked if he could meet her before she went home, perhaps on the drive home, so she agreed and they met at Oudekraal. Klaus told her that his friend would do the job, but he was heavily booked for the next two months. Klaus had pushed him and he had agreed to start them straight away. Of course it would cost twice as much, but he had agreed to take some stones in exchange for the work. He had estimated that it would take him two weeks of non-stop working. He had also told Klaus that the stones were very good quality and it would be a challenge to get the best out of them. Jessy thanked Klaus over and over again. She said her goodbyes and told him she wouldn't contact him again until they were ready. She went home, feeling that the day hadn't been a complete mess up. She thought about Jacques as she drove home and her heart lifted. The love she felt for him was enormous and she was overwhelmed with great happiness.

Chapter Sixteen

Jacques wasn't there when Jessy arrived home and she wondered where he had gone. Betty had been in to clean and the food was in the hostess trolley, but no sign of Jacques. She even checked the garden, but still nothing. She decided she needed to have a long, hot, bubble bath. She poured herself a sherry and jumped into her Victorian tub. The bubbles overflowed onto the tiled floor, soaking away all the woes and cares of the day.

It was sometime later that she heard Scanty bark and the front door close.

'Hello, anyone at home?' came Jacques' voice from a distance.

'I'm in the tub,' she called out. Jacques heard her, so he made his way into the bathroom where he found her soaking in the water, bubbles up to her neck.

'That looks like fun,' he said and bent down and kissed her. Before he knew it, she had pulled him by his shirt and pulled him into the tub with her. It was a large, over-sized Victorian tub so there was plenty of space for both of them. They started laughing and Jacques proceeded to undress and join her. They talked about his day which seemed so much more enjoyable in comparison to hers. Then he finally asked, 'How was your lunch with Michael, or shouldn't I ask?' It had been on his mind all afternoon.

'Well, a bit more exciting than yours. I'm afraid I couldn't break up with him,' she said, watching the puzzled look on Jacques' face.

'So, have you changed your mind?' he asked, trying to conceal the jealousy that was surging through his veins.

'No, not at all, but he knew about you and us having dinner together last night. He, of course, immediately drew the conclusion that it was because of you that I am not accepting his proposal. He started to get rather nasty, a side of him I have never seen before, except in business. He actually frightened me. He said it would be easy to find out more about you if I were still going ahead with the break-up. All he would have to do is phone Pierre in Mauritius and then he would know that I was lying. If that happened, I know he wouldn't be able to rest until he found out everything about you. It just isn't worth it, not until we get the diamonds out the way.'

'When I get out of this bath, the first thing I must do is phone Pierre and tell him that you are indeed a friend of his, and that he sent you to me. You see, I told Michael that it was none of his business who you were, because you weren't the reason for our lack of compatibility. I confessed that there was no chemistry between us. That's when he got nasty and wouldn't accept no for an answer. He thinks we were made for each other. If you could have seen the look in his eyes, it really scared me. So I had to try and calm him down. I said I wasn't ready to make such a final decision about marriage. He, of course, softened a little and said that he understood and he would give me a bit more time. I really am quite relieved, now that I have decided not to marry him. After lunch today, heaven knows what vented emotions and anger, lies deep within him. It's almost as if he has to possess me and that the thought of anyone else having me is just too much for him. I really don't know what to do,' she said feeling wretched and playing with the bubbles absent-mindedly.

Jacques had listened carefully. It looked like this Michael was going to be trouble and this sort of trouble would be the end of his parents' lives. He would have to think this through carefully. It was good that Jessy had calmed him down and not broken up with him because that would keep him at bay for a while. All the problems she was having because of him; she certainly didn't deserve any of this. Now she was stuck with Michael and it was obvious that she was starting to fear him. He really wanted to just take her away from all of this, but he knew, for now, that that was not possible.

'I'm sorry Jessy about all the trouble I have caused you, but whatever I can do to help, please just tell me. First of all, we must make sure that Michael never meets me. I think you must tell him that I have gone back. I will move out of your house and go somewhere else because if he is feeling threatened, there's no telling what he will do. He might even hire a private investigator. All they need is a photo of me and then it will be over,' he said cautiously.

Jessy listened to him and wondered what he meant by 'all over'. Surely it would mean Jacques would find out who he was; so why should that be negative? The only nagging issue was the diamonds. Perhaps throwing them into the sea wasn't a bad idea after all. All this hiding, ducking and diving was just too much for her. But where had he got the stones from? If in fact he had been part of a diamond heist, then that would mean jail for life. She couldn't take that chance. Even if they disposed of them, he would still be party to it despite his loss of memory. She really didn't want to think about it any further. It was all becoming more and more perplexing. Anyhow, worrying never solved anything, but only opens the door for more negativity to enter.

'Good idea. I know just the place. It's Patricia's cottage in Constantia. It's perfect. Michael knows I have a twin sister, but he has never met her and he thinks she is still in Johannesburg, which she is. She left a key with me so that I can go in every now and again to check up on things. She won't mind at all, and besides, it's tucked away in the forest and is very secluded. The more I think about it, the more perfect I think it is. What do you think?' she asked, her voice becoming more and more excited, convincing herself and Jacques that this was a brilliant idea.

'That would be wonderful. Great idea and I think I should move in today because we can't afford to wait,' he said, not relishing the thought of being there when Patricia came back. There was something about her that he just didn't trust, something that made him feel uneasy while in her presence. Although she looked identical to Jessy, they were oceans apart. Jessy and Jacques were now both feeling a lot more comfortable with their new plan and started to relax. They didn't stay in the tub too long as Jessy would have to take Jacques over to Patricia's and then be at Michael's at seven-thirty. Jessy dressed and went straight to the phone and called Pierre.

''ello?' the voice on the other side said with a French accent.

'Bonjour Pierre, c'est Jessy. Ca va bien?' she asked.

'Oh mais oui, Jessy, it is wonderful to hear from you. How are you? This really is a surprise, but today has been a day full of surprises,' he said. She wasn't quite sure what he was talking about.

'I'm well, thank you. Pierre, I have a favor to ask please. If you should get a call from Michael, I would like you to tell him that you sent a friend of yours, called Jacques, to stay with me while on business for you. Would you do that for me, please Pierre?' she requested.

'Of course I would have, but Michael phoned me early this morning, even woke me up and asked if I had a friend called Jacques and had he gone to Cape Town. Well, I was still half asleep and I didn't know what he was getting at. He never mentioned your name. I told him I have many friends called Jacques. I have many friends and colleagues with that name, which one did he mean? So I told him to ring me back this evening when I had all my faculties about me. So when he does phone, I will tell him that I *did* send a colleague over to do some business for me. For you! Anything my Jessy. When are you coming over to see me again?' he asked.

'Well, sometime soon I hope and thank you so much for doing that for me Pierre. One more thing, if he asks *what* business, tell him to mind his own business. Obviously you won't word it like that but you know what I mean,' she said. Pierre wasn't the inquisitive kind and asked no further questions. They chatted for about ten minutes and then Jessy said she had to rush off. She had also mentioned that he must not tell Michael that Jessy had been in touch with him which he agreed to do.

Jacques had come in and was standing beside her. He could tell by the expression on her face that things weren't too good. She looked up at Jacques with fire in her eyes.

'You won't believe it, but Michael phoned Pierre early this morning to check up on you! So he knew at lunch that he had already checked up on you and that he was going to phone Pierre back later to verify if my story was true or not. What is this man up to? I think you're right, we must get you out of here as quickly as possible. Go and get your things and I'll take you to Patricia's. We must make sure that we aren't being followed,' she said, trying to think things through in her mind.

Michael was up to something, but she didn't know what. She was going to have to go very carefully and watch his every move. She felt trapped and that didn't go down too well with her. She was a free spirit and didn't like the feeling of being possessed or cornered.

Jacques went to his room and put a few clothes in a small tote bag that Jessy had loaned him. They made their way out to the car and were vigilant, checking regularly to see if there were any unusual cars in the area. Jessy thought that if someone was following them, they would more than likely be at the top of the entry and exit road. That would be the best spot. As they approached the top road, Jessy looked both right and left but didn't see any cars parked or unattended. She felt a little relieved and turned right at the intersection. During the drive she noticed that a black car had been behind her all the way up to Constantia Nek.

'Jacques, there is a car behind us but I'm not sure when it started following us. What shall I do?' she asked with alarm in her voice. He turned around and had a look, trying not to be too paranoid.

'Pull over onto the next side road and see if it follows you,' he replied. They were both starting to feel rather uneasy. Jessy indicated and turned onto the next side road and they both watched very carefully to see what the black car was going to do. It carried on past them. They turned to look at each other and burst out laughing.

'I think we are becoming rather neurotic. We've been watching too many detective movies,' Jessy said in between her outbursts of laughter.

When they had pulled themselves together and wiped the tears from their cheeks, she turned the car around and went back to the main road. There was no sign of the black car. Really, that was the only road to the top so she was just being neurotic. She had to keep calm.

They made their way down the meandering road until they reached the exit road which led to Patricia's cottage. As they approached, Jessy wondered why Patricia had not come straight to her own home the night she arrived back in Cape Town. Instead, she had come straight to her, but thought no more about it. She had more important things to think about.

'This is it,' she announced to Jacques. It was quaint, built from stone and the garden was full of winter flowers.

'This is lovely, Jessica! You are right; it's perfect,' Jacques said as he got out of the car and made his way along a stone garden path. Jessy reached into her handbag and searched for the house keys to unlock the door. The house smelled musty, which was to be expected after being closed up for more than a few days. It was quite small, but it had a stone fireplace with a large, old wooden beam as a mantelpiece. There were also enormous wooden beams that held up the ceilings. There was a tranquil feeling about it but it wasn't the sort of place Jacques pictured Patricia living in, perhaps Jessy, but certainly not Patricia. It was chilly, so Jacques made a fire while Jessy went into the kitchen to see if there was anything to eat. But alas, the fridge was switched off and the pantry was empty.

'Jacques there's no food in the house. There's a take-away restaurant just down the road. I'll go and get us some food while you make the fire,' she said as she picked up her car keys and headed out the door. Jessy wasn't gone long and Jacques could hear her car as it came down the dusty old road. Perhaps that was a good thing because it meant he would be able to monitor the comings and goings of everyone who came to the cottage. They ate in front of the fire and sat in silence, watching the flames dance up and down. Jessy thought it was time that she gave Jacques some good news.

'Oh, by the way, I spoke to Klaus today and he has managed to get his friend to agree to cut the stones for us. He said he could only do it in two months time, but Klaus knows him very well and persuaded him to cut them sooner. They will be ready in a few weeks. He has also agreed to take a few stones in exchange. It is going to cost twice as much as he normally charges, but if you want them done quickly, that was the only way to get them cut. I told him to go ahead as you didn't want to wait, did you?' she asked, looking at him for reassurance.

'Of course not; the quicker they are ready, the better. That's great news,' he said, but he wasn't as excited about it as Jessy had expected. Jacques was very pleased, but he also knew that meant that when they were finished, it would be time to catch the ship. Perhaps he could stay until the second trip. But he knew that would only mean torture for both Jessy and himself. No, he would have to leave on the first of August.

'Won't it be wonderful when all this is behind us and we can start off fresh with no Michael or diamonds?' she asked. It would mean that they would both have to move somewhere else and start afresh. That didn't bother her, as long as she was with Jacques; that's all that mattered.

'I think you know that will never happen, Jessica. Michael will want to know who I am, and until I discover who I am, we must keep hiding from him. I'm sure you don't want to spend the rest of your life running and hiding,' he said with torture in his eyes.

'Yes, I know that, but somehow we'll find a solution, won't we?' she asked innocently.

'Sure, we'll work it out,' he said and kissed her warmly. He held her close to him, sensing her uneasiness.

Jacques reached out to her hair and slowly removed each hairclip that held it up and off her beautiful face. It fell gently onto her shoulders and back. He ran his hands through her soft, silky hair. She felt the shivers up her spine. His very touch made her feel weak all over. He removed her clothes slowly and deliberately. She removed his clothes, stroking his warm, hard body. He moved his hand down to her breasts that were pert and hard. He kissed her lips, her neck, and then ran his tongue around her nipples. He moved down over her body, kissing each part of it as he made his way to her stomach. He got to her thighs and the soft baby-like skin. He kissed her tenderly, enjoying the taste that only a woman has. She purred with each caress, loving the attention her body was receiving.

She moved her hand down and found he was aroused. Their foreplay was always so much fun and they both loved every minute of it. By the time Jacques entered her, they were filled with passion and love. They melted into one another, feeling whole and complete. After a long while, Jessy remembered where she still had to go, but she did not want to spoil the moment.

'Jacques, I must go back to my house; I can't stay here too long. I have some things I have to do, but I will phone you in the morning,' she said, stroking the side of his face tenderly.

Jacques thought it was rather strange that she was leaving so early but she had had a rough day and perhaps needed to be on her own, so he didn't question her and instead, just smiled.

She hadn't told him about going to the theater with Michael. It had slipped her mind and now didn't seem like the right moment. They lay there for a short time and then Jessy got up, dressed and made her way home. She was sure that she hadn't been followed even though the roads were busy. She arrived home, took a quick shower and changed into something more formal. She had a heavy, sick feeling in the pit of her stomach. How was she going to be able to face this man, knowing that he was suspicious of Jacques and her?

She got to Michael's at seven-forty and Melodie had already phoned. Michael told her that she sounded very upset and that he recommended that Jessy phone her back, suggesting she make it quick because otherwise they would be late for the show. Jessy made the call, being extra careful to speak loud enough so that Michael could hear what she was saying, with feigned dramatic emphasis on the, 'Oh no!' and 'Don't worry!' When she hung up the phone, she walked over to Michael and told him that she would have to go straight from the theater to see Melodie. She had some personal problems and needed her help. Michael wasn't too pleased about it. He had planned on taking Jessy out for a romantic dinner and then had hoped to spend the rest of the evening with her. He moaned a bit, but realized that there was nothing he could do. It wasn't often that Melodie asked Jessy for help, so he reluctantly agreed.

The show seemed to go on for hours and hours. Jessy really wasn't paying too much attention and she didn't enjoy it. Michael had sat there, loving every moment. He could spend every day at the theater; it was part of his soul. At half-time they went for cocktails and while there, bumped into some mutual friends. On the way back he took Jessy's hand.

'By the way, when is Jacques returning to Mauritius?' he asked in a matter-of-fact manner, not looking at her, just walking and talking as normal. Jessy felt the blood rush to her head. Why wasn't he telling her that he had checked up on Jacques?

'He left today but he hasn't gone back to Mauritius, he has gone to Europe,' she said, trying to lead the trail away from Mauritius. She sounded just as casual as he did.

'Oh really, that's good news; perhaps now we can get on with our lives,' he said, squeezing her hand in his.

For the first time, Jessy looked at him with disdain. *Who did he think he was?* She had been introduced to a new Michael, one she didn't like. His comments didn't even warrant a reply, so she just walked next to him in silence, hating every moment she was with him. She was glad when the show was finished and she could get away. She made her way towards Melodie's, just in case he was having her followed. She stayed there for a while and then went home. She had an early night and was glad when she fell asleep.

She phoned Jacques as soon as she woke up and was happy to hear his familiar voice. She told him about what had happened and how she hated being with Michael. He listened and tried to console her as much as he could. They arranged for her to come over after work. He would help her forget her evening with Michael. She was grateful that she had Jacques around because he always seemed to say the right things at the right time.

Chapter Seventeen

During the day, Jessy received a call from Patricia. She was back and said she wanted to see her. Jessy told her briefly that Jacques was staying in her cottage and that they could all meet there for dinner. Patricia agreed and reassured Jessy that she didn't mind at all and that she liked Jacques.

Jessy phoned Jacques and told him to expect Patricia. She was back in town and she was going to cook dinner for them. He wasn't too pleased at the prospect of Patricia, but he didn't say anything to Jessy as he really didn't want to hurt her feelings. She was having a rough enough time.

At about four o'clock, Jacques heard a car coming up the driveway and he looked out the window. Sure enough, it was Patricia in her flashy Porsche. He went to the door to let her in, and went to the car to help her carry some groceries inside. They chatted as he watched her cook.

'You have a lovely cottage,' he said.

'Yes, it is lovely. It makes me forget the outside world and brings me back home,' she said casually.

Jacques thought, *What a profound statement to make. It was almost as if she were one person when she walked out of the door and when she came home she was another.* The longer he spent with her, the more he realized that it was true. She was a completely different person from the one he had met at Jessy's. She was more like Jessy and he wondered why this was happening to her. She was obviously aware of it so she could stop it at any time, but why had she chosen to live as she did? He found himself actually enjoying her company. If he didn't know better, he would have thought she *was* Jessy. Physically, he couldn't tell them apart. Patricia dressed differently from Jessy and wore different jewelry, but if they swapped clothes, what a lot of trouble they could get into.

Patricia told him about her life and how much she loved Jessy but had always known that she was different to her, and how she had been jealous of Jessy for most of her life. She spoke so freely and truthfully that Jacques couldn't help feeling that there was hope for her yet. Jacques began to admire her. He appreciated her openness with regard to her emotions and her honesty about her weaknesses.

Jessy arrived later and they all sat around the table, eating, drinking and enjoying the meal with each other's company. There was plenty of laughter and many stories were recounted.

'Patricia, how long are you going to be in town?' Jessy asked.

'Well, funny you should ask, but I have packed in my job and I am moving back home. I've had enough of Johannesburg. I miss Cape Town and my friends,' she said.

Jessy was taken aback for a second, but nothing surprised her about Patricia. She was always changing jobs and moving around.

As Patricia sat, watched and listened to Jacques and Jessy, she realized how much in love they were. It seemed such a shame that they couldn't spend a few weeks together, without having to worry about Michael. Jessy was one of the few people Patricia knew who always had a fairytale romance about her. Jessy believed in the enormous power of love and now she had finally found it. Michael was standing in the way. *How could she help them?* Unexpectedly, she had the most brilliant idea. She thought about it for a while and knew it would work, if Jess agreed to it. Jacques and Jessy were both looking at her. Patricia's face had suddenly lit up and a smile appeared across it.

'Are you okay, Patricia?' asked Jessy.

'Yes, I'm fine, I couldn't be better. Jessy, do you remember when we were kids and we would change places, and nobody ever suspected us because they hadn't known we had done it?' she asked.

'Sure I do, and I remember how you loved doing it,' replied Jessy, smiling at the memory of those halcyon days.

'Well, if I told you that I wanted to do that again, what would you say?' Patricia asked breathlessly.

'Well, I would have to know what you have in mind. What are you getting at?' she asked, wondering what Patricia was up to now.

'I know you have been going out with Michael and that he has asked you to marry him, but I know you don't love him. I also know that he's having trouble facing that and you don't really want to be in his company,' she said. Jessy was wondering what was about to come; she wasn't sure where this was going.

'Well, I really don't have much to do, so I could certainly do with a little fun being spoiled and pampered. Jess, how would you feel if I told you that I would take your place and be *you* for a few weeks? That way, it would give you two time to spend together and also, I could have lots and lots of fun, and don't worry, I would keep him very occupied,' Patricia said. Jessy looked over in Jacques' direction, waiting for some reaction from him.

'Let me get this straight. You want to go out with my boyfriend and pretend that you are me. I suppose that means sleeping with him as well?' Jessy enquired. She was feeling rather thrilled by the whole idea. She didn't want to seem too keen, but it would give her the freedom to be with Jacques.

'Well yes, I know you might think it's a tad far-fetched but he will never know the difference and I will be treated like a queen. I'll look after him, you can be sure of that. I'll pamper his every need. It's not as if I'm giving up my virginity, now is it?' she said, smiling at Jessy who knew how many men her sister had slept with over the years.

'Well, it sounds fine, but don't you think that he will be able to tell the difference between us, especially with regards to the sex side of things?' asked Jessy.

'Well, if he says anything I will just say that I am feeling wonderful and mischievous and with that comes a lot of new energies. He won't think anymore about it. Our bodies are the same so there won't be anything that he can wonder about, and I was always good at playing you. I can change my whole personality when I want to,' Patricia said animated.

'How long do you two need to be together, to work out how you are going to handle Michael?' she asked.

'Well, Jacques and I have a few things that we want to do and we need a few weeks to get things sorted out,' she said, not offering too much information. Jessy sat in silence for a while, just watching the candlelight. Then she gave Patricia's idea the thumbs up!

'What do you think, Jacques?' she asked, as she turned to look at him. He hesitated a moment.

'It sounds like it could work and if Patricia is happy doing it, I think it would be amazing,' he said, while all the time looking at Patricia, trying to get a feel of what was going on in her mind. He had never heard of anything so outrageous, and yet so brilliant.

'Okay, I agree, but I am going to have to show you pictures of all my friends just to make sure you know them,' Jessy said. Jacques sat and listened to the two of them planning the whole sham, and talking so openly about the one sleeping with the other's boyfriend. He couldn't believe it. But he knew it could work. He had witnessed first-hand how much Patricia had become like Jessy and it would give him and Jessy time to be together.

'You can stay in my house, I'll show you the photos of my friends and you can just pretend you are me. It will be so much fun!' Jessy said throwing back her head and laughing happily.

She found it rather strange that Patricia had offered to do such a thing, but she didn't think about it too much because she knew what Patricia was like. This sort of thing would appeal to her strange sense of humor. Perhaps it was the thrill and playful side of her that made her agree to such a sham, but whatever it was, she was thankful that she had suggested it.

'What about going to your shop? Surely you don't want me to do that, do you?' she asked, with a frown on her face.

'Well, not every day, but if Michael says he'll phone you at work, or that you have a lunch date, then perhaps you could go in and take it easy, look through magazines, which is what I often do. I will tell Melodie what we plan on doing. She will understand and keep the others from disturbing you. Melodie knows I have a lot on my mind, and she will keep the place running and not bother you. Do you think you can handle that? If it gets to be too much, just walk out and tell them you'll be back later,' Jessy said reassuringly.

'I suppose I can do that,' said Patricia reluctantly.

'What do you really think about this plan of ours?' Jessy asked as she turned to face Jacques who hadn't said a word since he had agreed that it could work.

'Well, it seems impossible, but I believe Patricia can do it and it certainly would be nice for you to have a break,' he said, taking her hand in his.

'I can see that the two of you are in love. It stands out a mile. I sensed it that first night I met you at Jessy's. But this is just a short-term plan and whatever you want to do together, do it soon. I will enjoy it for a while, but not forever, and besides, I want to go on a cruise next month, so jump around and look smart,' said Patricia.

'Thank you Trish. You don't know how much it means to us, and obviously you won't tell anyone about this, will you?' she said pleadingly.

'Are you crazy? If Michael ever found out he would certainly have me arrested. I won't say a word to a soul,' replied Patricia, shuddering at the very thought of him finding out.

'*Why* are you doing this for me?' asked Jessy, growing suspicious of the easy-go-lucky attitude of Patricia, knowing that she didn't just do something like this for nothing. *What was her motive? There must be one.*

'Well, I don't have anything to do, and besides, we haven't played this game for ages. It will be fun to see if I can still get away with it, even under such peculiar conditions,' she said smiling.

Jessy and Jacques just accepted that she was doing it for the excitement and left it at that.

'There's just one more thing; you must make sure you aren't being followed when you come here because if he suspects that Jacques and I are having an affair, there will be serious trouble. I don't trust him so he may have

227

hired a private investigator to keep an eye on me. I told him that Jacques has gone over to Europe just to keep him from growing suspicious. But I'm sure you'll think of something to amuse him,' Jessy said.

'You don't have to worry about that. I will keep him so busy with other things, he won't have either the time or the inclination to think about Jacques,' she said with a twinkle in her eye, and Jessy believed her. Jessy had been told by many men that Patricia was a "wild thing" in bed and that she wore them out, which would be a good thing because then Michael wouldn't doubt that she was still in love with him.

'I will phone you tomorrow and we can go through some of the photographs so that you are not surprised by anyone's appearance,' Jessy said.

That night, Patricia left and went to Jessy's house and the game began. Patricia had her part to play and she was thankful that she could do something to help Jacques and Jessy. She must just keep Michael at bay for two weeks.

Jessy thought about what Patricia was doing and wondered what a coincidence it was that she just happened to give up her job to come and visit her at the perfect time. She wondered if coincidences were just that or were they signs from the universe, a bit like a signpost that reads: *Take heed of this sign and think about what you are doing.* It's the same as getting a strong feeling for something and then ignoring it. Are we then given free will to choose or to take no notice? What impact do these signs have on our lives? Especially when we ignore them? Of course the subject of predestination comes into play. Does that then mean that we really *don't* have free will because everything is already known and planned by God? She had a hard time believing that viewpoint. Wouldn't that then obviate the necessity for free will? She had learned over the years to listen to her gut feelings and the so-called coincidences, and because of that, her life seemed to be more in harmony with the universe than ever before. Life itself is really quite simple; it's we humans who complicate it. It would appear that there is an abundance of whatever it is that we need; an eternal, unlimited flow of love and energy that the universe offers to all of us. The question is, why do we not know it exists, and use it, on a daily basis? Why are we still stuck in the philosophy which believes that we are not worthy of an abundant life?

Jessy had learned so much from meditating and discovered that in the silence was peace. It was as if she had touched or awoken the God in herself, and whenever she needed to return to God, she could. She started looking at life through different eyes. She started to see the beauty in everything around her. Even in times of disharmony, she still saw the harmonious side of the situation. These days she awoke giving thanks to the universe for life and went to bed feeling the same way.

Jessy and Jacques, in the meantime, were happy with their new situation and just hoped that Patricia was careful when around Michael. The next few days were ones of anticipation for them. Patricia had had a few dates with Michael and they couldn't wait to hear how they had gone. Eventually the phone rang on the third day and it was Patricia.

'Hi there Jess. Well, things haven't really changed. He doesn't suspect a thing. He says our sex life has improved and there has been no mention of Jacques. Am I good or am I good?' she asked, with a menacing tone of voice.

'That's wonderful news, Patricia. Keep us posted and have fun. Oh, and yes, you are good!' replied Jessy.

'We are going away for the weekend so I won't speak to you until Monday. Michael hasn't said where we are going, but he assures me that we haven't been there before and that it is a very special place,' Patricia said.

'Don't let your guard down, Patricia, and don't have too much to drink because that's when you might let something out,' warned Jessy.

'Don't worry. I am being very careful. Bye for now and the two of you have a lovely weekend. I'll be thinking about you,' she said as she hung up the phone. Jessy went over to sit next to Jacques and told him what Patricia had said. So far so good; she really was good at that sort of thing, and most of all she never felt guilty about it. She loved doing it. Jessy was the one who had always been aware of what she was doing so she never did anything which would hurt the feelings of others.

'It looks like we have a week or so until we hear from Klaus, and Michael has been taken care of, so that just leaves you and me,' said Jessy, looking at Jacques, feeling happy that she didn't have to take care of Michael's sexual needs.

'That sounds wonderful. What can you recommend for passing time?' he asked.

'I think it's time that I showed you around Cape

Town instead of hiding you away. I think we'll start with a trip out to Franschhoek and Stellenbosch to taste the local wines and have lunch under the oak trees, followed by a drive in the country. How does that sound? Do you feel up to it?' she asked jokingly, knowing fine and well that Jacques must feel like a cooped up wild cat.

'Well, don't just talk about it, let's go,' he said, getting up and heading straight for the door.

'Okay. You go out to the car; I must just grab a few things,' she said. So that's how they spent the next week, going to the different sites around the Cape, loving each moment together and forgetting who they were. They went for long walks along the far stretching beach of Muizenberg and swam in the warm waters of the Indian Ocean. Jacques found it very strange that where Jessy lived, the waters of the Atlantic Ocean were freezing while just over the mountain was the warm Indian Ocean. At Cape Point, they merged into one ocean. They spent a day at Cape Point, climbing down to the small beaches and watched the thunderous waves caused by the meeting of the two oceans and mingling currents. It was a rather beautiful area which had been turned into a Nature Reserve and they even managed to see some wild animals as they drove. Another day was spent driving out to Gordon's Bay, which was a favorite place for watching the sharks. It was there that many great white sharks were seen. Another day was spent hiking. They started from Constantia Nek and climbed up and over the mountain, then through the Tokai forests and up Chapman's Peak Drive, from where they descended. Being up so high, looking out over the ocean was really a magnificent sight and they both reveled in its beauty. They sat and had a picnic before making their way down the mountainside and home. Some evenings they would sit by the fire and Jacques would read to Jessy. He had found a leather-bound book on Jessy's bookshelf. Jessy was mesmerized by his voice and the story. It was a love story and being a romantic, fell straight into the story, absorbed by the characters.

Then on another evening, the phone rang and it was Patricia.

'Well, how are the two of you enjoying your free-dom?' she asked gaily.

'We are having a lovely time and it's really all thanks to you,' said Jessy sincerely.

'All's well on this end. Michael still seems convinced that I am you, but I think someone has been following me. The last couple of days I have noticed a grey car at the top of your street. When I arrived home the other day, the same car was parked a few houses down. It could just be a coincidence. Do you think I should say something to Michael?' she asked.

'No, don't mention it to him; once he knows that he is getting all your attention, and that there is no sign of anyone around, he will call him off. I know how Michael thinks. Really, don't worry about it, he is just reassuring himself that he is the only man in your life, so don't go and do anything silly like picking up some strange man and taking him home with you,' Jessy said.

'Really Jessy, you can't think much about me to think

that I would do something like that. Perhaps in the old days, but I haven't done that for years and years. Anyhow, it really doesn't bother me; I feel like I'm part of a spy movie where the husband has the wife followed. It's all rather exciting. Oh, by the way, Klaus phoned today and said that he wanted to meet you tomorrow for lunch, same place. I wasn't sure what he was talking about, so I said sure, so don't forget to go at one-thirty,' she said, almost forgetting that that was the reason she had phoned Jessy in the first place.

'Thanks Patricia, I'll be there. Is everything all right at the shop?' Jessy asked.

'Just fine, I don't spend a lot of time there, but you were right, nobody is asking questions and they are leaving me to myself. Well, I must fly. Your two weeks is nearly over,' she said.

'Yes, I know, bye,' Jessy replied.

When she put the phone down she told Jacques about Patricia being followed and that Klaus wanted to see her at lunch tomorrow. They both looked at each other. Time had gone so quickly. They didn't want it to end, but neither of them voiced their dismay. The next day Jessy met Klaus for lunch and he told her what had happened.

'The stones will be ready tomorrow, so perhaps we should meet at the parking lot on Saturday morning and I can give them to you. He says that they have come out beautifully and that there are some really fine specimens amongst them. He also said he didn't want to know too much about where they had come from as he estimated that they were worth between five and six million US dollars. He has taken his payment for the work and, to tell you the truth, he enjoyed cutting them,' Klaus said.

'Thanks Klaus, I don't know how I can ever repay you,' said Jessy gratefully.

'You can repay me by being careful with them. I don't know what you have planned for selling them, but keep your eyes and ears open. By the way, I was talking to a friend of mine the other day and he heard about a diamond heist that took place in South West Africa a few weeks ago. I'm not saying that these have anything to do with that, but just be aware that the authorities will be on the hunt. Often they will appear as civilians, but are undercover agents, so be on the alert Jessy, that's all I ask of you,' he said, showing deep concern on his face.

Jessy listened to his every word. *Was Jacques involved in the heist?* How could she find out without drawing any attention to herself? She knew that she wouldn't be able to rest until she knew for certain.

'Don't worry Klaus, I will be careful, I promise. Can you get any more information about this heist, who was involved, what they looked like; their names?' she asked, knowing that there was a possibility that she was involved because of her mysterious friend.

'It was in all the papers in South West Africa and I know that my friend will have kept the article, so I will ask him to send me a copy of it. He will have to post it from there so it will be here next week sometime,' he said.

'There's no hurry; I am just interested to see what they say,' she said, trying to sound casual about it. Then she changed the conversation to something lighter. They ate their lunch and then said their goodbyes.

On the way home, Jessy couldn't stop thinking about what Klaus had told her. *Should she tell Jacques what he had said?* Something inside her told her not to, but how could she not. He may have been involved in it and just couldn't remember. When this was all over, she was going to suggest that he visit a doctor friend of hers to see what could be done about regaining his memory. Then of course there was Michael. If Jacques was involved with the heist, Michael would keep snooping until he found out the truth. It only meant one thing; they would have to disappear if they hoped for a normal life together. She would have to sell her shop but very quietly. That wouldn't be a problem because one of her friends had been dying to buy it from her. She would have to discuss this with Jacques and see what he thought.

If only Patricia would fall in love with Michael, then perhaps that would take care of that. Anything was possible with Patricia.

When she arrived home, Jacques was sitting out under the oaks reading his book. It was a beautiful winter's day. The air was fresh and crisp, with the sun creating a captivating light. Jacques had heard Jessy arrive and watched her walk past the window. She hadn't seen him as she was preoccupied.

'Hi there beautiful,' he said. She turned to see where his voice was coming from and walked over to join him.

'Is everything all right? You seem perturbed about something?' he asked, sensing her change in mood.

'I'm fine. Klaus will have the stones for me on Saturday so I must meet him at the same place and pick them up. He told me that the cutter had commented on the clarity and facets of the diamonds. They were excellent stones and he was very pleased with the outcome,' she said, with no excitement in her voice.

This wasn't what Jacques had been expecting; he thought that she would have been happy. There was something else that she wasn't telling him.

'That's wonderful, but what else is bothering you?' he asked. She moved away from him, walked a few steps back, hesitated a moment and then walked back to him.

'Klaus told me that he had heard about a diamond heist on one of the South West African mines. He didn't suggest that you were involved because he doesn't even know who you are, but he said I must be extra vigilant because they were checking up on all leads, phones or street talk. I have asked him to get a copy of the article from his friend in South West Africa which should be here sometime next week. There may even be a picture of whoever was in-volved and there are details about the whole heist,' she said, looking at him and watching his expression very carefully. Jacques remained poker-faced which made Jessy think that he really didn't know anything about the heist.

'I suppose once the article arrives we will know, once and for all, whether or not I was part of it,' he said to her, in a down-to-earth tone of voice. She seemed more concerned, than he was. Why wasn't he bothered?

'Well, what are we going to do if you *were* part of it?' she asked, a troubled expression on her face.

'Let's worry about that if it is true. Until then we must just sit and wait,' he said calmly.

'Jacques, I've been thinking. If the article arrives and you aren't involved, then we must get you to a doctor and see if there is anything that could trigger your memory. We can't live like this, not knowing who you are and where those diamonds came from. Can you promise me that you will do that for me?' she asked.

'Sure Jessica, if it makes you happy. I don't want to live like this either. I want to be free to come and go as I choose,' he responded.

The diamonds would be there on Saturday, which was the twenty-ninth of July. That would only give him until Tuesday and then he would be out of there. Should the article arrive *before* Tuesday, then Jessy would know everything, and what would she do? He wanted so badly just to take the stones and Jessy and to disappear forever, start again, but ... He had to do something so that she would know where to find him. He had to leave some tall tales without jeopardizing his safety.

Jessy picked up the stones on Saturday and they were truly magnificent. There was one particular one that she loved. It had a tinge of pink to it and the clarity was amazing and it was well over two carats in size, quite the most beautiful stone she had ever seen. They went through them carefully, counting them and comparing them to her list. They were all accounted for except for four of them. Those had been the ones that Klaus' friend had taken in exchange for the work he did.

'Jessica, I have borrowed money from you and I would

like to borrow another couple of thousand. So please total up what I owe you and then you must take a stone to cover the cost,' he said to her. She was quiet for a while and then moved her hand over and picked up a medium stone.

'This will cover everything,' she said, looking at Jacques.

'Jessica, I would like you to take this one,' he said, moving his hand towards the pink one that she loved so much.

'Jacques, that is an exquisite stone and worth ten times what you owe me. I can't take it,' she replied looking shocked.

'Please Jessica, you have done so much for me and I have done nothing for you. Please, it would make me happy, please take it,' he said, begging her, but she wouldn't. The subject was dropped and they carried on looking at the stones.

Jessy gave Jacques the money he had asked for and they spent the next few days in anticipation. Jessy had gone out on the Monday to visit her mother and when she got back Jacques was gone. He returned later that day in a taxi. He said that he had had to get out and went sight-seeing around Cape Town. Jessy thought nothing of it. They occupied most of their time making love and being together, as one. Jessy hadn't phoned Patricia to tell her that she could come home. She thought she would wait until Patricia phoned her and told her that she had had enough. The diamonds were never mentioned again and Jessy and Jacques just fell straight back into their own little bubble, unaware of the world around them.

Chapter Eighteen

THE TIME ARRIVED FOR JACQUES to leave. He made sure that Jessy was asleep. Normally, Jacques was awake long before her. As he walked away, he felt his heart was being ripped apart. He was being pulled in two between his parents and Jessy. He was already missing her.

He pushed all these thoughts out of his head and made his way to the dark side of the road. He had arranged to be there at twelve o'clock, giving the others enough time to get to Llandudno, and walk to Sandy Bay. It was only a twenty-minute drive, but he didn't want to be late. Sure enough, the taxi was there waiting, so he jumped in and they drove away. He asked the driver to stop at the home that was closest to the entrance to Sandy Bay. He paid the taxi driver and then stood until he watched him drive away.

Jacques made his way along the sandy path that he had so often walked since his arrival in Cape Town. He had only been there a while, but he had grown to love it. It was a special place and he would always hold it close to his heart.

When he arrived at the beach, he sat on one of the rocks close to the water and watched for any signs of a small boat. Time seemed to be dragging, giving his mind the opportunity to meander back into Jessy's world. He tried to convince himself that he had no choice, or did he? Sure he did. He had three choices. They were; love, life or diamonds! Which one? He still had time to change his mind. But he knew he had to save his parents. He kept looking at his watch, twelve forty-five, twelve fifty-six, one fifteen, one thirty-five and still no sign of the boat. He started to wonder if something had gone wrong on the other side. Why weren't they there to pick him up? Then he saw something bobbing around in the water. He couldn't see it too clearly as it was dark. Then he heard a voice call out.

'Pierre, are you there?' came the voice over the noisy waves.

'I'm over here,' he shouted back. He went down to the water's edge and watched the boat move closer, close enough for him to grab hold of the side, turn the boat around and jump in. It was Dave and as their eyes met, they nodded to one another and not another word was spoken. They maneuvered the boat over the waves which nearly sent them crashing against some of the nearby rocks. But with all their strength they rowed and guided the boat out of harm's way; only then did they talk.

'I trust you got your job completed,' said Dave, dying

to know how everything went. Pierre turned to face him.

'Yes, I got the job done,' he replied. Dave sensed an unhappy air about the man. He should have been excited about seeing his parents again and finally his freedom, but there were no signs of excitement.

'I don't know how you managed it because I must admit, I had my reservations about you pulling it off, but well done,' he said in a condescending tone of voice. His ticket to the "good life" had finally come, thanks to the man sitting opposite him.

'Thanks. Are my parents okay?' Pierre asked.

'Just fine; I think they will be happy to be onshore again. They've been at sea a long time and your mother has been getting seasick a lot, but we gave her some tablets and that seemed to settle her down,' he replied.

'When do you think we'll make Australia?' he asked.

'It will take us two to three weeks to get there, but there is still a bit of work to do. We will have to get your passport photos changed. The authorities are creeping all over the place. They have been aboard the ship. Your mother was put into the kitchen cooking and your father was helping with the cleaning. Luckily for us they never questioned them because they would have picked up their accent. Their documents were all in order so they gave the boat a clean bill and left. I wasn't on board, but I heard about it from Stan, the chap who owns the boat. We are very lucky to have him; he really is a character. Nothing seems to ever bother him; he just takes everything as it comes and he is always the same, happy-go-lucky chap. He is known and respected by many government officials. A good guy to have on our side,' Dave said. Pierre's ears pricked up at the word 'authorities', but he was relieved to hear what was said next.

'So, are they looking for me?' he asked.

'Yes, they have posted photos of you at all the docks, as well as a full description. You will have to grow a beard, moustache and your hair will have to be dyed. Perhaps blond or red. You will also have to practice speaking with an English accent. I will teach you and your parents. A Cockney accent would be a good idea. It's really very easy to pick up and most people can change their voice once they get the hang of it. So when we arrive in Australia, you must speak as little as possible at the passport desk, and be very aware of your accent. There will be no problem with your documents. They have all been taken care of. You and your parents will be free to do as you please,' Dave said.

'That sounds great,' said Pierre, still devoid of any emotion in his voice. Dave couldn't help wondering what was wrong; perhaps he was just relieved it was over and hadn't yet fully realized what was still ahead for them, but he thought no more about it and they rowed on into the silence of the night.

The moon was shining on the water, giving them some kind of light, but they didn't want too much because it would then be easy for a coast guard patrol to see them.

'There she is,' Dave said, pointing to the left of him.

Pierre turned and saw the ship. They changed their direction slightly and headed towards it.

The boat wasn't allowed to flash them with Morse code because that could also be picked up by others, so they only had the moon and their senses to guide them safely back to the ship. As they sat in silence, Pierre found himself drifting back to thoughts of Jessy. She was probably still asleep, all cuddled up under the blankets, looking like an angel. His heart crumbled a little more each time he thought of her. He was going to have to block her out and forget her. She would be receiving the newspaper cuttings and then what would she think? It was bad enough that he had just left without a word of goodbye or an explanation. He knew that she would be heartbroken and feel betrayed by his love, but what could he do? He couldn't take the chance of something going wrong and having his parents killed. He had often wondered if they really would have killed them. He doubted that Arthur would, but he had his reservations about Dave and it was Dave who was here now.

'Well, here we are,' said Dave as they arrived very close to the ship. He had noticed that Pierre was deep in thought and wondered if he was even aware of the approaching vessel.

Pierre's thoughts were cut short by Dave's voice, and a good thing that was, for he was just in time to grab a rope that had been thrown over the side of the ship. Their boat was hoisted up onto the ship and they jumped out and went straight down to the cabin where his parents were being held. As they got to the door, Dave turned to him, 'I won't come in. Your parents will be asleep. They haven't been told you were being picked up so they aren't expecting you. We'll talk in the morning. There's just one thing before I go,' he said as he held out his hand. He didn't have to say anything. Pierre knew exactly what he wanted and reached for the leather pouch from around his neck and handed it over to him. Once Dave had the pouch in his hand, he put it around his neck and tucked it under his shirt, he then held out his hand to Pierre. Pierre looked at him hesitantly for a second and then put out his hand too. They shook hands.

'I would just like to say well done again, and thanks,' said Dave before he turned towards the door and un-locked it. He turned back and walked towards the way they had just come.

Pierre opened the door very slowly, being careful not to make a noise. As he entered the cabin, he saw that his parents were fast asleep; his Dad snoring. He wanted to just bend over and kiss his mother on the cheek, but he knew that would wake her up. He stood and looked at them for a while and then took his weary mind and body off to bed. He was woken by a knocking on the door and then a scream from his mother.

'Father, look! Our son is back!' She was shouting and screaming. She jumped out of bed and then ran over to her son, putting her arms around him and kissing him all over his face, just as she used to do when he was a little boy. Pierre hugged her too and didn't get a chance to kiss her back as she was doing enough kissing for both of them. His father got out of bed and walked over to greet his son, a little more reserved than his wife's approach. Pierre shook his father's hand, then they embraced in a man's bear hug.

'Welcome back my son, it is good to see you,' his father said, in his broken French accent and Pierre knew by the tremor in his voice that he had been extremely worried about him.

'Why didn't you wake us up when you got in?' his mother asked, her eyes sparkling as she looked up at him lovingly.

'It was late and you were both sound asleep, and I was tired too, so I thought it would be better if I left it until morning,' he replied.

While all this was going on, Geoff had walked in and placed their breakfast on the table. He just stood to one side, waiting to greet Pierre. When he noticed a brief break, Geoff quickly stepped in and walked up to Pierre.

'Welcome back Pierre. I'm glad to see you are safe and sound, well done,' he said and held out his hand for Pierre.

'Thank you Geoff and thanks for taking care of my parents,' he said as he stood between them, looking down at each of them as he said the words and giving them a gentle squeeze.

'It was my pleasure. They really have been no trouble, in fact, they showed me how to play a few new card games. Well, I must go; enjoy your breakfast. I can see there is much catching up to do,' he said, smiling and left the cabin.

When Geoff left, they sat around the table, ate their breakfast and talked about what they had experienced with the authorities coming aboard ship. Someone had shown Pierre's mother a flyer that was given to them by one of the men who had come aboard the ship, asking her if she had seen "this man". Of course she just nodded and pretended that she was just a poor kitchen hand with little or no education. It was a picture of Pierre, with a brief description of what had taken place and how he had broken out of the mines and stolen a lot of uncut diamonds. Pierre listened to his mother and when she had finished, she sat there waiting for an explanation or some kind of response.

'All that you have told me is true, but I was made an offer I couldn't refuse,' he said, and then he went on to tell them his story. He thought it was time that they knew the truth. He even told them about Jessica and how he had fallen madly in love with her, how he had used her to get the diamonds cut, and how she had trusted him. He held his head down towards the table as he told them about what he had done to her. The shame was great and they could see it. When he had finished and told them about the house they were going to buy in Australia, his mother looked at him, and taking his face between her hands said, 'Pierre you have done some things that were wrong and may God forgive you, but you have given us our freedom back which was taken from us unjustly. You have nothing to be ashamed of; you didn't have a choice; you did what you had to do and we both thank you from the bottom of our hearts, don't we Father?' she said, in a soft gentle voice.

'What about Jessica? What I did to her was unforgivable,' he cried painfully.

'Yes, what you did to her was bad, but when you were with her, you gave her your love. That is obvious by the way you have spoken of her. She will remember that and won't ever forget it. It will be enough to keep her going and maybe one day, your paths will cross again. If that is the plan for the two of you, then one way or another it will happen,' she said, hoping that he would realize that what she had just said was right, and perhaps they would be together in the end.

'Thanks Mom, I will try and remember that, but it just rips my heart apart every time I think about her,' said Pierre, feeling better now that he had told them how he felt. He had to get it off his chest and it felt good to share it with someone. His Father had listened quietly and patted his son on the back, as if to say, 'We are by your side should you need some comfort.'

They moved on to more pleasant topics, such as what kind of house they would get and where they should live. They didn't know much about Australia, but Pierre had said that he wanted to live in Perth. He had heard it was isolated, but very beautiful. They all decided that the house should be on the coast so that they could walk down to the beach and his father could fish. As the days passed, they started to plan their new lives, while Dave taught them how to speak with an English accent. Pierre and his father started to grow beards and moustaches and they dyed their hair. They were now ready to finally reclaim their freedom.

Chapter Nineteen

Jessy had woken up that Tuesday morning around eight o'clock. She usually heard Jacques pottering around in the kitchen and the smell of the coffee would come wafting through to the bedroom. But this morning there was no smell of coffee, and there was silence. She got up out of bed and tottered into the kitchen and through to the lounge, calling his name as she walked, but no response. Then she spotted a box on the kitchen counter. She walked over, opened it, and immediately felt a warm burning inside her. It was the most beautiful ring she had ever seen. It was the pink diamond that she had loved so much. It had been set in a very simple setting. She was going to kill him. As she looked at it, she wondered if it were an engagement ring. Was this his way of proposing? A note sat beside the box which read,

My darling, this is a token of my love for you. Please wear it and every time you look at it, remember how much I love you. All my love forever, Jacques.

She had reflected on why he had been so attentive last night and how he could not stop telling her how much he loved her. Their lovemaking had been magic; it was gentle and full of love and passion. She eagerly took the ring out of the box and placed it on her engagement finger, looked at it and thought it was a bit presumptuous to wear it on that finger. So she took it off and placed it on her right hand. It fit perfectly and looked stunning. She remembered when they had been at the beach and Jacques had scooped her up into his arms. He looked into her eyes and told her that 'he loved her'. He had never said that before. She had responded by kissing him tenderly and telling him that 'she loved him too'. Their deep love bound them together as one.

She called out to him again. Maybe he was in the garden feeding the birds. She wanted to smother him to death with kisses and hugs but still there was no response. *Where could he possibly have gone?* She checked to see if the car was there, and it was, so he hadn't popped out to the shops for anything. Well, perhaps he had gone for a morning walk. Jessy decided to make some coffee – he couldn't be too long. She made the coffee and drank hers, and still there was no sign of him. Then the phone rang, so she ran to it expecting it to be him.

'Where are you? I've been looking all over for you,' she said. But there was silence on the other side and then she heard a woman's voice.

'Hello Jessy, is that you?' asked Patricia. Jessy recognized her voice.

'Oh, hi Patricia, I was expecting it to be Jacques. When I woke up this morning he wasn't here. The car is still here, so I suppose he has gone for a morning walk. I thought that you might have been him, wanting me to pick him up or something,' she said.

'Oh, I'm sorry I disappointed you, but I just wanted to tell you that your time is up and we need to make new plans. I am ready to move on,' she told her.

Jessy thought for a while and then replied, 'Sure that's fine. Have you made any arrangements with Michael for tonight or tomorrow?' she asked.

'No, I didn't know if you wanted to see him, so when I left this morning I told him I would call him during the day. You must just decide what you want to do because I am going away on a cruise for a couple of months before I start looking for another job. I really need a break and this is the perfect time. No boyfriends, no job, it is just right,' said Patricia.

'Oh Patricia, that sounds wonderful. When are you leaving?' Jessy asked.

'I am flying to Durban in eight days and then catching a ship to Australia, America, Europe and back to Cape Town. I am *so* excited about it all, I can't wait. Listen, you and Jacques are welcome to stay in my cottage while I'm away, if you would like to,' she offered.

'Thanks Patricia, I'll talk to Jacques and get back to you. Can you stay in my house until you go? It would be safer for Jacques to stay here, but we will let you know.

I'll phone you tonight,' Jessy said. She was dying to tell Patricia about her ring, but she thought she had better just confirm that it actually *was* a proposal, so she controlled herself and said nothing.

'That's great; just leave a message if I'm not there. I have a lot of organizing to do, so I won't be in that much, bye!' she said. Jessy put the phone down and then sat in the chair in the lounge and waited for Jacques to come home.

She sat there all morning, and still there was no news or contact. She hung around the house all day and all night. *What was going on? Where was he?* She phoned Patricia to see if he had perhaps gone through there for some reason, but the answering machine was on, so she left a message for her to phone her.

Then it suddenly hit her. Perhaps his memory had come back and he had gone home. She felt sick to her stomach. *Was this ring a farewell gift? Was he never coming back?* She tried to put those thoughts out of her mind and remain positive. He would be back, of course he would. She didn't know how long she sat there as time seemed to have no meaning. She had sunk into a place that she had never known before. It was a very sad, dark and lonely place.

Jessy sat in a corner of the room, in the darkness and stillness of the days and nights, not eating or drinking, just thinking of Jacques and waiting for him to return. She was lost in her own sadness. The phone rang but she ignored it; she had lost herself. She didn't know how long she had been sitting there, the days and nights just slipped by with no sign of him.

Then she heard a car pull up and the front door

opened. She knew it wasn't Jacques, so why even get up. It was dark and there weren't any lights on, so she couldn't see. Then the switch was flicked and the lights came on. She hid from the shocking glare of them. They blinded her. She shielded her eyes with her hands.

'What are you doing? I've been trying to get hold of you! You left a message for me to phone and I have been trying for days now, what is going on?' asked the voice. It was Patricia. Jessy didn't look up; she just sat on the floor, still with her head buried in her hands.

Patricia walked over to her and knelt down beside her. She had never seen her sister like this and it shocked her. She took her by her hands and moved them away from her face. Jessy slowly lifted her face and then it hit Patricia.

'What has happened Jessy? Your face is so swollen from crying and you're sitting in the dark. What is going on, how long have you been here?' she asked, trying to be gentle with her.

'He's gone. Jacques has gone. There's no sign of him, no message, nothing; he has just disappeared into thin air. I feel that I can't go on; I don't want to go on,' she cried. Patricia hugged her and then sat and listened as Jessy began to recite their wonderful love story. It brought tears to Patricia's eyes. All her life she had dreamed of finding such love but had never really believed that it actually existed, and had never met anyone who had ever known it either. She had always envied Jessy, but right now, she wouldn't have changed places with her for the world; it was breaking her heart. Patricia felt her heart being pulled on and tugged at. She wanted to make her sister's pain go away, but she couldn't. She was watching the very life in Jessy slowly drain from her.

Patricia managed to get Jessy up from the floor and ran her a hot bath. She also managed to persuade her to climb into the bath while she made her something to eat. It was obvious that she hadn't eaten for days, and it showed on her body. She would have to spend her last couple of days with her sister, try to get her back on her feet, and get some life back into her. Time would heal the pain she was feeling and hoped it would eventually disappear. She had to try and make Jessy see that. When Jessy was out of the bath, she came into the kitchen to join Patricia. She looked a little better, but still the sorrow lingered in her swollen eyes. Patricia sat and listened to more stories about the two of them and once again her heart felt heavy. When she had finally finished, she looked at Patricia and tried to smile at her.

'I was admiring your diamond ring Jessy, I have never seen it before. Is that one of the diamonds? It looks like it has a tinge of pink. I didn't know that diamonds came in different colors?' she asked.

'They are rare, but you do get pinks,' she replied softly.

'It is exquisite and obviously Jacques loved you very much. It must have been something very important for him to just disappear like this,' commented Patricia.

'Thank you for saying that and listening to all my woes. I feel a little better now that I have told someone. I didn't know who I could turn to. You see, this whole thing is a mystery to me. The only thing I can think of, is that his memory came back and he has gone back to the life he had left behind. But I suppose I should be thankful that I have been so lucky to have loved so completely, albeit for a short while. I will never forget that,' she said. Patricia felt confident that with those last words spoken, Jessy was on the mend, thank goodness.

'That's right Jess, some people go through their whole lives and never love as you have. Just look at me! I'm a typical example. But I'm glad you have said that and now it is time to move on. Time will heal the hurt,' she said carefully.

'I know in my heart that it will never heal; it is as if he is part of me and I am of him. It's something I can't explain, but it is very real. What about you and Michael? I was hoping that perhaps you would fall for him,' she said, now wanting to change the subject. She had been pouring her heart out for hours while Patricia had sat there patiently just listening.

'He's a nice guy and maybe if I had met him years ago, who knows, but I'm off and nothing will change my mind about this trip. What are you going to do about him? I mean, now that Jacques has gone, do you think that there is a chance that you could marry him? He is very much in love with you, I know that,' she said.

'No never. I had really decided not to even before Jacques came into my life. If I did, it would be on the rebound and that would never work,' Jessy replied.

'Well, whatever you decide, please phone him. He has left a million messages for you and now that Jacques has gone you don't have to duck and dive anymore. At least your life can become your own again. There's always that thought,' Patricia said. But as the words came out of her mouth, she knew that she had said the wrong thing. Jessy would have given it all up for Jacques because without him she didn't have a life. Well, not a life that she would call whole.

'I will pluck up the courage to phone him and tell him it's over,' she said.

'That poor guy must think you are going crazy. First you break it off with him, then you just about throw yourself at him, pampering his every need, now you don't want him anymore. He is not going to take this too lightly. Rather you than me, breaking the news to him,' she said.

'I haven't really thanked you for all that you did for us. Without you we wouldn't have had so much special time together. Thank you again,' said Jessy. Her eyes filled up again. Every few minutes she would be fine and then the tears would appear, only to be wiped away and her face dried.

'I'm glad I could do something for you. All our lives it's always been you who has been the strong one, always knowing what you wanted and where you were going. So it feels good to have finally done something to help repay all those times you bailed me out of my messes,' she said as she hugged Jessy.

'You couldn't have showed up at a better time. It was such a coincidence and I thank you again,' Jessy said.

'Now, I am staying with you tonight and tomorrow we are going shopping for clothes for my holiday. Who knows what we'll find for you? But right now, you must get to bed and get some sleep,' she stated as she walked towards the bathroom, coming back with some tablets in her hand. She opened the plastic container and pulled out two, small, white tablets and handed them to Jessy.

'What are these?' Jessy asked before taking them from her.

'They are sleeping tablets as I need to know that you are sleeping and not just lying there, crying,' she said, stretching her hand out to reach Jessy.

'I have never taken a sleeping tablet in my life,' she said. She was about to open her mouth to say something else but Patricia stopped her in her tracks.

'I don't want to hear it. You can take one, that will be enough for you, especially if you have never taken one before,' she said while putting one back and giving the other one to Jessy. She also handed her a glass of water to take it with. She stood there and watched her, making sure that it went down.

'Now, I don't want to hear any more buts, I want you in bed,' she said as she grabbed Jessy by the hand and led her to the room which was an absolute mess. The two of them made the bed and Jessy got into it and before she could start thinking about Jacques, she suddenly felt very tired. Patricia sat by her side until she knew she was asleep and then she went to bed herself.

Patricia woke up before Jessy and cleaned the cottage which was badly in need of it. The maid must have come, saw the car in the driveway and when nobody answered the door, had left. Patricia once told her that if she arrived at the cottage and nobody answers, then she was to leave.

It was eleven-thirty when Jessy awoke from her deep sleep. She felt a little better having had such a good rest. The last time she had slept so well was the last night she had spent with Jacques. For a few seconds, when she woke and smelled the coffee, she thought it was Jacques in the kitchen, and then reality hit her. She was filled with melancholy but forced herself to get out of bed. As she walked into the kitchen, she spotted Patricia wiping off the counter.

'Good morning sis, did you sleep well?' Patricia asked her, looking up from her work.

'Yes, brilliant thanks,' Jessy replied. Patricia walked towards the coffee machine took out a cup and saucer, and poured Jessy a cup. She knew she only drank her coffee from a tea cup, never a mug, like most people.

'Thanks, that smells great,' said Jessy, getting a whiff of the coffee as Patricia handed it to her.

They chatted for a while, neither of them mentioning Jacques. They decided that it was time for Jessy to move back into her own house. There were too many memories in the cottage and Patricia stayed with her until she left for her cruise.

Jessy had numerous messages on her answering machine and one was from Klaus, advising he had the article that she had asked for. He also told her that he had been trying to get hold of her for days. All the others were from Michael, asking if they were still on for dinner tonight. She looked over at Patricia.

'I thought I had better keep in touch with him, otherwise he would be pestering you again,' smiled Patricia.

'You are absolutely right, but do you think you could go tonight?' she asked.

'I had already decided that I would go, because I can see you are in no condition,' replied Patricia.

Jessy then picked up the phone to call Klaus, apologizing for not getting back to him sooner, but she had had a lot on her mind. They met and he handed a piece of the newspaper to her. She read it while she was sitting there, but before she did, she saw a picture of Jacques. There he was. She must have gone quite white because Klaus asked her if she was all right. She mumbled as she read on. When she had finished, she put it in her bag, thanked Klaus and never mentioned it to him again. She showed it to Patricia when she got home and asked her to read it.

'What do you think about it? That is Jacques. Surely to goodness he couldn't go back to that. I'm not sure what to make of it,' she said, wanting and hoping that Patricia might come up with some possible scenario that would make sense of it all.

'Well Jessy, what can I say? He was party to it as he was the one who stole the diamonds. It is all here. But whether or not he has run away because he remembered who and what he had done, I can't tell you. However, I think you have to forget about it and just get on with your life or you will surely make yourself ill,' Patricia commented.

'Do you think that I should go to the authorities and tell them my story?' she asked. Obviously she wasn't thinking, because if she did that she would go to jail as well as Jacques, if they ever caught him. She was an accomplice and she even had one of the diamonds.

'Don't be silly Jessy, you would be in as much trouble as he is; they will throw you in jail. You aren't thinking rationally. Doing that is not going to bring him back, can you understand that?' she said, hoping that Jessy would come to her senses.

'Yes you're right, I am just being silly. It was a stupid thing to say, but I can't help thinking that there is more to this than I am seeing,' she said.

'Of course there is, that's why you are sitting around wondering what has happened to Jacques, but you must move on. Whatever he has done and wherever he has gone, your life has to carry on,' Patricia said, firmly.

So that was the end of that. Perhaps she would never know the answer to any of her questions. Jessy read the article over and over again, trying to see what it was that she was missing. But there was nothing there that enlightened her. She managed to pull herself together and get back to work, hiding the pain she still felt inside and not showing it to anyone. She had been grateful that Patricia had been there. She was careful not to mention Jacques again, making Patricia believe that she was back to normal. She didn't want her to cancel her cruise; she had waited such a long time for a holiday like this. So Patricia went off on her cruise and Jessy was alone again with only her thoughts of Jacques.

Jessy took off the ring he had left for her and placed it in her bedside table. She couldn't stand to be reminded of his love because if he truly loved her, he would never have misled her. It was obviously a set-up and he had used her to get the diamonds cut. So was his love a lie too? Was the entire time they spent together, their lovemaking, all of it, a lie? She had to stop thinking about it because these were all questions she couldn't answer and it was driving her crazy. All she knew was that her love for him was real and even though she tried to fool herself into believing that she had moved on with her life, in actual fact, she was heartbroken and would love him until the day she died.

Chapter Twenty

Jessy started to see Michael again on Patricia's recommendation, hoping that it would take her mind off Jacques. It felt good to be loved by someone but there had been no physical contact. He had said that he didn't know how much longer he could take this hot and cold treatment that she was dishing out. Jessy wasn't really in any mood to agree or disagree with him. She knew exactly what he was talking about, but of course he couldn't tell Michael that he had been seeing and sleeping with her twin sister, Patricia.

Michael was patient with her, at a loss as to what was going through her mind, but waiting and hoping that she would come right. She had forgotten how he had treated her while Jacques was around, for he was now very gentle and caring with her and also very, very tolerant. Jessy found herself starting to like the man again.

The days rolled on and the weeks rolled by and

then one day, as she was going through the books on her bookshelf, she saw the book that Jacques was always reading. She reached to pull it out, and just as she touched it, the memories came flooding back to her. She wanted to take it out, but she couldn't. She was torn between the love she felt and the depression that hit her so often when she was reminded of him. She hesitated, just staring at it, but then an uncontrollable urge had her 'taking it out'. Jessy removed it from the bookcase and walked over to a comfortable chair. She opened it up and started to read it. It was rather large in size with a good few hundred pages, leather bound and still in good condition. Jessy tried to focus on reading but after a few pages she put it back. Jacques had read some of the story to her and he had said how it reminded him of them. With that thought, she picked it up again. Perhaps there was something in it that would give her some understanding of why he left. She had questioned him about why he thought that, but all he had said was, 'One day, you will pick this book up and then you will know what I am talking about.'

She had forgotten all about the book until now, so she forced herself to read it, even though she wasn't in the mood. She remembered how he had even taken it to the cottage. It must have been put into one of the bags that Patricia had packed, to bring back to the house. There were things that just didn't make sense to her, but she had been over them so often that she was beginning to torture herself. She decided to put the book back into the bookcase, made a promise to herself to forget him and to never look at the book again. It was now time to move forward with her life.

She took Scanty for a walk. They went to Sandy Bay. She knew she had to go there, just one more time. When she was sitting on a rock, she thought she heard a soft voice whispering in the wind. 'Jessy I love you, I am waiting for you.' She sat and listened to the whispering winds, feeling Jacques' presence, and for a moment it seemed surreal. He was actually calling her and telling her he still loved her.

But how could this be so? The feeling was so powerful, that she knew he was out there somewhere, but where? She shook her head the first time she heard it. Then she heard it again and again. She thought she was going mad. She left and swore she would never return as the pain was too much. She ignored her instinct and gut feeling. It was too painful to take heed of. This sign, she would have to ignore. She wondered what consequences she would have to deal with because of her ignorance but at this moment, it seemed easier than being reminded of him.

As time went by she slipped back into her normal routine of life and everything seemed to be as it was before Jacques. Patricia had gone on her trip. Jessy received a postcard from Australia saying that she was having so much fun and that she hoped that Jessy was "back to normal". She was happy for her sister; it was about time she took a positive look at life and started to live and love it.

The months slipped by and Jessy found herself facing the world with one face and living inside with another.

It was eating her up, until finally, one day, she just broke down in the middle of the shop, collapsing on the floor. Melodie was more in tune with what Jessy was displaying to the world. She knew there was something terribly wrong, but no matter how hard she tried to make her talk about it, Jessy denied it and got on with her work. Melodie called for some help while the others picked her up and put her in a chair. She got a wet cloth and tried to cool her down; she thought that Jessy had fainted and usually a bit of cold water did the trick. Nothing was working, so one of the men carried her to Melodie's car and they rushed her to hospital. They took her in and did all sorts of tests but there seemed to be nothing wrong. The doctors couldn't understand it. She had fallen into a coma for no apparent reason. Then, on the tenth day, she came out of it, only to see Michael sitting by her side. The nurses told her that he had been there day and night and how lucky she was to have such a caring man. Melodie came in later and told Jessy what had happened but as there did not seem to be anything wrong with her blood and the other tests proved inconclusive, the hospital released her after a few days. Michael insisted that she stay with him so that he could look after her.

Michael was just so wonderful to her. Jessy had lost the will to live. She knew that the coma had been brought about by her breaking heart, but how could she tell the doctors that? Medicine had no cure for what she had – a broken heart – and she wasn't going to tell them either, so the secret remained hers. She wanted to die, even though she would never admit that to anyone else.

As the weeks and months passed she remained with Michael, and then one day he asked her to marry him. Before she knew what she was saying she said "yes". He put a ring on her finger and started planning their engagement party. He was ecstatic and of course, Jessy played the part of a loving fiancé. It seemed like Michael had invited the whole world; her mother, brothers, friends, including Zeke, whom she was very happy to see. They sat and chattered for a long time, then Zeke looked her in the eye.

'Now Jessy, you might be able to fool everyone else, but this man is not for you, and I can see in your eyes that there is a great sadness, what's wrong? What is it? I really want to help you, but I can't if you don't tell me,' he said in a caring way, which was a rare occurrence.

'I don't know what you are talking about! Michael and I have a lot in common. I will be happy with him and he loves me dearly,' she said unconvincingly.

'Don't fool yourself. What do you two have in common? Name one thing,' he said. Jessy was quiet for a while.

'Well, my head is too full of this engagement thing. I can't think right now, but I will and I'll let you know,' she said weakly.

'Jess, what has happened? It's only been six months since I saw you last, and you were full of enthusiasm, with a great passion for life. Now look at yourself. There is none of that. Where has it gone and why?' he asked with genuine concern.

She had to turn away from him because she could feel

the sorrow building up inside her. She mustn't cry as this was supposed to be a happy occasion.

'Zeke, I can't talk to you anymore; I must mingle,' she said and walked away from him, leaving him confused and with a heavy heart.

He knew that she didn't love this man, but more than that, there was something very wrong. How could he help her? He was great pals with her brothers, so he questioned them. But they said they didn't know what he was talking about, she seemed fine to them. Of course that was typical of them, never seeing much outside the world of sport. Jessy pulled herself together and tried to ensure that everyone had a good time. Then it was time to go and as Zeke came to the door to say goodbye, he leaned over, kissed her gently on her cheek and whispered in her ear, 'If you need a shoulder to cry on and someone to open your heart to, just pick up the phone and no matter what I am doing, or where I am, I will come. Please don't forget that. I love you Jess,' he said. He had never actually told her that he loved her before; they had just always known it.

'Thanks Zeke, I'll remember that and I love you too,' she said as she watched him turn and walk away.

She so badly wanted to call him back and tell him everything, but she didn't have the strength to face Michael and everyone else. She watched him as he walked down the stairs and headed for his car. He was a very special soul and she loved him dearly.

The wedding date was set for six weeks time and Jessy had sent word to Patricia. She really wanted her to be there. She had received an engagement card from her, saying she couldn't make the engagement party, but she wouldn't miss the wedding for anything. She also mentioned that she had met someone "wonderful" and that she might bring him along, if that was all right with her. Michael seemed please that she could make it. Because as far as he knew, he had never met her and was looking forward to it! He had heard so much about her from friends and relatives.

Jessy had moved in with Michael, but she still went back to her house every now and again for clothes and a little peace and quiet. One day, while she was there, she spotted Jacques' book again. She kept being drawn to it, so she picked it up once again, even though she had promised herself she wouldn't. She sat down and started pulling the pages out of it, one by one. It was almost like the death of Jacques, once and for all. She had never desecrated a book before but she knew she had to do this and when she had just about finished, she threw it against the wall on the far side of the room. As she did, she noticed that something dropped out of it, so she walked over and picked it up. It was a blank envelope but there was something inside. As she started opening it, she tried to remember if she herself had put something in it for safekeeping. It was a terrible habit of hers, putting things in a safe place and then forgetting all about them. But nothing came to mind; this time she really had confused herself. Then she opened it and pulled out an airline ticket. Now she knew that she had not put an airline ticket away as that would have been a stupid thing to do, and as she opened it up, she saw that it was in her name. It was an open ticket valid for a year, flying to Perth, Australia.

Now she was really confused. Had she bought a ticket for herself? She couldn't remember. Did she do this in one of her depressed moods and forget? It was purchased from the travel agent around the corner from her. She would have to go and enquire if she had bought it from them. Oh dear, she felt as if she really was losing her mind. This was even a bit too scary for her. *Whatever next*, she mused. She put the ticket in her bag and didn't give it another thought until the next day at work when she opened her bag. She slipped it out and popped in to see her travel agent.

'Sarah, did I buy this ticket from you?' she asked, feeling a bit stupid, not knowing whether she had bought a ticket or not. Sarah took the ticket from Jessy, opened it and then just smiled.

'No, don't be silly. Someone else bought it for you,' she said. Jessy felt relieved, but also confused. *Who would buy an airline ticket for her?*

'Who bought it for me?' she asked.

'I'm not too sure. I received a phone call from a man and he said that he wanted to surprise you with a trip to Australia. He wanted it left open for a year because he didn't know when you wanted to go. I never actually met the man. He sent some woman in to pay for it and collect it,' she said.

'So is this ticket still valid? It says a year on it and it was purchased eight months ago,' Jessy said.

'Yes, it should be, just let me run a check,' she said, turning to her computer and calling up the ticket details.

She hesitated for a second and a frown appeared across her forehead.

'What is wrong?' asked Jessy.

'This is very strange. I have received information that the ticket has been renewed for another year and will continue to be renewed until you use it. This is something I have never seen before. It is possible to do, but only if the person who bought the ticket carries on paying the additional costs,' she said.

'Is there any way of finding out who is doing that? It's very important,' she said.

'No. Not really. It isn't our policy to keep records of who is paying for a ticket. The only information we need is whose name is on the ticket,' she said.

Jessy was absolutely baffled. It surely wouldn't be Michael; it would be a return ticket. Perhaps it had been Patricia; she had just been over there. But why wouldn't she have told Jessy? She didn't know what was going on.

'I would appreciate it if you didn't tell anyone about this, especially Michael,' she requested.

'Sure, not a word will pass my lips, but it is certainly nice of someone to give you a ticket like that. I wish it were me,' she said to Jessy, as she watched her get up from the chair and walk out the door.

Jessy returned to the office, more baffled than ever. There were still so many things about Jacques that were unanswered. *Could it have been him who bought the ticket? Dare she think such a thing?* No, surely it wasn't, as he would have told her. Never once did he mention Australia or that it was a dream of his. *What was going on?* Jessy wanted to know who had left the ticket there, but she was also very tired of all these strange things happening to her, and after the "Jacques" episode, she just couldn't be bothered. She decided to think no more about it. It was placed on her bedside table and forgotten about.

Patricia had written to her to say that she would arrive two weeks before the wedding. She wanted to buy Jessy's wedding gown and she wasn't taking 'no' for an answer.

There was great enthusiasm about the wedding. Over five hundred guests had been invited and it was being held at the most beautiful old hotel in Franschhoek. Jessy was dying to see Patricia again and to hear about her time in Australia, America and Europe. It was a perfect time for a wedding as everything was so green, the sun was hot and the air so crisp.

Under normal circumstances Jessy would have been in her element making the wedding arrangements but there were so many others; the wedding planners and Michael's mother, taking care of everything, that she left it up to them. Then Patricia arrived. She had not brought her new man with her as she wanted to spend as much time with Jessy as she could. He would be arriving in ten days, just in time for the wedding. Jessy picked her up from the airport and they didn't stop talking all the way home. Patricia did most of the talking. She was so full of Europe and all the wonderful things she had done there. Jessy had recognized some of the places she had been to many years before and so could relate and share Patricia's passion.

Patricia decided to stay with Jessy instead of at her cottage. Jessy told Michael that she wanted to spend the last few weeks in her own house because after they were married she was either going to have to rent it out, or sell it. She hadn't quite decided what to do. The two sisters went out for dinner and still Patricia kept talking. When they got home, Patricia was still talking. It was the following morning when she actually ran out of things to say, that it dawned on her that she had not asked Jessy what had been happening in her life.

'I'm sorry Jess, I've gone on so much about myself, where I've been and what I've seen, that I haven't even bothered to ask how you have been,' she said apologetically.

'Well, I don't really have much to say. I'm getting married and everything is just fine. Besides, I've enjoyed reminiscing with you,' she responded. Patricia found it a bit strange that Jessy wasn't making a big fuss about this wedding. She had always said that when she got married, the sky would be filled with stars and the moon would shine down on the two of them. She always made it sound like a fairytale story, but now there was none of that so she questioned her.

'What happened to the sky being filled with bright stars?' asked Patricia.

'Oh, that stuff, that's just fairytales. That doesn't happen in real life,' Jessy said, still in a monotone voice. Patricia didn't say any more about it, but she sensed that there was something drastically wrong.

'Let's go out this morning and pick up a dress for you. I'm surprised that you didn't have one specially made,' she said.

'I didn't feel like going to all those fittings, and after all, people get married all the time, so I decided to buy one. Well, you're paying for it,' Jessy replied, trying to smile.

'I just want to stop at the cottage to check up on everything. Shall we do that on the way there or on the way back?' Patricia asked her.

'I'll tell you what, why don't you go there first. I have a few things to do at the shop. Then I can meet you for lunch and we can go and buy a dress,' said Jessy.

'That sounds great. I'll see you at your shop around lunchtime,' she said and walked towards the front door.

As Patricia drove along the twisty road, she couldn't help thinking that there was a dramatic change in Jessy. She had lost her zest for life. She used to be so vivacious and ready to take on the world. But now, it seemed as if she were a robot, going about doing the things she had to do without feeling anything. What had happened?

Patricia drove up the driveway to her cottage. It didn't look any different. She really did love this place and she would never sell it, even if she were going to be away a lot. She went inside and walked around. It looked clean but smelt a bit musty, so she opened a few windows. As she walked past her answering machine, she could see the red light flashing. *Who could have left a message for her?* She'd been gone a long time. She chuckled to herself as she walked over to it and pressed the answer button, wondering how long the message had been there.

Chapter Twenty-One

'HI PATRICIA. IT'S ZEKE, JESSY'S friend. I hope you remember me. Jessy told me you were coming back for the wedding and I need to talk to you. Please Patricia, it is very, very important. My number is 249-7384 at work or 790-4827 at home. Please phone me as soon as you get this message; it's urgent. Please don't tell Jessy I called you.' Then the answering machine clicked off.

Patricia remembered Zeke. How could she forget him? He was a crazy guy, but Jessy loved him to bits and the feelings were reciprocated. What in heaven's name would he be phoning her for, and what was all the secrecy she wondered? She picked up the phone and dialed his work number.

'Good morning, Mathew and Sons,' answered the receptionist.

'Hello, may I speak to Zeke please?' Patricia asked.

'Certainly, I will put you through,' she replied as she switched the call through to Zeke's office.

'Hello, Zeke speaking,' said the voice on the other end of the phone.

'Hello Zeke. It is Patricia, Jessy's sister. I am returning your call.'

'Hi there Patricia, thank you for phoning me. I have something to tell you, but I can't do it over the phone. Can we meet?' he asked.

'I'm at home right now, but I'm going to town to meet Jess for lunch and to pick out a wedding dress for her,' she said.

'It's really urgent. Could I come around to your house now?' he asked, wasting no time at all to see her.

'Sure! Do you remember that little cottage I bought years ago? The one in Constantia? You came to the house-warming party I had,' she reminded him.

'Yes, I remember. I will leave town now, so I should be there in twenty minutes. Will that be all right with you?' he asked.

'That's fine; it will give me a chance to air out the cottage. See you then,' Patricia said and replaced the receiver.

She racked her brains to think of a good enough reason to make Zeke take time off work and come all the way to Constantia immediately, to see her. But there wasn't a single, logical reason. She would have to wait and see. She stopped thinking about why he was coming and busied herself around the cottage, until she heard him drive up the road. Patricia watched him get out of his car and walk up to the front door, but before he could ring the door bell, Patricia had opened it.

'Come in Zeke, it's nice to see you again,' she said as he walked inside.

'Good to see you too Patricia,' he said and gave her a quick peck on her cheek.

'Why don't we sit over here?' Patricia suggested as she walked towards two comfortable chairs. Zeke just nodded and walked behind her, making himself comfortable in one of them.

'Now Zeke, I have been racking my brains trying to think of a reason why you would want to see me so urgently, but I came up with nothing. My curiosity has got the better of me. What is going on?' she asked quizzically.

'Well, it's hard to say exactly, but I am just going to come right out with it. I have spoken to all of your brothers but none of them agree with me. I am just hoping that you can do something to help Jessy, before it's too late,' he said earnestly. But before he could go any further, Patricia butted in.

'Why, what's wrong with Jessy? I have only just left her and she seemed fine to me,' she said, wondering if something had happened between then and now.

'No, she's fine. I'm not talking about her body. I'm talking about her soul, her being. Now, please, don't interrupt me until I am finished,' he said.

Patricia acknowledged him with a nod, then sat and listened.

'I saw Jessy at her exhibition about nine months ago and she was full of life and very happy. She said that she had something to tell me, but she couldn't at that time and that I would have to wait. I said it must be a man, not Michael, it must be someone else, and she didn't say anything. She just smiled and I knew there was someone very special in her life. I could see it in the twinkle of her eyes. I have never seen her so happy; she was just full of love, like a shining light.

'Then, I never heard from her, but a friend of ours phoned me and told me that she had been taken to the hospital and that she was in a coma. This must have been a month or two ago. I went every day to the hospital to see her, but Michael was always there, so I never got a chance to speak to her, obviously. On the tenth day she finally came round, and I managed to go into her room. Michael had just slipped out to the men's room and I asked her how she was, but she just said "fine". All that love that she had been filled with was gone, and so was she. She is here in body only because she seems to have lost life.

'I don't know what happened and she wouldn't talk to me about it. When we talked again at her engagement party, she would still not say anything. I know Jess well. There is something terribly wrong and I would give anything to bring her back and show her that nothing is worth giving up on. But I can't help her because she won't let me. I have phoned her and asked if I can meet her, but she always makes excuses. You might think that she just doesn't want to see me, but Patricia, you know as well as I do that we would die for each other, and right now I would do that if it would bring her back. She is marrying this Michael but I know she doesn't love him. She is doing it because she has lost her love of life.

'Please, Patricia, if there is anything that you can tell me, or anything that you can do, please help her. I am begging you to help her. She will be making a grave mistake if she marries this man. At the engagement party I could tell that she had to get away from me because I was starting to make her feel something. I could see it in her eyes, but she avoided eye contact and would turn away from me. I could also hear in her voice that she wanted to cry, and they weren't tears of love and happiness, they were of sadness,' he said, his own eyes filled with despair.

Patricia could see that he was passionate about her sister. He truly loved Jessy and if anyone knew Jess, it was Zeke and herself. She thought for a minute about what he had said. Jess looked the same, but it *was* strange that she wasn't excited about anything. But she couldn't be sure if it was as bad as he was making it out to be. Was it true or not?

'Zeke, I hear what you are saying, but I have only just arrived back so I haven't really spent much time with her. I did sense a lack of excitement about everything. But I will watch her very carefully and see if she will open up to me,' said Patricia consolingly.

'Thanks Patricia. Will you let me know if there is any change and what transpires, or if there is anything *I* can do to help? Please keep me posted,' pleaded Zeke.

'Sure, I'll do that, but give me a few days.' They both got up and walked towards the door.

When Zeke had gone, she closed up everything and went to town to meet Jess, who was waiting in her office.

They had lunch and then went to pick out a dress. Patricia said nothing of her meeting with Zeke, but she listened and watched Jess very closely. She tried on quite a few dresses, saying that they were all "fine", but it was Patricia who suddenly said, 'That's the one!' Jessy just agreed and they bought it.

What Zeke had said was true. This was not the Jessy she knew. Then it dawned on her that perhaps the coma, and lack of zest for life, was because of Jacques. Perhaps she had never gotten over him. How could she have been so blind as not to have known that? She remembered the story that Jessy had told her about the two of them and how it sounded like a fairytale. Where was that fairytale now?

The days went by. She could no longer keep quiet about what she knew. Jessy was sitting on the chair in the lounge, so Patricia took the opportunity and sat down next to her.

'Jessy, I am going to ask you something now and I want you to tell me the truth. Are you as madly in love with Michael as you were with Jacques?' she asked, watching Jessy's face change at the mention of Jacques' name.

'Don't be silly, of course I love Michael,' she answered nervously, twisting her hands together.

'No Jessy, that's not what I asked you. I want to know if you love Michael as much as you loved Jacques?' she repeated.

Jessy sat in silence and then looked up at Patricia. She could feel the whole of her insides crying in pain and before she knew it, she was sobbing. She couldn't stop. Patricia held her in her arms and rocked her to and fro, glad that she was letting it all out. It was obvious that she hadn't cried for a long time and that she was still hurting. Patricia got up and went to the bathroom, brought back a box of tissues and handed them to Jess.

'You cry as much as you want, and when you are finished I want you to answer my question, truthfully,' Patricia said. Even though she knew the answer, she wanted to hear it from Jessy's mouth, just to make sure. Jessy cried until there were no more tears to cry and then she looked at Patricia.

'I could never love anyone like that again. He was my life, my very being. It was as if we were one, I still love him and will never stop loving him. For the last nine months I have blocked off all feelings of love that I have for him. I have wandered around this planet being incomplete. My heart has been cut out of me. I feel as if I have died inside. You don't know how many times I have wanted to take my own life and put an end to this pain that I carry around with me,' Jessy said in between the sobs and tears.

Patricia was crying as well. She felt so bad. She wanted her sister to be with Jacques again and for them to live happily ever after. They held each other and wept together, something they hadn't done since they were little girls. Then Patricia pulled away and looked at Jessy, knowing that what she was about to tell her might put a rift between them for life.

'Jess, I want you to listen to me very carefully. No

matter what you think of me, it doesn't matter, because I can't stand seeing you like this anymore,' she said, and then taking a deep breath, she proceeded to tell Jessy the whole story.

'It all happened in Johannesburg. I met a guy called Dave and we had a wild affair. As we got to know each other I mentioned that I had a twin sister and that she lived in Cape Town. I told him she was a jeweler. I found it strange at the time because he kept asking questions about you, and then he made me a proposition. He told me that he, and a friend, who was a manager on one of the diamond mines in South West Africa, had an idea to make some good money so that they could retire. I, of course, became interested at the mention of good money and was all ears.

'He went on to tell me that they had been planning this for years and were just waiting for the right opportunity to come along. He thought that perhaps we could use my sister, you, as the bait. I listened to his whole plan, and contemplated it. It seemed like a good plan and I thought it might work and nobody would get hurt. It would be an indirect way of getting the diamonds cut because you had the contacts. So I went along with it and I agreed to help, for, of course, a large sum of money, but I never dreamed you would get hurt. You see Jess, you weren't supposed to fall in love with Jacques.

'His real name is Pierre, and they used him as bait, because they held his parents as hostages. His job was to get the stones cut, and in exchange, he and his parents would go free. They planned his escape from the mines and set the whole thing up. He knew this was his only way out and the only way he could help his parents. Apparently, his mother was gradually getting weaker and weaker and it is rumored that they were put in the mines for a crime they never committed. They were immigrants from France and were set up in a drug heist, arrested, sentenced and sent to the mines to work. So you see, Jacques had no choice. He couldn't tell you anything because they had threatened to kill his parents if he didn't get the job done or went to the authorities. Jess, I'm so, so sorry.

'I really didn't mean for you or him to get hurt, but when I met Dave in Durban to pick up my share, he told me about Jacques and how he had told his parents about you and how much he loved you. Please forgive me Jess, but seeing you like this, I just had to tell you. You see, I thought that you had gotten over him and that you were happy marrying Michael, but I can see that isn't true and that you have lost your zest for life,' she said with tears running down her cheeks.

Jessy was stunned and speechless. *Could this all just be a nightmare? Was she dreaming? How could her own sister set her up like that, just for money? Was that really the root of all evil?*

'Where is he now? Do you know? Why hasn't he contacted me if he was so madly in love with me?' she asked panicking.

'It was part of the deal. He and his parents gained their freedom, and some money to get themselves settled, in exchange for getting the diamonds cut. Jessy, any one of us would have done the same thing if our parents' lives were at stake,' Patricia implored.

'How could you do this to me, Patricia? It is so hard to understand. Just for money?' she cried, looking injured and shocked.

'I'm so sorry Jess,' was Patricia's reply as she bent her head in shame.

Jessy wanted to hit her, kick her and scratch her eyes out, but she didn't. There was suddenly a new emotion swelling up inside of her. Jacques hadn't gone back to his other life, because he never had one. He had never lost his memory. Perhaps all those times she had heard the whispering winds, telling her that he still loved her, it was him who was calling her. She hadn't been hearing things, it was Jacques.

Everything was slowly falling into place, and the love she felt for him was all coming back. She was so happy that Patricia had told her; how could she possibly be cross with her? She looked over to her and lifted her head in her hands and looked her in the eyes.

'Patricia, it is now something in the past. I *would* like to scratch out your eyes, but I forgive you because you have just given me back my life and I thank you,' she said.   Patricia couldn't believe her ears. *How could Jessy forgive her so quickly after all the dreadful things she had done to her?* Patricia was so ashamed but in awe of her. Neither spoke, they smiled and held each other in a hug.

'Now, tell me where he is? Where is Jacques or Pierre, or whatever he is called?' she asked, the old excitement back in her voice.

'They gave them new passports and took them to Perth, Australia. But I really can't say if they stayed there, or whether they have moved on. I really don't know Jess, I promise you,' she said.

As Jessy heard those words, 'Perth, Australia', she jumped up from her chair and ran into her bedroom, opened her bedside table and pulled out the airline ticket. She went back to Patricia, flapping it in her hand as she ran.

'Look Patricia! I found this in one of the books that Jacques used to read. It's a one-way ticket to Perth. I didn't know where it came from. It was Jacques who must have put it there! He's still in Perth, I know he is. I went to the travel agent and she couldn't tell me who bought it for me, but she has had instructions to renew it every year until it is used.'

Jessy smiled, remembering his words to her that "one day, she would understand *why* that book reminded him of the two of them". He had left her a ticket; that way he didn't have to say anything. All he had to do was hope that she found the ticket, put two and two together and caught the first available flight to Perth. Jessy jumped up out of her chair and swung around in a few circles, her lovely blond hair blowing wildly. She looked down at Patricia.

'I could kill you and Jacques. But I want to thank you for confessing and not letting me marry Michael. Thank you Patricia! There is a good streak in you after all. So, that's why you showed up on my doorstep when Jacques arrived and why you agreed to take my place with Michael. Suddenly it is all starting to fall into place. You guys planned it very well. You had us all on the hook, with no idea of what was going on. Does Jacques know about you too?' Jessy asked.

'No, he was never told about me, so he never suspected anything. But it was perfect because I could keep an eye on him. I also managed to help get Michael off your backs, and that made me feel like I earned my share,' Patricia said.

'Well, I suppose you made enough to keep you going for a long time. Those were really good stones,' Jessy said.

'They were hand-picked by the guy who handles them every week. They should have been good ones,' Patricia said with a smile on her face.

'Come and help me pack,' she said as she walked to the bedroom.

'What are you doing? What about the wedding, and Michael?' Patricia asked.

'Forget Michael. I'm off to Perth. I have my ticket so I am going to catch the next available flight and follow my heart,' she said.

Then she headed towards the phone and called Sarah. Sarah confirmed that her flight was leaving in the morning, direct to Perth. She made Sarah promise that she wouldn't tell a soul where she had gone. She agreed, and then Jessy hung up and screamed with joy.

'I'm booked on a flight tomorrow morning at nine-thirty. Will you take me to the airport?' she asked Patricia.

'Sure, but what are you going to do when you get there? How will you find him? Maybe he's not even there anymore,' cautioned Patricia.

'Yes he is. This is an open ticket and I know he is there. This might sound strange to you, but he has been calling me, mentally that is. Doesn't that just sound so crazy? But you know what, I believe it,' said Jessy passionately.

'I'm so happy for you, and don't forget to invite me to your wedding, but this time *you* buy your own wedding dress,' said Patricia sarcastically to Jess.

Jessy opened one of her draws and pulled out a ring box. She then took off the ring that Michael had given her and replaced it with the ring that was in the box. Then she held it up to show Patricia.

'It's beautiful Jessy,' Patricia sighed.

'Yes it is. This was my favorite stone out of the bunch and he wanted to give it to me, but I said I couldn't take it. You see, I lent him money while he was here and he wanted to give me this as payment, but it was just worth too much, so I said no. The next thing, it appears set in a ring and left on the kitchen counter. I found it there the morning he disappeared. I just love it. I suppose that cut your profits down a bit,' she said with a cheeky smile on her face.

'They didn't miss it, and it has been worth it, just to restore my faith in love,' said Patricia.

They hurriedly packed two suitcases and then chatted about the amazing, wonderful turn of events. Jessy told Patricia about the night she had knocked on the door and that she and Jacques had all the uncut diamonds spread all over the lounge coffee table. They both nearly jumped out of their skins with fright.

'Jessy, I must just tell you that it was Zeke who put me in the picture. He came to see me the other day to tell me how worried he was about you and that you weren't yourself. He also said it would be a huge mistake if you married Michael. He really was very worried about you. He said that you just kept avoiding him. He really loves you,' said Patricia wistfully.

'It's true what he says. I couldn't tell anyone else about the whole episode. It was bad enough that you knew, but as it turns out it didn't matter. You see, I can't fool Zeke as he reads me like a book. He knows when I am avoiding the truth, or not facing something. If I had agreed to see him, I know that I would have spilled the beans, and that would also put him in danger as well, so I only had myself to talk to,' she said.

When she had finished, she walked over to the phone and phoned Zeke.

'Hi there! It's me. Don't ask any questions. Everything will be explained tomorrow morning at the airport. Meet us there at eight-thirty, in the international departure lounge. Don't be late; see you then,' she said, and before he could say anything she put down the phone.

Patricia then turned to Jessy and in a serious tone said, 'Jessy, there is something else I need to tell you. When I was with Michael he confessed to me that if I hadn't have come back to him, he had decided that no matter what it cost him and how long it took him, he was going to find this Jacques chap and ruin his life, one way or another. The look of hatred and revenge was terrifying. So now that you are going to leave him at the altar, heaven knows what he is going to do. Please just keep your wits about you, because I think that man is capable of murder, remember that.'

'I know what you are talking about. I remember when I met with Michael to tell him that I wasn't going to marry him; he had heard about Jacques and the look in his eyes frightened me too. We will be careful, I promise. Now no more talk of this, I am too happy and I am not going to let fear keep me from this journey,' replied Jessy.

So the subject was dropped and the two of them sat up most of the night talking. Jessy asked Patricia to apologize to her parents and friends, to tell Michael that she had called off the wedding, and that Patricia didn't know where she had gone, only that she had left. Patricia wasn't quite sure how she was going to pull it off, but she would break the news as gently as possible. She told Jessy not to worry about it. They eventually got to bed at four-thirty, only to be woken up at six-thirty by the alarm clock.

The two girls showered, dressed and headed out to the car. It was a twenty-minute drive and they had told Zeke to be there at eight-thirty. Patricia dropped Jessy off with her luggage and went and parked the car. When she got into the airport, Jessy had already checked her luggage in. They went to the lounge and ordered some breakfast and coffee. They saw Zeke arriving. He looked as if he had just jumped out of bed and was still half asleep, walking along with that ever casual stride of his. They waved to him and he walked towards them.

'Well, you girls are full of surprises. What is going on?'

he asked as he was about to sit down. But he was hugged by Jessy before he got a chance to sit. She grabbed hold of him, and if she could have, she would have squeezed the life out of him.

'That's just for knowing me so well and telling Patricia to help sort me out. If you had never said a word to her, I might still be that "nothingness" that I had become,' she said with love in her heart.

'Well, it's nice to have you back to normal, my Jess. I really didn't like seeing you like that, and I suppose you still aren't going to tell me what's up. Why do I have that feeling?' he said, shrugging his shoulders and shaking his head.

'How did you know? We really can't, but all you have to know is that I have found myself again and I have also found someone whom I love with all my heart and it's not Michael. I can't tell you where I'm going and you are not to tell anyone that you came to the airport to see me off, not even my brothers, nobody,' she said in a solemn voice.

'I suppose I am lucky to be here, seeing as you don't seem to have any other guests seeing you off, so I'll have to settle for small blessings. But I hope that one day you will shed a little light on this situation and if all goes well, it will be before I die! It sounds like it could be a good story, and I'm a sucker for a good love story,' he said, feeling a bit sorry that he couldn't hear it now.

'Someday you *will* meet this man I am in love with. Maybe I'll invite you to the wedding,' she said teasingly.

'You don't know how good it feels to have you back

to your normal self – full of cheek. I know I keep telling you that, but I am just so happy for you Jess, I really am,' he said with all his heart.

Patricia could feel the tears welling up in her eyes. When her flight number was called, Jessy hugged them both and thanked them for their help. She told them she loved them, and then she turned and walked away, ready to board the plane to finally be with the love of her life.

They watched her walk down the long corridor with such determination and confidence. They turned to look at each other and smile; both of them knowing they were going to miss her, but elated that they had helped in some way. Jessy didn't look back to wave; she just walked ahead, her eyes full of tears, tears of sadness and joy.

She had left everything behind her. Her house, her business, everything, and she was going to Perth, not knowing where she was going to stay, but confident in the knowledge that somehow, he would be there to meet her and love her forever. It was that same confidence that kept her going. She took a deep breath and never looked back, happy to once again, feel alive.

Chapter Twenty-Two

THE SHIP HAD NEARLY REACHED Perth and Pierre and his parents were ready. They had learned the English accent as well as they could. Their hair had been dyed and they all looked quite different.

'What happened to Arthur? Is he still at the mine? Did they suspect him at all?' asked Pierre.

'Well, he's still there, but he is hoping to leave in the next couple of months. He took his annual leave last month and has gone back to tell them he has fallen in love and wants to get married. He got someone to take photographs of himself and a beautiful woman. She is of course very young but Arthur is going to tell everyone that this is his chance for a happy marriage. It means he will have to resign because she refuses to go and live in South West Africa. He is hoping that that will be his way out, without drawing too much attention to himself. I have brought you something too,' Dave said, pulling out an envelope which was bulging.

'I'm relieved Arthur is safe and well. I liked the man and oh, thank you, what is this?' he asked taking the envelope from Dave.

'It's your share of the money. We will be there in the next couple of days, so I just wanted to give it to you now. We managed to get a very good price for the stones, all thanks to you,' he said gratefully.

'Is that why we stopped at Durban?' asked Pierre.

'Yes, our contact was waiting for me there. It had all been arranged beforehand but of course he couldn't make a commitment until he saw the stones. But, when he saw them, he jumped at the opportunity of buying them below market value, so everything worked out well. There should be enough money there to get you and your parents settled, but of course it won't last forever; you will still have to work. It is all in US dollars, which you can spend anywhere in the world. Here are work permits for you and your father, as well as your entry documents. With any luck there will be no questions asked. You must just say you have come over from England. Try not to say anything unless they ask you. They might have a picture of you, but with your English accent, and the way you look, I don't think you'll have any trouble getting through,' he said.

'Thank you for everything,' Pierre said, taking the other documents from him.

'It's been nice meeting you. Remember, this must remain our secret. Don't ever slip up and tell anyone because it will be very easy to trace you back to the mine. So for the rest of your life, you must forget about your past and never mention it,' said Dave in a grave voice.

'Don't worry, we have already forgotten it,' Pierre said.

The two men shook hands and said goodbye. Once Dave had left the room, Pierre opened the envelope and pulled out the money that was inside. It was all in one hundred dollar bills and he sat down and counted it. There was a total of $500,000 dollars, all new and clean bills. Pierre and his parents sat staring at the money. They had never seen so much all at once, and they certainly had never handled that much before. They looked at each other, started to smile which then turned into hysterical laughter. They were free at last and could now start living their lives again.

'That was very generous of them,' Pierre's mother commented.

'You are right Mother, they really didn't have to give us that much, but I think they are very fair men and we stuck to our side of the bargain, so they stuck to theirs,' Pierre replied.

'You know what this means Mother? We can buy a little cottage by the sea and I can fish and you can sew, garden and never have to worry about a thing again. We have finally found what we left France to find – peace and prosperity,' said Pierre's father as he looked lovingly at his wife, holding her hand as he spoke.

It made Pierre feel very happy to see the peaceful look on their faces. It had been worth the trouble, just to witness this moment. He saw the tears roll down his mother's face and his father wipe them away gently with his handkerchief. Pierre wondered if he would ever feel that love again, and for a few seconds was reminded of

Jessica and the love that he still felt for her. *Had she found the airline ticket?* It was so well hidden that it was possible she would *never* find it. He just hoped that she would remember his words. Then again, perhaps she had already forgotten him. He could never forget her.

The next few days flew by and they amused themselves by talking about their new lives and all that lay in front of them. Then, on the third day, Geoff came to collect them, to advise that they would be docking in an hour's time. They had been looking out of their one little porthole and could see the land getting closer and closer. Dave had brought them a suitcase each, and there were some new clothes inside for each of them.

The money was split up between the three and placed in well-hidden areas because cash, in large amounts, was not allowed.

Pierre and his parents went up to the top deck and then walked along the gangway with some of the others who were getting off too. They queued in a line and waited anxiously, but tried not to look too nervous. Finally, it was their turn. Pierre handed the passport officer their passports and work permits. He took them from him and studied them closely.

'G'day, is this your first time to Australia?' he asked Pierre.

'Yes, it's our first time,' he replied in a very strong English accent. It would have been difficult even for another Englishman to detect that he wasn't from England. The officer looked at all three of them again and got up from his chair.

'Please just wait here a minute,' he said and walked over towards another officer who was standing a few yards away.

Pierre felt sick. Surely nothing could go wrong now, not after all they had been through. To get so far and have your freedom taken from you again; he couldn't stand it. He watched them talking to each other and then the officer came back on his own and sat down in his chair.

'I'm sorry about that but I just had to check something,' he said as he lifted his rubber stamp, stamped each one of their passports and handed them back to Pierre.

'We hope that you will be happy here, good luck,' he said in his Australian accent. The three of them held their breath and then breathed a sigh of relief as Pierre took the passports and documents back.

'Thank you,' he said and they walked off casually towards the baggage collection section.

The urge to jump and shout for joy was overwhelming but they had to keep calm and not draw attention to themselves. They smiled knowingly at each other, still not talking, in case someone overheard them. Once they had their luggage, Pierre called for a taxi and asked the driver if he could recommend a good hotel, near the sea. It was a beautiful hotel, not too big and it overlooked the ocean. They checked into their rooms and then went straight down to the beach for a delicious swim. The water was warm and clear and it felt like the most beautiful day of their lives.

For a while Pierre forgot about Jessica and joined in the happiness that his parents were experiencing, and it felt good. They stayed there a week to acclimatize, and forgot that anything existed outside their small hotel.

At the end of the first week, they decided to have a look at some property, so the next few weeks were spent looking at a variety of different houses. Some were magnificent, and at a good price, but they really wanted a small cottage.

Pierre had changed his name to Jacques. With each of them having different names, they had to learn to call each other by their new names. They slipped up often, but only when they were on their own, never in company. It would take a while to get used to them, but they had no choice. Their new names were now part of their new life; a better life.

Jacques spent a lot of time going through the job section of the local newspaper. He didn't have to work straightaway, but he felt he needed to do something to keep his mind occupied. He attended a few interviews and his parents went to see more properties. His mother was in her element. She would come back after the day's trip and be full of every little detail about the houses she liked. It was only after three weeks that she came home and told him that they had found just what they wanted. But they wanted him to have a look at it first.

It was in a good area and right on the beach. A wonderful stone cottage, no roses creeping around the windows, but they could plant some. It was just perfect for them, not too big. His mother didn't really want to spend her days cleaning a large house and the size was ideal; so they bought it.

It had two bedrooms, so Jacques said he would stay with them for a while, just until they were settled and accustomed to their new surroundings. He wanted to get his own home. They were a bit disappointed, but they knew he was a grown man and wanted his own privacy. They understood and respected that and didn't argue with him.

They had all dyed their hair back to its normal color. Jacques and his father shaved off the moustaches and beards and it felt good to be themselves again. Jacques had tried to keep some of his English accent and when people asked where he came from in England, he said he was from London, but that he had lived in France for a while. The chances of anybody ever finding out who he was, was a million to one. Nobody knew about the diamond heist and nobody was even interested.

Jacques was offered a job working for a small architectural company that hadn't been going long, but they were serious about their work and he was impressed with the designs they turned out. He loved his work, and after a month he was called into the office and congratulated on the standard of work he was producing. That gave him even more confidence and made him push himself even more.

He bought himself a really lovely house, also by the sea. It was modern, with a lot of glass, giving him an unobstructed view of the ocean. You could say he had it all; a lovely home, an excellent job, happy parents, and lots of women who were constantly chasing him.

He had been to the travel agent and had asked the lady there to renew Jessy's ticket, and that she was to continue to do that every year. He paid the difference and had asked her to phone him the minute the ticket was used. For her service, he sent her flowers every month. He made a point of phoning her regularly, to see if there were any changes.

The months rolled on and he was beginning to think that Jessica was never going to find the ticket. He couldn't go back and get her. He couldn't even take the chance of phoning or writing to her. So he just waited patiently, hoping that one day she would turn up. Even if it took ten years, he would wait. He knew that they were meant to be together.

Every day he walked along the beach. He would think about her and tell her he was waiting for her and that he loved her with all his heart. He wasn't sure why he did that, but if there was any chance at all, that they were somehow connected, he hoped that she would pick it up and know that he was waiting.

Then one day, while sitting at his desk working, the phone rang.

'Hello, is that Jacques?' the voice on the phone asked.

'Yes it is. Who is this please?' he asked, not recognizing the woman's voice.

'It's Susan from the travel agency,' she replied.

'Oh! Hello Susan. This is a nice surprise,' he said, dying to know what she had to tell him.

'I'm sorry to disturb you at work, but you said that I should let you know when Jessica had used her ticket,' she said.

'Yes I did,' he said, feeling quite numb.

'She caught the morning flight from Cape Town, via Durban this morning and she should be arriving there tomorrow morning at ten-thirty,' she said. There was silence and Susan said, 'Hello, are you still there?' she asked.

'Yes. I'm sorry. I just can't believe it, thank you very much. I really appreciate it,' he said, with great emotion in his voice.

'It's a pleasure. She must be very special to you and the world is a sucker for a good love story,' she said. Jacques thanked her again and hung up the phone.

He sat back in his chair. She was coming, she was coming. He was suddenly filled with all the thoughts of the wonderful times they had together. He couldn't work the rest of the day. He asked his boss if he could take a few days off because a good friend of his was arriving in town, and he had to go to pick her up from the airport.

He had been there nearly seven months and hadn't missed a day of work yet. His boss agreed and just told him to get back as soon as he could. Jacques was working on a few projects that had deadlines, but he assured his boss that he would have them ready on time, even if it meant he had to work day and night.

He went home, phoned his parents and told them what had happened, and that he would bring her around to meet them. He walked around the rest of the day in a daydream, not really knowing whether he was coming or going. He tossed and turned all night, and finally got up and watched a movie, to try and relax and take his mind off Jessica. By the time he finally got to sleep it was three-thirty in the morning and he was exhausted. But he was awake at six-thirty, which was the normal time he got up for work. He forced himself to eat some breakfast and then made his way to the airport, of course getting there two hours too early, but he just couldn't wait any longer. Maybe her flight would come in early. He wanted to be there, but of course, he knew it would never arrive two hours before the expected time. He sat in the restaurant looking out across the airstrip, watching the arrival and departure of the flights. Time seemed to stand still. He must have looked at his watch fifty times.

It was still only nine-thirty, he bought a magazine and read it. It helped to pass the time. He must have drunk ten cups of coffee. Then it was ten-fifteen and now he had to decide if he wanted to watch her flight arrive and then go down to the arrival zone, or just go straight there now. He decided to stay and watch her get out of the plane, because once she was out, she still had to go through customs.

He sat with his eyes glued to the window, watching every plane that arrived and checking everyone who came out. Then suddenly, she was there. He felt his heart skip a beat. He was like a man sitting outside a maternity ward waiting for his first child to be born.

There she was.

She was the most beautiful woman who ever walked the face of the earth. He watched her as she made her way towards the building until he couldn't see her anymore, then ran down the stairs and headed towards the arrival room. It was full of people waiting to meet their friends, lovers, relatives and business associates.

He wasn't going to stand at the back. He wanted to see and touch her as soon as she got through the door. He kept saying "excuse me" and made his way through the crowd right up to the front. He overheard one woman say, 'Who does he think he is pushing around like that?' But he really didn't care; he had to get there. He waited and waited until the passengers slowly started to trickle through. But Jessica wasn't one of the first, so he stood around and watched the crowd get smaller and smaller. *Where was she? He just hoped that she didn't have any trouble getting through customs, but why would she?* Then there she was.

She saw him and walked towards the enclosed ropes which kept them apart. She felt her heart miss a beat and the earth move from under her feet. She dropped the overnight case she was carrying and flew into his arms. They held each other closely, kissing and hugging. Then they looked into each other's eyes and felt, once again, the enormous love flowing between them.

'Jessica, will you marry me?' he asked her.

'Yes, yes, yes, I will,' she said. The crowd, enthralled, watching the lovers with delight, started to clap and cheer. They hadn't realized that anyone was taking any notice of them as they were so caught up with each other. At the sound of the shouting and cheering they looked around and saw a large crowd encircling them, cheering them on happily. They smiled at each other. The crowd slowly started to disperse and then Jacques looked at Jessica.

'Jessica, before you agree to marry me, I have

something to tell you. I am so glad you came, I love you, I love you, I love you,' he said.

'You don't have to explain anything. Patricia told me the whole story. She was also part of it, so I will tell you her story sometime,' she replied as she held up her hand and showed him the ring which was on her engagement finger.

'There wasn't a day that went by when I wished you would find that ticket and feel my love for you. You see, when love like ours exists, we become one. I've come to appreciate that to find a love like ours is everyone's dream and so often it never happens. I feel so blessed to have found you,' he said. Jessica felt tears of unconditional love and joy welling up inside; she was whole again.

They both knew that there was no stronger force than love and it was this love that had sustained them, even under extreme duress.

THE END

About the Author

I was born in Zambia, Africa where I lived until I left in my late teens to travel. My grandfather was a diamond prospector in Kimberley, South Africa; hence the theme for my story.

He would often tell us great stories about his mining and we loved to see the jam jar that he kept on his mantelpiece, filled with uncut diamonds. Once the jar was full he would use it for his holiday money.

I lived in Australia for seven years, England for four years and have been living in America for the last sixteen years. I have four children and four grandchildren.

I have a passion for the universe at large and a great love for life.